MELANIE JACOBSON

SCROOGE
AND THE
GIRLS
NEXT DOOR

To Jenny Proctor
For all the things. All of them.

Chapter One

Paige

CAN I LIVE IN a haunted house?

I mean, there are some variables at play here. Nice ghost or mean? Is it mostly active at night? I'm a single mom—I *need* my sleep. Is it trying to avenge anything? That's a hard no. Creepy little kid? Also no. Tragic widow? Maaaaaybe. I could also deal with a grumpy but harmless ghost. Like an old man ghost or something.

Which kind of ghost lives in 341 Orchard Street? From the sidewalk, I eye the small house's peeling yellow paint on its faded exterior. Half the windows are missing shutters, and several of the remaining ones hang askew. While someone has kept the shrubbery trimmed, brown leaves blanket the yard and the sagging front porch.

There's no way its only residents are spiders and mice.

It's possible the Halloween decorations on the stately porches and well-groomed yards of the rest of Orchard Street are contributing to the vibes, but I have a feeling this derelict cottage would look haunted no matter what.

The thing is, this house has one irresistible quality: a For Sale sign, the only house that's ever come up in Creekville in my price range. I can see its potential, and I haven't been able to get it out of my mind in the three days since it was listed.

I called my mortgage broker's office this morning and applied for loan preapproval; it was waiting for me by lunchtime, *and* he'd found a grant program that would allow me to do a smaller down payment. That would give me a cushion for some initial renovations.

I glance up and down the street; it's empty of people. I'm on my lunch break, and I can't resist the urge to get a closer look. Three concrete steps take me up to the warped wood porch, and when I peer through the cloudy glass of the cheap front door, I spot some old furniture and dust motes floating in the muted light.

"Can I help you?" a male voice asks.

I whirl to find a pale middle-aged man standing on the walkway of the leaf-covered yard. He's wearing khakis and a brown sweater. With his dark hair and brown-rimmed glasses, he's crayon-like in his head-to-toe brownness.

"Just looking inside to get a sense of the place," I say. "Do you live here?"

His eyebrow goes up. "Does it look like *anyone* lives here?"

Ew. He's—what does Cary Grant call the sheriff in *His Girl Friday*? Oh, an insignificant, square-toed, pimple-headed spy. I summon my inner customer service patience fairy and offer him a pleasant smile. "I meant on Orchard."

He nods toward the house next door, the largest and most elegant house on the street, but says nothing else.

"Well, I'm thinking of making an offer, so if things go well, we'll be neighbors." It's a test for me to see how I feel about saying it. I don't feel pukey. That's a good sign. In the past, I've felt pukey when I was on the verge of making decisions that would burn my life down.

"You don't want that place." He says it so surely. So flatly. So infuriatingly.

"But I do." I'm not sure about that yet, but I *am* sure I don't want *him* telling me whether I do or not.

"Too small."

"Three bedrooms," I counter. I've pored over that listing. "That's perfect."

"Are you single?" he asks. This is not a creepy come-on ask. This is a judgy ask. Any answer I give here will be wrong. I can feel it.

"Why does that matter?"

"There's not much to offer here for single people."

I stare at him. "In a college town?"

"On Orchard Street."

It's clear he thinks I belong anywhere but next door to him. I am so tired of dudes talking down to me. They did it when I waited tables until Evie was five. They do it now in the hardware store I manage, which makes it extra fun when I point out that they actually need to use a pocket screw, not a corner brace. I don't know what it is about me that screams DUMB, but I'm over it.

I walk down from the porch and stop a few feet from him. Now that I'm closer, he's much younger than I thought at first, probably in his mid-thirties. Still very brown up close, all except for his sun-starved skin. Even his eyes are dark brown.

"Well, neighbor," I say, emphasizing the word slightly, "I have a kid. Seems like Orchard Street will be perfect for us."

"So you're married."

"Nope." Let him judge me for that. I'm an A+ mom.

That stops him, and he looks like a trout for a split second before he regroups. "It's all old people on this street. Your kid will hate it."

I let my eyes wander leisurely over the manicured yards and Halloween decorations. Then, without another word, I pull my phone from my pocket and dial a number.

"Hello, is this Arshneel?" I ask, reading the realtor's name on the For Sale sign. "My name is Paige, and I'd love to schedule a showing of the Orchard Street house, today if possible." I listen for a minute. "Seven o'clock is perfect, thanks."

Mr. Brown's mouth thins and tightens as he listens. I put my phone away and smile. "Nice meeting you, neighbor. But just so you know, anything you need to borrow, I won't have."

I walk past him and continue down the street, around the corner, and four blocks back to Handy's Hardware, where I have to break the news of my potential house purchase to my boss, who is going to *hate* it.

Chapter Two

Paige

I WISH I WASN'T such a good person. Then I wouldn't mind crushing people so much. But I am, so I do.

It's a weird feeling to hold two opposite emotions at once—in this case, joy and dread.

Then again, however good of a person I joke about being, there's not a better human on the earth than my boss, Bill Winters.

I enter Handy Hardware through the back, hoping to give myself a chance to pull it together. Maybe I could roleplay this? Practice it?

A scarecrow stands in the backroom, and I stop to consider him. I pulled Scarecrow John from storage last week and brought him over so I could try out some window concepts for November. Right now, he's standing there in a plaid shirt with a stupid grin on his face.

I've definitely dated dumber guys than Scarecrow John. Might as well try the roleplay. He's got nothing but time, and he'll be a non-judgy audience.

I clear my throat. "So, Bill, I need to tell you something that might upset you."

The scarecrow's head lolls forward.

"You're already taking it badly."

The head drops to the ground and bounces once.

"Drama queen, much?"

Maybe I should try something else, like shoving a bag full of Bill's favorite candy at him and breaking the news when he can't hear me over the crunch of his toffee.

Except even Evie, my seven-year-old daughter, would see through that. No point in stalling since my stalling tactics suck.

I set my purse on the office desk, tie my black canvas apron around my waist, and pin on my name tag, the white letters spelling out, "Paige, Manager." The title gives me the same glow of satisfaction it did when Bill promoted me three months ago. Everything about this place makes me happy, which might be strange for a woman who dreamed of becoming a theater set designer.

From the vanilla and pine smell of the lumber section to the sharp scent of an open can of paint, I love it all. In some ways, it reminds me of working on the sets for our high school plays, back when my life was uncomplicated.

I also love that this is a place where people come to fix things that are broken or to breathe life into their project plans. And I love that I've put my own stamp on Handy's by making the front windows a seasonal attraction. I switch up themes to entice customers to treat themselves to everything from a new grill to a tray of flower bulbs.

When I step out on the sales floor, I spot Bill behind the checkout desk. His hair shows as much gray as brown, and his weathered skin betrays how much time he spends outdoors puttering in his garden, but he's not yet sixty, and he looks like a man with plenty of energy to enjoy life.

"Morning," I say, trying to keep a smile on my face that says, *I'm not about to break your heart.*

"Morning, kid," he answers, smiling up at me.

You'd think a grown woman of twenty-six would resent being called a kid, but I love it. It's what he calls his daughters too, and they're both older than me. But when he and his wife, Lisa, declared they were adopting Evie as their honorary grandchild two years ago, it turned out I was part of the package. Now they tell everyone they have three daughters.

"I have some news," I say.

His forehead furrows. "Your face says I'm going to hate it."

"My face doesn't say that." I stretch my smile wider. "See? It's happy."

His eyes narrow. "Are you quitting?"

"No, I love it here." And I do. It's fun. Plus, I can walk Evie to school every morning before work, and I'm home by 6:30 most days. Every Sunday off, and the pay is generous. So generous, in fact, that it's making the news I'm about to break possible.

"You sick?" He looks even more alarmed.

"No!" Bill was coming out of a nasty battle for his health when I met him, and I hate that he had to go there for even an instant, so I blurt it out. "I'm buying a house. Probably."

His face sags in relief. "Is that all? I was waiting for the worst."

I pause a beat to see if he'll process the implications. When he doesn't, I add, "It means Evie and I are moving out."

The rest of him sags now. "Oh. Yeah, I guess it does."

Evie and I have lived in the small apartment above Bill and Lisa's garage for two years. In a lot of ways, it's been perfect. They love having Evie run up and down from our place to theirs as much as she loves doing it. She wanders out to work with Bill in his garden most Saturday mornings. She also spends plenty of time with Lisa in the kitchen, learning how to cook and bake, "just like Auntie Tab did, and now she's *famous*," Evie likes to tell people.

If ever I had doubted Bill's affection for Evie, his sad face would convince me now. I hurry to make it better. "I will never, ever be able to thank you enough for giving us a place to live while I finished school. But it's time to move out, and it'll make it so much easier when Grace or Tabitha come back to visit. Tab won't have to stay at the B&B."

"They don't mind," he says.

"I know. But they'll like staying with y'all even more." Grace, their younger daughter, is married to my brother, and they always stay in Tabitha's old bedroom; it's the only spare room available.

"When did you decide all this?" he asks.

"Maybe ten minutes ago?" At his startled look, I explain. "I saw the listing go up a few days ago. I got preapproved for a loan this morning, and it's in my budget. I walked over to look at it just now, and . . . yeah. I want it."

"But . . ." Bill looks like he's gathering more arguments, but I head them off.

"This is a good thing, Bill. The only reason it can happen is because of all the help you and Lisa have given me." A generous salary, a cozy apartment for only the cost of utilities, more free babysitting than I can ever repay. "It's time for us to start the next phase of our lives, and you and Lisa will be a huge part of that."

He sighs and settles his chin in his hand. "Tell me where this house is, and I'll try to be happy about it."

"This part is good news," I tell him. "It's on Orchard." That's only one block away from them.

He thinks for a moment. "Wait, the fixer-upper that just got listed?"

I nod, grinning.

"But, honey, it's a du—" He breaks off and clears his throat. "It's got potential."

He was about to say "dump," and I don't blame him. I'd called the real estate agent back for information on the walk to the store. The place was built in 1920, and it's only had two owners. The most recent one died five years ago, and the house sat empty until the heirs pulled themselves together enough to list it.

I've fantasized about a place Evie and I could call our own since she was a baby. I've bought and decorated a few dozen homes in my imagination, never dreaming it could be a reality. Until two years ago, I'd worked as a waitress for Evie's entire life, and a single mom on a server's salary couldn't afford even a single-wide trailer these days.

But I finished a bachelor's in business this summer, and I have a regular salary, plus the money I've scrimped and saved. It's been two years of shopping at grocery outlets, thrifting all our clothes, and going without a car because we can walk everywhere—work, church, and school—and it's added up.

"I know it's the worst house in Creekville," I say. "But the mortgage broker found a grant that means I can keep some of the down payment back for repairs."

Bill sighs. It's a long, tired sound. "Until we all get our angel wings, Lisa and I are your parents now. I wish you'd stay a little longer, save a bigger down payment, and make sure this is what you want to do."

It's so sincere that a tiny lump lodges in my throat. I already had one set of amazing parents, even if I lost them way too early. "I got luckier than anyone should when I got you as bonus parents. But there's a point where I have to stand on my own two feet, and I'm really proud of buying this house. I want you to be happy for me."

He gives me a smile. "I am. And Lisa will be thrilled too. But *you* have to tell her you're moving out."

I wrinkle my nose.

He gives me a knowing look.

"I will, I will."

"Tell you what, when Evie's done with school, let's close the store for an hour and go check out your new place. Does she know about it?"

"What do you think?" I ask.

He laughs. "No, or I'd have heard about it already."

"Exactly." Evie has started countless sentences with the words, "Here's a secret I'm not s'posed to tell you."

"All right, I'm going to call Lisa to come on over, you're going to surprise her, then we'll all surprise Evie together. Sound good?"

"Sounds perfect."

It's taken a long time to get used to Bill and Lisa being a part of everything we do. It had been Noah, Evie, and me against the world for five years before Grace came along. Now she and Noah are living in South Carolina, but only because Noah trusts the Winters to have our backs.

They definitely do. Evie's got her "Nana and Poppa Dub," as she likes to call them, short for the "W" in Winters. That's Evie's way of adopting people: nicknaming them as she collects them.

A half hour before Evie's school lets out, Lisa walks into the store and parks herself in front of the register.

"Hey, sweetie. Bill says you have a surprise for me."

Bill, who'd been organizing the paint chips, clears his throat and mouths, "Good luck."

"I do," I say, smiling at her. She has the same dark hair as Grace's but hazel eyes like Tabitha. She's dressed in black slacks and a pale blue blouse. She must have been working with a real estate client today, and if there's one thing that's going to keep me out of trouble with her, it's her job. At least, it will if I play this right.

I swallow hard and announce, "I'm buying a house."

She blinks at me. "Sorry, what?"

"I'm buying a house. For me and Evie."

"That can't be right. Because if you were buying a house, you would have talked to me about it, and I'd have helped you get everything together for your offer."

"I still need you to do that," I say. "I wanted to do all the preliminary stuff by myself in case I couldn't even get loan approval. But I have all that, and now I'm hoping you'll represent me on this purchase."

She considers that for a long moment of silence, and then the rapid-fire questions begin. Which house? *That* house? Am I sure? Am I really, *really* sure?

I answer all of it, then she mulls. Finally, she breaks into a smile. "Congratulations, honey. I'm proud of you! How about you move into the house, and we keep Evie?"

"Ha ha," I say. "Good luck getting rid of her. We'll only be a block away."

"Speaking of Evie . . . " Bill walks over and flips the sign to Closed and sets the hands on the "Back in ___ minutes" sign to show an hour. "We're going to walk her over to the house and surprise her," he tells Lisa.

"Let's go." She beelines for the door. "But I still have a million more questions for you."

"I'm counting on it," I answer, smiling. Lisa's love language is fussing.

Evie's face splits with a grin when her second-grade class spills out at dismissal and she spots us waiting on the sidewalk. "Hey, Dubs!" she calls. "Hey, Mama!"

"Hey, baby. We've got a surprise for you. Come on!"

She rushes over to meet us, slipping one hand into Bill's and the other into Lisa's. "Is it a puppy?"

"NO," we all say. Grace and Tab gave Lisa a puppy almost two years ago, and he still hasn't outgrown his wear-everyone-out phase.

"What is it?" Evie asks.

"Have to wait," I tell her.

She peppers us with guesses until we turn onto Orchard. Evie quiets, curious about why we're here. We've walked Coal, Lisa's poodle, down this street many times, waving and smiling at the older people sitting on their porches.

Halfway down, I stop in front of the cottage. "Evie, we're going to get our own house."

Evie's eyes widen and she looks around, craning her neck at all the lovely homes lining the sidewalks. "Which one?"

I point straight in front of us. "This one."

She stares at it, puzzled. "We're getting the haunted house?"

I settle my hands on her shoulders and drop a kiss on her hair. "Would I buy us a haunted house?"

"Prolly not on purpose," she concedes.

Bill chokes on a laugh.

"Trust me, E. When we get through with it, it's going to be the prettiest house in Creekville, no ghosts."

Lisa sighs. "At least it's a Cape Cod and not a Victorian. Those are hard to restore."

A sedate blue Camry turns into the driveway next to us, crunching over the leaves that have blown over from my yard. Soon-to-be my yard, anyway. Mr. Brown is behind the wheel. He frowns at our group and drives around to the back of his house.

"Friendly," I say. "I met him this morning, and he had pretty much the same look."

"That's the Ellis house," Lisa says. "Their grandson inherited it a couple of years ago. Wonder if that's him."

"Miss Lily will know," Bill says. "Ask her next time she comes into the store."

It's true. Lily Greene will know. She's not a gossip, but somehow, all news and information finds its way to her. She often chooses not to share, but if it's something that can be told without doing anyone an unkindness, she'll tell.

"Right now, I want to worry about *our* house." I crouch beside Evie. "We need to use our imaginations, kiddo. Picture this place after we fix it up. New yellow paint, pale green shutters, window boxes with flowers. No ghost will want to live in a house that cheerful."

"*We* fix it up?" she says. "I can help?"

"Of course."

"Okay. I like it."

And just like that, she's into it. There will be future drama when she realizes it means moving away from her Dubs, but we'll deal with that when we get there. Right now, all I can see is the potential of this place, and I don't want any more metaphorical rain on it.

"All right, then," Lisa says. "Let's put your offer together. You've got a home to make."

Chapter Three

Henry

I STIFLE A GROAN when I turn into my driveway. A small knot of people stands in front of the house next door, and the snappish woman from earlier is right in the middle of them.

I'll have to call Arshneel. He said he'd let me know when there's an offer on the property so I can submit a bid. I'd been hoping it would stay empty forever. I can't afford it, exactly. I inherited my grandparents' place with a clear title, but the utility bill is the size of a mortgage payment every month, and associate professor salaries only go so far.

The woman waves at me with a sarcastic smile, and I frown. She's young. Probably her parents buying a place for her and her kid. The best thing about Orchard Street is that it doesn't draw families with children. They want to be in the suburbs with other young families.

I have old, quiet neighbors. I'm bad with kids. I'm an only child, and I wasn't good at being a kid then. The few times I tried never went well.

I have even less idea what to do with children now. Mostly they remind me of dogs: noise covered in dirt. Both sense my fear, and both take advantage of it.

I park beneath the carport behind the house and enter through the kitchen, set my satchel on the counter and head straight for the fridge and a beer. I've been saving a Belgian ale from a Roanoke craft brewery for a couple of weeks, but if ever there was a day when I deserved to drown my sorrows in hops, today is it.

I crack it open and collapse onto the living room sofa. Despite my grandparents' house looking fancy outside, inside it's cozy, filled with all the same furniture it had held when I visited as a kid. The couch is comfortable, the day has already been long, and I need a cold one before I tackle the new problem of buying a house I don't want.

I'll rent it out. It's a bit far from either of the universities bordering Creekville to attract student renters, but that's fine. Maybe I can find another professor looking for a place.

I rest my head against the sofa and try to let my mind go blank, but this is a day that doesn't want to die. I should have expected it. After returning midterm papers for three sections, my office hours had been a parade of students wondering why they didn't get better grades.

The answer, of course, is they needed to write better papers. But that concept regularly escapes students at our elite liberal arts college. They've been coddled into believing that all of their ideas are interesting and worthwhile, and there's a distinct lack of rigor in their work.

Even the long line of complainers wouldn't have been so bad if it hadn't been capped off by a student who spent twenty minutes arguing for the return of five points to make his assignment grade an A.

If he wanted an A, he should have reviewed his citation guidelines.

For an institution full of supposedly bright students, academia is stupid sometimes.

The thing is, they're capable. With enough pushing, they do things they didn't know they could. Watching them realize this is the best part of my job. Pushing them to get there is the most exhausting.

The tension slowly seeps out of me, but it takes longer than usual because I can hear the people on the sidewalk. The child's high voice penetrates my windows, exclaiming over things as they make their way around the exterior of the house.

When it finally quiets, I pull out my phone and call Arshneel. "I saw a buyer at the house next door today," I say after we dispense with pleasantries. "Should I be prepared to make an offer?"

"I think so," he says. "I've been talking to her agent this afternoon, and although it's possible she'll change her mind after seeing the interior, she sounds pretty motivated. Apparently, she's fairly skilled with renovation."

"Is she a house flipper?" That wouldn't be so bad. If she's getting in and out, I won't have to worry about a noisy kid.

"No. It's her first home purchase."

Great. She's thinking long-term then. We talk for a couple more minutes, then I hang up and nurse my beer, thinking about how I said I'd make an offer like it's nothing. But the reality is, even a cheap mortgage will be an uncomfortable stretch. I consider all the different things I can do with the place. There has to be a way to make it work as a rental, right? Maybe an Airbnb?

That might not be too bad if there's a way to cyberstalk potential guests and determine whether they're the kind who throw rowdy parties. But that's not really who visits Creekville. People come for the antiques and Civil War history. Not to throw keggers.

I'll figure it out. I have to. I need this part of my life to stay quiet. Quiet just like it is right now. I polish off my beer and slouch against the sofa, soaking in the silence.

Even more than the quiet, I need the control. I keep my life well-ordered. Bad neighbors? Noisy neighbors? I know from experience in apartment living that it can have an enormous effect on day-to-day quality of life.

Eventually, small details from the new unit we'll begin in my two Intro to Anthropology sections dribble into the pleasant blankness, and I know the signs too well to bother resisting: it's time to get up and finalize my next lecture on the deceptively simple question, "What Is Culture?"

I work for a long time, stopping only when lights suddenly shine from the unobstructed windows next door. I've been in this house since January, and it's the first time there's been a light over there. Arshneel must have had the utilities connected in anticipation of showings.

Clearly, I was naïve to think a house that looks creepy enough to get its own *Ghosthunters* episode would languish on the market.

The light is on for about half an hour before the house goes dark again. I go to bed out of sorts and wake up no better.

I've barely settled into my closet-sized office on the Jefferson University campus when Arshneel calls the next morning.

"Hello." I keep my voice low so I don't disturb my office mate, Leigh.

"Are you ready with an offer?" he asks.

"She made one then?"

"It came in about ten minutes ago. If the interior fazed her, she didn't show it."

"Is it a full-price offer?"

"I can't tell you, but I wouldn't offer less than that."

"All right," I say. "I'll get preapproved and see what I can reasonably counteroffer."

"Sounds good," he says. "I'll need it by close of business today if you're serious."

As soon as we hang up, I call a mortgage broker. I explain what I need, they send me a link to follow and fill out, and twenty minutes later, I get a call back telling me they should have an answer for me by mid-afternoon.

"You're buying a house?" Leigh asks, her voice amused. "How many do you need?"

I clear my throat, a nervous habit I hate. I'm not even nervous that often, but Leigh is stunning. In academia, the scale for attractiveness is different. Our ten is about a seven everywhere else, but Leigh would be a ten anywhere. "House next door," I say. I'm about to explain possibly using it as an investment property, but she says, "Cool" and goes right back to work.

I haven't dated since I moved to Creekville, too busy trying to design and keep up with courses. But this semester, the Intro to Anthro courses are repeats, and I've found chunks of free time appearing like loose change in the sofa.

I don't know where one goes to find dates in this town. I don't like the idea of dating apps. Leigh is the only single female I know my age, but I'd be interested in her even if there were bushels of single women around.

So why haven't I made an overture?

Leigh is rather intimidating. She looks like Gal Godot. She teaches abnormal psychology. And human sexuality.

How does a dusty anthropologist ask a sexologist on a date?

He doesn't.

He shares his office with her because there aren't enough offices to go around, and he thanks the gods of every culture he's ever studied for that fact. That's what he does.

Perhaps one day I'll figure out how to have a normal conversation with her. But until that day, I'd best shut my mouth and appreciate being in her orbit.

I finish my lecture notes and teach my two Thursday sections without incident. I don't have office hours on Thursday afternoon, so I head home, stopping at the small specialty foods market on Main for dinner provisions.

The store only has a couple other customers, but one of them is an elderly woman standing in the pasta aisle. I stifle a sigh. Why is that the people who have the least time left in life are the ones who take all the time in the world making a decision? Maybe I can edge around her to get to the . . .

"Hello," she says. Her blues eyes are alert and crinkle at the corners like she's done a lot of smiling. I'm not good at guessing older people's ages, but given her straight posture, I estimate she's probably under a hundred. But her short hair is snowy white, so who knows?

I give her a tight smile and try to edge past her. I'm so close to the . . .

"Any recommendations?" she asks. "My housekeeper usually cooks, but she's out of town. I thought I'd make my own dinner, but I'm out of practice."

Sometimes there's no way to avoid a conversation. I resign myself to polite chitchat. I'm a student enough of my own culture to know that this is what's expected in small-town markets.

"You're cooking for one this evening?" I do a lot of that. I might actually have a suggestion.

"Yes. I'm a pretty decent cook, believe it or not, but rarely for one."

I wonder if she's suffered a recent loss. Or maybe she's simply lonely. I resolve to be patient. "I'm making gnocchi. It's a potato pasta."

"I've had it." Her eyes twinkle at me, like she's enjoying a private joke.

"Yes, well, it's a nice change from regular pasta sometimes, but it's hardly worth making from scratch for myself. The one they sell here is acceptable, and if you make a fresh pesto, it's simple enough, and it makes the boxed pasta feel indulgent. But that's the only good boxed gnocchi." I point to it.

"Clever. I like it." She reaches for the gnocchi and hands me a box before settling one in her own basket. "I'm Lily Greene, by the way. I don't believe we've met."

"Henry Hill." I shake the hand she offers.

Her eyes sharpen with interest. "You're Marley and George Ellis's grandson, aren't you?"

The question surprises me. "Yes. Most people remember my grandfather, but hardly anyone mentions my grandmother."

"I've lived in Creekville almost sixty years," she says. "I came here as a young newlywed, and I'm past eighty now. I was near your grandparents' age. I'm sorry for your losses."

Again, it's a surprise to hear condolences on my grandmother's passing because it was so long ago. What isn't a surprise is the pang of guilt I still feel almost thirty years later. "Thank you," I tell her. "That's kind."

"I hear you've moved into their home," she says. "It's a beautiful place."

"It is," I agree. "More house than I know what to do with, but it's certainly a good house."

We chat a bit more, and I like her warm demeanor. She asks quite a few questions, but it feels like interest, not curiosity. By the time we drift in opposite directions down the aisle, she's ascertained my age, job, and marital status.

I shake my head as I peruse the fresh basil a couple minutes later. She pulled my info from me so easily, I never felt the tug. That's a talent.

Ten minutes later, I turn into my driveway and contemplate whether thirty-five years old is too young to make dinner at 4:00. Since I can't bring myself to say, "4:00 *in the evening*," I conclude that yes, I'm too young to eat dinner so early.

My phone rings as I kill the engine, and it's the mortgage broker informing me that I've been preapproved for enough to counter the snippy woman's offer. Barely. But it's still enough.

My phone rings again as I set my satchel on the counter. Arshneel this time.

"Good timing. I just got my preapproval. I'll counter with the asking price."

"I don't think that's a good idea."

"It's fine. I can swing it." I can cut back on expenses. There *has* to be someone on faculty, some future visiting professor who will want a low-key, low-charm, but low-fuss place like the house next door when it's renovated.

Arshneel clears his throat. "That's not the only consideration. The expense of the repairs—"

"Arshneel." If he keeps going, my anxiety will climb, and this is really the only solution. "Just counter the offer."

"But—"

"I know what I want in a neighbor, and that situation is not it. Go back to the sellers with the offer."

His answer is a long sigh. "Mate, it's a bad idea."

I say nothing.

"All right," he says. "I'll keep you posted."

We hang up, and I stare through the dining room window at the shabby cottage. Nothing stirs except the dry fall leaves, a breeze kicking them up a bit. Everything else is silent.

Exactly as I like it.

Chapter Four

Paige

"Can we go see our house, Mama?" Evie asks, dancing up the driveway to our apartment.

"Not tonight, honey. Soon."

"I want a rainbow room."

"We can do that. Hey, Lisa," I say, spotting her on the back patio. She's in the glider, a pitcher of tea and a juice box waiting for us. "Evie wants a rainbow room. Pretty sure I know where to find some paint."

Evie rolls her eyes but giggles.

"That sounds pretty, Evie. Why don't you go check on Poppa Dub and make sure he's not getting too worked up over the football game?"

"Okay," Evie says, and darts through the back door to find Bill.

"We may have a problem," Lisa says, her smile fading. "There's a counteroffer for the house."

"What? I thought you said no one else would want it." I'd bid below asking price because she'd been so sure.

She holds up her hands with an expression of bewilderment. "I was shocked even you did. I did *not* see a bidding war coming."

"What do I do?"

"Wait for a better property to come up?" But she sighs when she sees my face. "I know. It's unlikely you'll find anything with such a good location in your budget."

"Exactly. I can't afford to go higher than the asking price." She knows every penny over that is a penny I can't spend on the reno.

She rubs her forehead. "The best move here is to counter with asking price but remove all contingencies. It'll increase your remodeling costs, but at least you can budget those out over time without adding anything to your monthly mortgage."

I don't love the solution, but I hate the idea of losing the house even more. Curse whoever made the counteroffer. "Let me think about it."

"All right. I'll get dinner started."

I head up to drop my purse and change clothes. My place is a very large room or a very small apartment, depending on your perspective.

Bill built it one summer with the help of Tabitha and Grace. It has a closet-sized bathroom with a skinny shower, a kitchenette with a cooktop but no oven, and a small bedroom. He'd hoped having their own place might entice one or both of them to stay in town and go to a local college.

But one of the schools is a military institute, which I can't imagine either sister in, and the other is Jefferson, a very exclusive—and expensive—liberal arts college. They'd both chosen cheaper but prestigious state schools, Grace at Virginia Tech and Tabitha at UVA.

Evie and I are outgrowing this tiny place, and I'm angry that someone else is bidding on the house meant for us. I shouldn't take it personally, but it's hard not to, given how badly I want it. I'd rather have a person to blame than believe the universe is conspiring against me.

I push it out of my mind and change into joggers and a long-sleeved Albemarle High T-shirt I stole from Noah, then settle down to rethink my renovation plan now that I have to raise my offer by five thousand dollars. I'll basically have to wait a year or two to replace some of the older appliances, but I can still take care of the most important stuff.

Is it worth it? I'm probably paying more than I should at this price. But I had felt so sure when I stood in front of it yesterday. Maybe I need to check and see if that was a fluke or a trustworthy instinct.

"Lisa?" I call as I go downstairs. "Would you mind if Evie hangs out for a bit? I'm going to walk to 341." I give her the house number so Evie doesn't hear "Orchard" and beg to come. I don't want her heart getting any more set on this house if it's not meant to be ours.

"Sure." Lisa comes out of the kitchen, wiping her hands against her apron. "Dinner will be ready in half an hour. That enough time?"

"More than enough, thanks."

I head to Orchard at a light jog. A couple minutes later, I'm standing in front of the cottage again, thinking. It's dark and hard to make out much, but its faults and potential are all etched into my mind anyway.

Just like yesterday, standing here feels right. Except yesterday, I had a chance of making my plans a reality, and now it's on the verge of slipping away.

Is it worth losing a chunk of my renovation budget to own it? I squint at the windows with damaged and missing shutters. The inside is old. It's musty and dusty. I don't think it was ever updated by the owner. It's going to take so much work.

But the bones are so good.

And I've never been afraid of hard work.

I bite my lip, thinking, trying to make sure what I want so badly isn't crowding out logic. But I think about Cary Grant in *Mr. Blandings Builds His Dream House,* the first movie ever made about a home renovation. And I remember when Cary Grant as Mr. Blandings finally makes his dream home a reality. Sure, there are minor and major disasters along the way. And yes, most of the laughs come at his expense. But in the end, Mr. Blandings gets his house, and it's everything.

I'm about to start up the path to the porch when the scuff of shoes on concrete draws my attention to the house next door, Mr. Brown's house. He's walking toward me in a pair of loafers, and it's too dark to tell what color his clothes are, but I'm betting he's got on a V-neck sweater and chinos.

"Back again?" His voice is cool.

"Sure. I made an offer on it. Exciting, isn't it?" I know full well that if he finds this at all exciting, it's not the good kind of excitement.

"I suppose so. I feel more impatient waiting to hear about my counteroffer."

I go still and stare at him. There's a streetlamp near us, but trees filter the light and I can't read his expression. "I'm bidding against you?"

He shrugs. "If you're the only other offer, then yes. You're bidding against me."

"Why do you want it? You already have a house."

"I'd rather turn it into an investment property and have some say over the tenants. Quiet ones. Adult ones."

"So you don't want it. You just don't want me to have it." He might as well push me over, kick dirt at me, and call me names. "You need to find a different agent if he's advising you to invest in this place. It's never going to earn enough as a rental because you'll have to spend too much to remodel it enough to attract renters."

"And yet *you* want it." His voice is still cool but now there's an edge to it.

"Because I want a home. It changes how much it's worth to me when I plan to be there for the next twenty years." If I hoped that would soften him, it was a deeply misguided hope.

"We pay for what matters to us." His voice is as careless as his shrug had been.

I peer through the darkness toward the cottage once more.

"Yes," I say quietly. "We do."

"Guess who we're bidding against?" I demand when I get back home. I answer before they can guess. "The next door neighbor."

"That cranky-pants guy you told us about?" Bill asks.

I nod. "Doesn't love the idea of a kid living next door. Or me."

"Wow. That's a real special guy. You sure you want to live next to him?" Lisa asks. "Just live here forever."

I smile at her. "We'll be here all the time anyway. But yes, I think we need our own space. Let's counter with asking price and no contingencies."

Her face says she doesn't like it.

"I can afford it," I say.

"But you already go without so much . . . "

"Nothing I need," I say. "And I've got some ideas for work-from-home part-time jobs now that my degree is done." They were only vague ideas and all things I could do between 8:00 PM and midnight when Evie was asleep. Phone surveys. Remote helpline for alarm companies. Nothing was firm yet, but whether I get this house or not, I'll still be trying to figure out how to work a second job so I can save for a reliable used car.

Lisa sighs. "Okay. I'll put in the offer. I can't decide if I want the seller to accept it or not, but either way, we'll be in a waiting game."

Evie pops out of the kitchen. "Hi, Mama. We made chicken and lemon."

"Sounds delicious," I say. "Is your homework done?"

"Almost. I'll finish it because the chicken has to cook more." She sits at the dining table where her open spelling book waits for her. It's such a small thing, but it's something we don't have room for upstairs, where she'd have to work on her bed or the couch with her books and paper in her lap.

I slide an arm around Lisa's waist. She's a couple inches taller than me, and I rest my head on her shoulder. "Want this for me, Lisa. Because I want it so much for us."

She hugs me back. "I'll want it for you. And I promise to be as nervous as you are until we hear back on your offer, but there's something we can try that might make a difference."

I straighten. "What is it?"

"Sometimes it can sway a seller if you write a heartfelt letter explaining why you want the place."

I hesitate. I hate telling other people my story because I don't like being the sum of my tragedies. But if it means getting the house . . .

"You think it will work?"

Lisa nods. "I think it's your only play if Cranky Pants counteroffers again."

"Then it looks like I have some homework to do too." I sit across from Evie and outline the broad strokes of my story until it's time to help set the table. After a dinner of roasted chicken, Bill and Evie help with dishes while Lisa waves me away to work on the letter.

I go up to work on my laptop, opening it and taking a deep breath. Then another. And then I begin to type, telling these sellers my story, a story I hope will offset whatever Mr. Brown can offer.

To whom it may concern,

My name is Paige Redmond, and I grew up just two towns away from Creekville. I'm twenty-six years old, and we've lived in this area for eight years, ever since I found out I was about to become a single mother at eighteen.

My parents had recently died in a car accident, and I'd left home after graduation, grieving and lost. But when I found out my daughter Evie was on her way, I remembered that I still had one piece of home: my big brother. So back I came, and I left a year-long trail of poor judgment and bad decisions behind me.

I haven't looked back. Moving here was the best thing I've ever done. For myself, yes. But most importantly for Evie.

I tell them about putting myself through college over the last two years with grants and scholarships, taking classes in Roanoke at night and online courses while Evie slept or on my lunch breaks, and cramming on my days off from the store. I talk about only having lived in cramped apartments, and about how much a home will mean to us.

I don't know if it's enough when it's finished, but I do know I've given it everything I have. I hit send to deliver it to Lisa and go back downstairs to get Evie.

"It's done," I tell Lisa. "I emailed it to you. What happens next?"

"I enclose it with your offer. And then we wait." She squeezes my wrist as if to reassure me that it will all work out, but it's hard to imagine that it will if they reject my offer. I just have to hope.

And so I do. Hard. Day and night for two days. Two loooooong days.

Two stressful days in which I imagine I'm hammering the neighbor's face when I teach the Builder Buddies workshop at the store on Saturday. And I blame him and growl when I can't fit my sweatshirt in the dresser Evie and I share. And I daydream about egging his stupid, beautiful house for trying to take my homely one.

On Monday, Lisa comes into the store, grinning. "You got it! He won't counter. You close in four weeks."

This leads to whooping and something that is maybe a square dance but is definitely not like any other dance as Lisa and I link arms and skip in a circle while Bill laughs.

It leads to ice cream with Evie after school and a flurry of crayon drawings as she designs her rainbow room.

It leads to list after revised list as I put together a three-year renovation plan, wishing I could do it sooner, but so, so glad I get to do it at all.

Evie and I get our *own* home.

Chapter Five

Henry

I COULDN'T DO IT. I had the money, but I couldn't outbid her on the house. Arshneel insisted I do a walkthrough with him to understand the full extent of the repairs needed. And he was right; I wouldn't get the monthly rent I'd need to make the house a reasonable investment. But in the end, I kept hearing her voice in my head saying, "I want a home."

I didn't bid again.

I catch glimpses of her now and then, walking past the property and scoping it out. I can't quite gauge her. She looks about the age of my students, or at least the seniors. Medium brown hair, average height, lean build, but I'll admit she makes jeans look good.

She's wearing a shirt for the local hardware store every time I see her, so perhaps that's why she reminds me of the attractive assistant on that old sitcom with Tim "The Toolman" Taylor and that neighbor who talked over the fence. I might even find her pretty if she hadn't already shown herself to be a harpy.

I hear her too—or more specifically, her child.

Today has so far been safe from such disruptions.

This is what I think exactly two seconds before a loud thunk sounds against the side of the house. I jump and curse, wondering if a branch has fallen, when a small face topped by light brown hair peeks over the windowsill.

"Sorry I hit your house. My ball slipped. It doesn't look broken. Your house, I mean. Balls bounce. They can't break." Then she giggles like it's the silliest idea she's ever heard and disappears.

I'm staring in befuddlement where her face appeared and vanished when I hear her shout, "Let's play catch, Mama. It's hard by myself!"

Even at a distance, the kid can speak at a frequency that vibrates my eardrum. It's as if it's custom-designed to pierce my windowpanes. The child should be studied for science.

These are not what I would call "good" vibrations.

I look down at the papers I'm grading. At least my students have somewhat straightened out. Irritating excuses about absences and late work have dropped by a half since their first essays were returned, as if they fear I'll have no more patience for those things than I did for their half-baked papers.

They're correct, of course. *They* may have no issue with wasting their parents' tuition money, but I'll certainly make them work for it.

The cat is the other interesting development. He—she? It. It is a feral black cat I've spotted lurking beneath my carport twice now when it rained. At least, I assume it's feral. I don't know much about cats. But it wears no tags or even collar. It looks a bit . . . tufty, his fur patchy in a couple of places, which makes me think it's male. A lady cat would care more about her grooming. He slinks rather than walks, and the handful of times I've seen him, I always barely catch sight of him from the corner of my eye.

When I get home from campus later the next afternoon, the autumn sun is shining like it's never seen a cloud, and Cat streaks past me, a fluid shadow, disappearing around the corner of the house. Each sighting feels like an achievement. This must be how birdwatchers feel when they spot something new. It's a bit of a thrill. Perhaps I should take up the hobby myself.

Cat is not fluffy. In fact, he's so skinny, he must be in charge of feeding himself. I drop my things inside and rustle in the refrigerator until I find some leftovers and set a bowl of shredded chicken out for him. I make a mental note to buy tuna.

When I leave the following morning for work, I walk out to a decapitated bird on my back doorstep.

The scientist in me is intrigued by this cultural exchange. I offer Cat shelter and food, and he returns the favor by hunting for me. Cat is quite the most interesting character I've met in Creekville so far. And as I glance over to the empty house whose quiet days are numbered, I decide he's also possibly the least annoying.

I need a game plan to limit the nuisance next door. I've been teaching undergrad courses since I started my PhD program almost ten years ago, and if there's anything I've learned about dealing with squirrelly people, it's to set clear expectations and boundaries and—here's the important part—*enforce* them.

I don't like being in other people's business. I'm content in my lane. But sometimes, other people's nonsense blows into that lane, and I'm forced to deal with it anyway. This is exactly what the new neighbor situation looks like it will shape up to do. So, much like I'm training Cat to expect food each day, I'll train the neighbor to behave as I wish. Orchard Street is a micro-society, and I'll have to be the enforcer until she gets it.

It will annoy both of us at first—calling out infractions, drawing her attention to all excessive noise, and leaving polite notes and reminders periodically. But it shouldn't take long for her to make sure that their behavior—and noise—fall within acceptable parameters. It will be uncomfortable short-term but worth it for all of us in the long run.

After the initial adjustment, I—and the rest of Orchard Street—can return to quiet evenings of crosswords and a glass of mid-range wine, evening shows and morning routines safe from disruption.

This is the single greatest appeal of living in Creekville. I hadn't been back since my grandmother's passing. The sense of guilt was too great despite my grandad's many reassurances and invitations. Even after he left the house to me in his will, I still couldn't make myself return for two years.

But tenured professors grow scarcer by the year in the cutthroat halls of academia, and my grandfather had possessed the one thing I needed most professionally: connections. He'd been the provost of Jefferson in the late nineties and continued on the board of trustees until shortly before his death.

One of the other trustees had reached out to inform me that she'd promised him to advocate for hiring me if a relevant position came open, which it had. The series of interviews I'd had last fall were the first time I'd returned to Creekville since childhood, and I had found it largely unchanged.

I like tradition, routine, and knowing what to expect, and I knew what to expect from a town like Creekville. When the dean of the College of Social Sciences had called to extend a tenure track position, the job offer plus my inherited house were far too good of an opportunity to pass up.

My situation is ideal. In spite of the energy that buzzes around my new neighbor and her child, I will not allow their chaos to infect the rest of us. They will learn, and in the end, they will both come to value peace and quiet the way the rest of Orchard Street does.

I guarantee it.

Chapter Six

Paige

THE NEXT FOUR WEEKS are a whirlwind while we wait for all the paperwork to process. I walk past the house often and make plans with Evie. Her room is my first priority. After that, I want to remodel the living room. Those are the two spaces we'll spend most of our time in, and I want them to feel like home.

A couple of times, I see Mr. Brown. Once, he frowns and doesn't make eye contact. The second time, he pretends not to see me. His uniform of khakis only varies with the color of his sweaters. Gray. Navy. He's still brown to me.

Finally, it's move-in day.

"You ready for this?" Lisa asks.

We're standing on the sidewalk in front of 341 Orchard Street, Evie holding my hand, Lisa and Bill on either side of us. It's a Friday afternoon, and once again, Bill has closed the store for a bit so we can all get Evie after school and walk her over.

"Ready!" Evie shouts. "I want to go IN."

"Ready." I'm not as loud as Evie, but I'm just as excited.

"Then I believe these belong to you." Lisa hands me the keys to the house.

There are only two, and even though she's attached them to a small brass "R" key fob (for Redmond), they still feel light in my hand. Way too light for how hugely this changes our lives.

I curl my fingers around them, take a deep breath, and smile down at Evie. "Let's go."

She turns the old brass knob and pushes the door open, and I know one of my first projects as I listen to it creak. We step inside, and despite the musty smell, it feels far less haunted than it looks outside. As in not-at-all haunted.

Maybe it helps that Halloween is behind us and we have two weeks until Thanksgiving. All the spooky decorations on Orchard are gone, and a few houses now boast fall-themed wreaths on their front doors.

The house—*our* house—is more worn than spooky. The heirs had cleaned out all the knickknacks but asked if I wanted the furnishings left behind, and I'd told them yes. I had plans for the old furniture.

Other than that, it's just us, faded walls, and dust bunnies.

Oh, and all of Evie's excitement, which the small house can barely contain. "Time for Rainbow Magic Paradise!" she cries, and beelines for the bedroom she staked out as hers on the one walk-through she was allowed before the closing.

The floors are old oak, and her footsteps make a muffled thump as she runs. I smile at the Dubs, who grin back.

"Guess I better get used to that," I say.

"She doesn't go anywhere at a walk," Bill agrees.

"Let's move you in," Lisa says.

Once we start, it takes less than an hour to move in every single thing Evie and I own. Lisa and Bill also present me with a microwave before they leave. "You'll get a fridge delivered tomorrow morning," Bill says. He holds up his hand before I can protest. "You need to let us have some peace of mind. At least we'll know that starting tomorrow, you can live on Hot Pockets if you need to."

They're Evie's favorite food.

Fine, I kind of love them too. "I promise we'll eat more than Hot Pockets."

"I know you will on Sundays because you better be at our place every week for family dinner," Lisa says.

I throw my arms around them, and Evie flies out of her room and barrels into the group hug.

After we walk Bill and Lisa out, she asks, "What now?"

"Discover all our new nooks and crannies?"

She scrunches her face. "What's a cranny?"

"I don't know, but in books, sometimes they hide cool stuff."

"Let's go!"

Our front door opens into a small living room with a galley kitchen off to the right. Straight ahead, a hallway leads to the three bedrooms. Mine is first on the left, Evie's is next to it, and a smaller third one sits past the bathroom on the right at the end of the hall. I don't know what it'll be yet, but it's fun to think about. A guest room? An office? An oversized closet for all the clothes I don't buy?

I laugh to myself and lead Evie to it. Oddly, it has a door leading outside, but I know what I'll find when I open it: the paint I left on the back stoop yesterday, all mixed and ready for me to get to work on Evie's room.

I throw open the back door and grin as she spots the paint cans, her eyes widening as she recognizes the colored dobs on each lid.

"My rainbow room?"

"Yes, ma'am."

She cheers and soon we have the drop cloth laid down. Eventually I'll need to refinish the floors, but for now, they'll be passable with a good polishing. There aren't any baseboards either, but thanks to Mr. Brown's bidding shenanigans, some of the finishing touches will have to wait a year or two, budget-wise.

Because of all the time I spent working on stage sets for our high school plays, I know I can put together a look that will thrill Evie within a couple of days. The question is whether I can work hard *and* smart.

"Let's take lots of pictures so we can see how much work we did," I tell her. Sometimes it helps when she gets bored with a project to remind her of how much progress she's made.

By the third wall, Evie's lost interest. If it was a matter of her *wanting* to paint, I'd keep coaching her, but she's itching to do other things.

"Hey, Evie, I think I can do the rest of this by myself, but you know what I can't get to?"

"What?"

"I wanted to scope out the yard and find a good spot for a veggie garden." She grimaces. "And flowers."

"I'll go!" She drops the roller where she stands and beelines out the back door.

"If you go around front, leave the door open so I can hear you!" I call after her.

"Okay, Mama!"

I'm halfway through priming the fourth wall when Evie bursts through the back door, her footsteps thumping toward me at a run. She pauses in the doorway long enough to announce, "I'm going out the front."

"Leave the door open."

"Okay."

And she's gone again. I'll check on her in a few minutes, but just to see what she's doing. Creekville is as safe as the small town I grew up in ten miles away, and I don't have an ounce of worry that anyone will do anything to her.

When I poke my head out after the last wall is done, she's pushing leaves into a pile. I'll need to see if there are any rakes lurking in the small shed out back. If not, I'll borrow Bill's. I could buy one discounted, but the idea makes my eye twitchy. These are the kinds of expenses I hadn't planned for when I figured my monthly budget. Discounted paint and curtains made from thrifted sheets? Yes. A $25 rake? No.

I'll have to start haunting the neighborhood Facebook sales and giveaway sites for household and yard stuff. Still, a smile creeps over my face as I head back to Evie's room, because I, Paige Redmond, am a grownup with a yard that needs raking.

"Heck, yes, sis," I say aloud. "You did the thing."

The primer on the first wall, the one destined for a rainbow glow up, is dry, so I measure and block out the wide stripes for each section of color. I picked up a rich, happy pink to start and end the spectrum.

Evie pops in. "Can I go see the Dubs?"

"Not right now, kiddo. I need to work on your room. I can't go with you."

"So?" Her tone is curious, not rude, like she can't figure out what me being busy has to do with anything.

Well . . . is it that big of a deal to let her go a block in a perfectly safe neighborhood by herself?

"You're right. You can go. Let me text Nana Dub that you're coming, and she can text me when you get there. Deal?"

"Bye!" she calls, already halfway down the hall.

I'll eventually need to put Evie to work, but there's truly not much she can do right now. Everything is waiting for something else to be done first. She can't move into her room until it's painted. She can't unpack silverware because the drawers need to be lined. By next weekend, I'll have enough to keep her busy, and Evie loves to be busy.

Lisa texts less than ten minutes later to let me know Evie made it, and I go out back to fetch the pink paint I need. I should be able to get down one coat of each color today. Our tiny back stoop has just enough room for two people to stand on it, then four concrete steps leading down. The handrail is missing, something I need to fix sooner than later, but right now, it makes it a convenient workbench if I stand on the ground beside the stairs. It makes the stoop waist-high.

I give the can with the pink dob a few hearty shakes before prying off the lid to stir it more. I pull out the stir stick, satisfied. It'll take two coats, but it's the perfect shade.

"You should fix that handrail," a male voice says behind me.

I yelp and spin, ready to stab with my stir stick, only to find Mr. Brown standing there in khakis and a gray sweater with a pink spatter line of fresh paint across the chest.

The hazard of most yards not having fences around here is people can sneak up on you. And the hazard of sneaking up on someone is getting painted.

He stares down, his mouth falling open slightly before his wide eyes meet mine.

Despite my best efforts, a sinking sensation fills my stomach at the exact same moment a laugh bubbles out of me. "I'm so sor—" I try to say, but he cuts me off.

"It's not funny." He looks down at his pink stripe again like he can't quite figure out what just happened.

It's the worst thing he could have said. It's only going to make the laughter worse, which is only going to make him angrier, which will only make me laugh harder, no matter what I do. I try, knowing it will be futile.

"Sorry, you just" —the word wobbles on another laugh— "surprised me. It was an accident." This makes me laugh again, and I can't even blame him when he glares at me. "I really am s-s-s-sorry," I stutter around more laughter.

His mouth opens then closes once, twice, and then presses it into a tight line before he turns on his heel with military precision and marches back to his big fancy house.

I try to pull myself together, but it only makes me laugh harder. I have to run up the stairs and step inside to let it roll for almost a full minute before I can force myself to take deep, even breaths until it subsides.

I didn't want to be friends with Mr. Brown. I'm sick of uptight men, and I'm still annoyed he forced me into six extra months of mortgage payments and soaked up half my repair budget with his stupid counteroffer. But I definitely didn't mean to paint him—another snorting giggle escapes me—on our first day as neighbors. Or anytime, really.

But honestly, his sweater looked a little better. At least the color gave it some life.

I lean against the wall with a sigh, the sign that the laughter is finally draining from me. Sometime in the last few years, I've developed the bad habit of laughing at inappropriate times. And the more inappropriate it is, the harder it is to stop. It's getting to the point where I feel a slight dread before I start work each day that something bad will happen and set off a laughing jag at the expense of some poor customer. Or Evie's teacher. Or Lisa or Bill. Or *anyone*.

As far as Chino Dude, there's not much I can do now. I apologized. It is what it is.

I pick up the paint can and head back to Evie's room, climbing on the ladder to start the uppermost stripe. I finish the first section and need to climb down to move the ladder and start the next one, but when I reach the floor, my conscience pricks me. Does it count as an apology if I mean it, but I laugh through the whole thing?

I really did mean it.

Ugh. I'm going to have to go over there and apologize for real.

But *after* I finish this pink.

I'm nearing the end of the stripe, happy with how it's turning out, when a text comes in.

BILL: It's Bill.

That's how all of his texts start. None of us have been able to break him of it.

BILL: I will bring back Evie plus a surprise.

I smile. It doesn't matter what it is; it will be far too generous as usual, but I've learned to pay back these kindnesses in other ways.

I should go do my real apology now. I sigh and climb down, turning toward the front door, ready to be a mature adult.

But . . .

I have *two* pink stripes to paint. I might as well work on the second one and wait to see Bill's surprise before heading next door. Then I'll go.

Probably.

Chapter Seven

Henry

I'D SUSPECTED IT WAS not going to be great when the neighbor moved in. Paige, I think? Day One of her residency begins with clatter and color, and no sooner do her helpers drive away than her back stoop sprouts with a junk pile of paint cans.

It would be one thing if she'd planned to do some exterior work and bring the house up to par with all the others on Orchard. But apparently, she's more worried about the interior than she is with the eyesore everyone's had to live with. I've been trimming the bushes, at least, because when they run wild, the whole house looks like an even bigger tragedy. For a man whose career is studying the decline and fall of civilizations, that's saying something.

She's lived here all of one afternoon, and it's been entirely disrupted by her daughter's chatter in the front yard. The child talked to every passing dog and owner, the leaves, the tree, the . . .

I don't know. Everything. She talked to all the things until she blessedly disappeared.

With the intent of setting the boundary early, I'd gone over to ask—*politely*—how often she intended to make her stoop a workbench, seeing as Orchard Street backyards don't have fences, so all of her neighbors must look at her clutter too.

I hadn't even gotten to the polite ask yet before she painted me.

I stare down at my fourth favorite sweater, now ruined with a garish pink stripe. It's hideous. Nothing deserves to be painted that color.

I peel the sweater off, careful not to let the paint contaminate anything else, then drop it in the trash. I go upstairs and get one of my other gray sweaters, then settle myself in the living room for more grading. I generally prefer to grade in my office on campus, but while I share it with Leigh, this has proven difficult. Instead of concentrating, I find myself noticing her smell and losing my place constantly.

As a result, I'm stuck doing it here, and now even that's disruptive.

I glare through my side window, but it's still quiet, so I settle in to see what my paleopathology students have to say about ancient epidemiology. I work for about an hour before the rattle of a pickup truck pulling in next door distracts me.

It's the same pickup truck as before, the back full of more boxes and . . . I squint. What is that? Boards? But in shapes? Like those ridiculous pictures where you stick your face in a hole and suddenly you're a superhero or a mermaid or a strongman. The sides facing me aren't painted, so I have no idea what they actually are.

When the engine stops, my neighbor's father climbs out, her little girl darting around to join him, practically skipping in circles as they walk to the front door and let themselves in.

I feel a dull, distant pang in my chest. I used to be like that with Grandad Ellis before . . . well. It's been a long time. I'm surprised I can even remember holding his hand that way.

They disappear inside and it's quiet for a few minutes before the kid tumbles outside again on a stream of chatter, followed by her grandfather and my neighbor.

"This is ridiculous," I announce to my house. It doesn't answer, which is good, considering I'm the only one in it. I scoop up my work and head to the study in the back, the room farthest away from my noisy neighbors.

I sit and listen. I can still hear them.

I gather up everything once more and head through the kitchen and out to my car, settle my laptop bag on the front seat, and pull out, hitting the road with only an annoyed look at my neighbor, who doesn't notice. There has to be somewhere quieter to work in town. Not Bixby's. Too busy in there. The idea of returning to campus doesn't appeal to me, but the public library is open until 8:00 today, and that will have to do.

I settle into a carrel that's quiet enough.

And yet . . .

Forty-five minutes later, I'm still wondering how the chaos next door is going. Not out of curiosity, of course. Out of stress over whatever it's going to do to disturb the peace. *My* peace.

I force myself through the remainder of my grading but leave next week's lesson prep for tomorrow. I've been disciplined enough for one day. It's time to go home and unwind a bit, maybe with the new documentary on Standing Rock. I did my dissertation on the conflict between indigenous communities and energy companies in Ecuador, but I wouldn't mind a relaxing deep dive look at the domestic angles of the problem.

It's dark when I walk out to my car. The time changed a couple weeks ago, and I like it. Especially now, since it means my neighbors will have to quit their yard activities. If I close my curtains on that side of the house, maybe I'll forget for an evening that I have neighbors.

Unfortunately, it's not quite dark enough when I pull into my driveway to fully obliterate the horror show waiting for me in the yard of 341 Orchard. Where once only slightly objectionable unraked leaves covered the modest lawn, the streetlight shows it is now blanketed by the only thing that could bother me more than a neighbor with a noisy child: a neighbor whose unironic love of Christmas is now blanketing her yard.

I brake at the foot of my driveway hard enough to send my laptop sliding to the floor and stare at the wooden cutouts, still far too visible even in the dark. Large sheets of plywood painted with Christmas scenes lie on their sides everywhere.

There is no mistake. In this next circle of Dante's hell, my new neighbor, she of the blue eyes and lightly freckled nose, she of the well-fitting jeans and perky—

Er, the woman next door is a Christmas lunatic.

Chapter Eight

Paige

"BUT WHEN CAN WE put them up, Mama?" Evie asks, peering out at the massive decoration drop Bill did on our lawn. He stowed most of it in the shed out back, but his hand-painted plywood pieces wait for me on the grass because Evie begged for us to start decorating *now*.

"Tomorrow, Eves." I'd normally wait until after Thanksgiving next week, but since we've had to wait literally Evie's entire life to have our own Christmas yard display, tackling it a week early this year won't hurt anything.

She dances impatiently as I serve up the beef and barley stew Lisa sent over with disposable dinnerware in case I hadn't yet found my plates.

I love Lisa's thoughtfulness, but with few enough belongings to fit in a single pickup truck bed, it was easy to find my box of recently thrifted dishes. They're a pleasingly heavy set of imitation Fiestaware in shades of turquoise, papaya, lime, and lemon. I used three of my fall sweaters to cushion them, and I'm glad to have the sweaters back for my wardrobe rotation. Maybe not the brown one though. I have a sudden aversion to brown sweaters.

Maybe I should give my neighbor a list of colors I prefer he not wear so he doesn't ruin any more for me.

My neighbor! Oh, shoot. I didn't go give him my revised apology.

I sigh.

"What's wrong, Mama?"

"Nothing, bug. I accidentally got some paint on our neighbor's sweater, and I need to go over and apologize."

"I don't really like apologizing," she says. "My teachers always make me say sorry even when I'm not. Like every time Connor annoys me." Connor is her tablemate. I've already heard more stories than I can count. "He snapped my pencil in half, so I pushed his to the floor, and Mrs. Dyson said we *both* had to apologize."

I keep a neutral expression even though what I *want* to say is, "Good job, girl." Instead, I ask, "That didn't feel fair to you?"

Evie scoffs. "No. He got his pencil back like nothing was wrong with it, and I had to borrow one. I don't know why I had to say sorry."

"Sounds like Mrs. Dyson was trying to be fair."

"Then Dumbhead Connor should have to give me another pencil."

Agreed. "I'm sure Mrs. Dyson made the best decision she could."

Evie shrugs, then lets it go. "Do you want to apologize to the neighbor?"

"I do. And you've given me a good idea. I need to offer to replace the sweater I ruined."

"Okay. After apologies, can we put up the decorations?"

"It's too dark now. But it will be fun to plan tonight, and maybe tomorrow we can figure out where they go."

The decorations aren't my style. They're more country farmhouse and I lean more toward whimsical boho, but for the Dubs, Christmas is their defining holiday. The whole town knows about their Christmas display. They put out enough lights to guide in a 747 for a landing, and their street is always full of cars cruising past, admiring the sheer volume of the Winters family's efforts.

Bill was so excited to pass them all down to me today. "I've had the fun long enough. It's time to pass the torch," he'd said, patting the head of the cartoony Santa driving his reindeer. All eight of them. In a row. A long row. Not even side by side. It was a lot of plywood. And cartoon art. "You're the perfect person for the job. You're the keepers of Christmas now!"

This had sent Evie into raptures of joy, so I'd given Bill my warmest smile and sincere thanks. It's a huge sign of his trust that he would pass this to me, and I get why he's doing it; after my work on the store windows over the last three years, he thinks I'm the woman for the big Christmas house job too. I don't want to disappoint him, so I guess I'll just have to make him proud.

Evie, content that we'll tackle Christmas soon enough, has started in on her soup. Our table is one the sellers left behind, small and round with sides that fold down to make a smaller square. It's not antique but it's made of good oak, and it's a prime candidate for refinishing, maybe something in soft green with an antiqued look.

I'll have to think about how to do that. There will be many, many YouTube tutorials in my future. This makes me happy. Breathing life into things is my jam.

"Done. Let's go apologize to the man, Mama." Evie tips her bowl my way to prove she's eaten everything, even the veggies. We've never been great at eating them, but Lisa always serves them, and we're slowly coming around. Or trying to.

"All right," I say. "But my mom always taught me that you never visit a neighbor empty-handed, and I'm sure that's double-true for apologies. How about we share our stew?" Teaching Evie about the grandparents she'll never meet is always bittersweet. I never know what's sticking and what isn't, but I hope she tucks some of these stories away so they'll become a part of her too.

I reseal the plastic soup container and scoop it up. "Let's go, kiddo."

We take the short walk next door. There are a few lights on, so Mr. Brown must be home. We climb the stairs, and I knock. Several seconds pass without a response, and this time I try the actual door knocker, a cast iron bird that I feel sort of bad about lifting and dropping. It's too charming to have been installed by Mr. Brown, so it must be left from his grandparents. I really do need to get his story from Lily Greene.

We hear distant footsteps descend, then cross the floor. I've rehearsed this apology a few times to make sure I can do it without laughing, although that shouldn't be a problem as long as he's changed out of the paint-damaged sweater.

When the door opens, I smile and say, "Hi, Mr. Brow—" Oh. No. He hasn't been polite enough to give me his name. Didn't Lisa call it the Ellis house once? I pivot quickly. "Um, Mr. Ellis. I'm sorry again about ruining your sweater. I hope you'll accept some beef and barley soup as an apology. I'll be sure to replace your sweater too." I should be able to find about five billion of them next time we go thrifting.

Then I stare. Is he wearing the *same* gray sweater? "Wait, were you able to get the paint out? You'll have to tell me your trick."

He stares down at his sweater and shifts from one foot to the other. "It's not the same sweater."

I don't know which one of us should be embarrassed by this. *Him*, I decide.

"Right. Well, I'll replace the other one if you'll give me your size." Probably a large. He's about six feet tall and thin but with broad-ish shoulders.

"It's okay." He looks uncomfortable. "I have more."

I wonder how many. Three? Five? A dozen? "That's nice of you to let me off the hook." Literally the only nice thing he's done, but okay, credit where credit is due. "Anyway, here's the soup, Mr. El—"

"Henry."

"Mr. Henry. I hope you enjoy it."

"No, I mean my first name is Henry. Not Mr. Henry."

"Oh, sorry. Enjoy your soup, Henry." I hand it to him, and he takes it, but then looks confused as to why he's holding a container of stew.

I turn to leave but he stops us with a question. "May I ask what the project on your lawn is about?"

"Christmas!" Evie whirls and announces. "Isn't it so awesome? The Dubs gave it to us, and we're going to have the best Christmas house in the whole town!"

His eyebrows draw together, and he looks from her to me. "You might want to wait until you see some of the other displays go up so you can calibrate yours to match. Orchard has a refined sensibility."

Hold up. This dude is calling me tacky.

I do not say the following words, but I think them very loudly: *Son, I'm talented enough to do the Manhattan Bloomingdale's windows and they'd be lucky to have me.*

I give him a noncommittal "Mmm, good thoughts." I take Evie's hand and skim down the stairs, stopping at the bottom like it's an afterthought. "I was going to wait until December, but given how crazy the actual holidays are for me at work, I think we'll start our decorating tomorrow. Have a good night."

He opens and closes his mouth soundlessly—Henry the Trout making a flustered reappearance.

We walk home with Evie oblivious to the fact that we have the most stuck-up neighbor in Creekville, and me satisfied that I shut him up.

Chapter Nine

Henry

I GET UP AROUND eight—a decent sleep-in for a weekend—and treat myself to an omelet with cremini mushrooms and caramelized onions. The time I allow for caramelizing is probably the most decadent part of the breakfast. I absent-mindedly push them around the skillet as I contemplate the problem of the new neighbor. What atrocity can I expect as they set about their decorating?

My shoulders tense. There will doubtless be more kid yelling and probably some hammering. I shudder. I can't do it. I can't spend all day listening to them crash around their yard.

It's been a while since I visited my parents. Today feels like a good day for a trip to Richmond. My grading is caught up, and I can think through my lecture notes while I drive. I'll text my parents that I'm coming, get in a morning run, take a shower, and then hit the road and leave the girls next door to their noise.

Two hours later, I've logged several more miles on my running shoes, and the neighbors still aren't out and about yet when I get back to my house. At least, they're not in the yard. I frown. I don't know much about raising kids, but the child doesn't seem old enough to be sleeping in this late.

Whatever. It's not my problem, and I'm getting out of here before they get to work outside on the painted Christmas cutouts. They're cornier in the daylight than I had even imagined. A grinning cartoon Santa Claus. And his reindeer. They're not cute in the best of times, but to have all of them in one loooooong row? The plaid bows painted on their harnesses make it worse, somehow. Menacing in a way that I can't explain. The white dots in their irises come off as demented instead of sparkling.

I shower quickly and choose a pair of khakis and a striped Oxford shirt my mom will like, and I'm in the car and on my way before I have to deal with the neighbors.

The two-hour drive to Richmond proves sufficient for planning my lectures. When I arrive at my parents' place, my dad orders me to join him for golf. Having expected this, I change into my golf shoes and fetch my clubs from their garage. This is a pastime only he and I share, not one I do with others, so it only makes sense to leave my clubs here.

We return home after eighteen holes, both in good spirits, my dad because he won, and me because I won't have to listen to him vent about losing. It's always worth fudging my numbers so he comes out with a better score. It means we both walk into the house smiling, and my mom returns it. She and my dad set to work preparing dinner. Even though I know what she'll say, I try to help.

"Sit, Henry," she says, shooing me toward a kitchen chair. "How are things going at Jefferson?"

It's a familiar routine. We'll talk about my classes. My dad will offer some advice on teaching from his years of experience as an economics professor, and my mom will eventually work her way around to asking me how the house is. I'll try to brace for the question but be deeply uncomfortable anyway when she asks.

I will wish that I could tell her honestly that I enjoy it, but I don't; I'm an interloper. That feeling won't change. So I'll lie, and she'll accept it because it's the answer she wants, and none of us will talk about why the house went to me or why I never wanted it.

I hope that part of the conversation comes sooner than later. It's always a relief when it's out of the way and we can move on to more pleasant topics, like politics and international wars.

We cap off the evening with the new Ken Burns documentary, and when it ends, I stand and stretch. "Thank you for dinner and the entertainment. I'd better head back."

"Very well, son," my dad says as he always does. "Good visit."

I hug each of them and head out to my car.

The drive home passes quickly as I listen to AnthroPod, a cultural anthropology podcast. It's about two hours and nine minutes from my parents' house to mine, and two hours, eight minutes, and thirty seconds of them are pleasant—right until I turn into my driveway and stop, staring at the neighbors' house in horror.

Flabbergasted horror.

Stunned, flabbergasted horror.

You would think that any change to the house could only be an improvement.

You would be wrong. So very wrong.

Before, the house was only an eyesore during the day. At night, one could assume it was as tidy and well-kept as all the other houses on Orchard.

But now . . . now it is lit up like the Las Vegas Strip, a place I've had the good fortune to never see in person, until my new neighbor decided to spend a Saturday recreating it on her front lawn.

The cutouts—while garish—had at least previously lain flat. Now they're upright with floodlights staked in front of each one to make sure no one can miss their cartoon brightness. The menacing reindeer, red-cheeked Santa, bright presents spilling from his bag in colors that I feel sure never existed before this painting, more panels with elves in aggressively colored outfits and striped stockings . . . and there's more.

More panels with more illustrations than my mind can process. More lights shining on them. More Christmas lights, period. They wind around her front posts, illuminating her windows and ramshackle shutters—or lack of them. They march along her front eaves to puddle in a senseless pile where they ran out of house to hang on.

There's strong evidence that the kid did some if not all of the decorating. Lights hang on the painted cutouts with no rhyme or reason, here wrapped around grinning Santa's neck as if he enjoys strangulation, there wrapped round and round a snowman with no regard for the laws of science and nature—he would melt, damn it. The lights would *melt* him.

It's beyond garish. It's a travesty.

And it's all far too early. There's almost two weeks to go until Thanksgiving, and even then, people of refined taste don't begin the Christmas season before the start of December.

I'm half-tempted to march up to her disgraceful porch and tell her all this myself, but I remember the slight narrowing of her eyes as she'd delivered her—admittedly tasty—soup last night, and I'd mentioned waiting to calibrate her display.

If this horror show is a reaction to my hint, how would she react to an outright criticism? My car would no doubt sport a new coat of bright pink paint come morning. The woman might be unhinged.

I run an eye over the vomitous display. "Might be" is generous. She's as unhinged as her shutters.

A civil conversation is out of the question, obviously. It's all well and good for her to offer an apology and soup, but if the tiniest suggestions upset her apple cart, it's better to take a different tack. There's not a beef and barley stew on earth good enough to put up with these current crimes against taste.

I pull around to my carport, already smiling. I know exactly what to do.

A half hour later, I snap my laptop shut in triumph. It took some clever searching through indescribably boring city ordinances, but I've found what I need, and I'll be able to shut down the chaos next door with a single phone call on Monday morning.

Now I can work a crossword in peace. Only, that doesn't feel celebratory enough for having found the solution to my headache. It's a night to indulge. This calls for a film. Perhaps even a scripted one instead of a documentary. I enjoy my vegetables, but it's healthy to treat oneself now and then, and Leigh had mentioned an independent film she'd enjoyed recently. Watching it might give us something to talk about.

It feels positively luxurious to turn on the television and open Netflix. I find the title and cue it up but pause before it plays. I'll take this one step further and enjoy some snacks while I watch. In the kitchen, I take out a box of cracked pepper crackers and a wedge of brie I'd been saving for when I finished grading midterms.

Racket from next door leaks through the windows as I arrange my mini charcuterie. I can't make out exactly what's happening through the reflection on my glass, but it's clear enough that the neighbor—Paige?—and the child are running around outside in the dark. Paige seemed to pride herself on her parenting, but I don't think this does her any credit. It's almost seven o'clock. Surely the girl should be asleep already?

I resolve to ignore them. "You do not get to intrude on my party," I say. But I don't have the interest or ability to pitch my voice to penetrate glass like the girl's does.

I settle on the sofa. I'll simply turn up the volume if they don't settle down next door. With a sigh of contentment, I pick up the remote, press "play," and plunge the house into immediate darkness.

Chapter Ten

Paige

Uh oh. Every light in our house and Scrooge's has winked out. House lights. Christmas lights. All of them, inside and out.

He's going to be so mad. Big mad. The kind of mad that beef and barley soup won't fix.

"Evie?" I call. "Did you plug in the lights on the side?"

"No," she calls, but it comes from that side of the house, and it's not very convincing.

I walk around to find her standing there, a dark shape staring at the ground with her hands behind her back.

I crouch in front of her, the extension cord from our Santa face leading to Henry's plug, stretched taut about eight inches above the ground all the way across his driveway, waiting to trip her up like the lie she's telling me. "You want to try that again, honey?"

We'd spent most of the afternoon creating a Santa face out of strings of bulbs—white for his beard, red for his hat—on the side of our house—the side that will stare straight into Henry's—but I'd need to figure out where to plug them before we could light them.

Evie had pointed to an external socket on Henry's house. I'd promptly ruled it out and promised to do some magic with extension cords tomorrow.

Now Evie sniffs. "I'm sorry, Mama. I wanted Santa to light up. I didn't know it would break everything."

A tear trembles on her eyelashes. I stifle a sigh. There will be time to talk to her tomorrow about why "I didn't know" isn't an excuse when an adult asks you not to do something. Right now, she's probably terrified she's ruined our house for good.

"I know, baby." I gather her into a hug just as I hear Henry's front door slam. I squeeze my eyes shut and draw a deep breath so I can deal with him. "It's okay. I can fix it."

"What is going on out here?" he demands, storming over. The effect is ruined by the fact that he's in socks.

"I'm sorry," Evie says, the tinge of a wail creeping into her voice.

Better head this off right now. I stand and face him, keeping her hand in mine. "We blew a fuse."

He crosses his arms, and though I can't see his face well, I'm sure he's glaring. Every time I see him, he's either glaring or looking like he's about to glare. Or more to the point, every time he sees us.

"This is unacceptable. Noise all day. Rampant commercialism on the lawn. And now you've caused a blackout."

Rampant commercialism? What the . . . ? I could have—and would have—been nice and sincerely apologetic—again—until that phrase came out of his mouth.

"Since when is an unsponsored holiday display commercialism? You act like we're in late-stage capitalism. It's just reindeer and Santa. Settle down." I say the last part to make sure he *doesn't* settle down. It works. His chest puffs up. It's broader than I realized.

"You. Caused. A. Blackout."

"No, dude. I blew a fuse. I can fix it."

"It was me!" Evie says, the truth bursting out of her. "Don't yell at my mom. I'm sorry!"

She shakes beside me, and it's a punch in the gut to realize that she thinks she's gotten me in trouble, and worse, that she senses a threat from Henry.

As if he realizes this too, he drops his arms and takes a quick step back, but I can't deal with him right now. I draw her against me. "It's okay, Evie. I really can fix it. And you can help me. Would that make you feel better?" She nods, her head pressed against my chest. "I like that you want to fix your mistakes. It makes me proud of you. Now, why don't you go unplug the cord from Mr. Henry's house to start?"

She sniffs, gives me a tight squeeze, then slips around me on the side opposite from Henry and scurries over to unplug the lights. Nothing happens, of course. I'll have to flip the breakers.

I turn to stare at Henry, hoping he can see the fury in my eyes even in the dark.

"I wasn't yelling," he says, sounding defensive.

"Evie has spent most of her time around my brother and her grandfather. They're both patient men." Just let him say one word about them needing to be stricter. *Try me, Scrooge.*

He clears his throat. "I didn't mean to scare her."

"Then what were you trying to do? Scare me?"

He shakes his head. "No, I—"

"Forget it," I say. "Bottom line is that we blew your fuses. Your breaker box is probably in your utility room. I need to check it. Do you mind?"

"No."

I start toward the back of his house. "Evie, go sit on the back steps and wait for me. I'll get our lights on in a minute."

"Actually," he calls, "could you show me how to do it? I probably need to know. I've never had to do it before." I pause, and he clears his throat. "And Evie, I'm sorry I scared you. I'm grouchy sometimes, but I'm not mean."

There's a long silence. "Okay," she says cautiously.

"Do you know how to do this?" he asks. "This breaker your mom is talking about?"

She shakes her head and says a soft, "No."

"I promise not to be scary if you want to come learn how to do it too."

He sounds awkward, like he's not used to talking to kids, but he's said exactly the right thing—if I were in a forgiving mood.

I hold out my hand to Evie. "What do you think, kiddo? Would you like to learn? I can show you on ours after I fix Mr. Henry's."

She walks over and takes my hand, nodding. I lead her to our back stoop and give her my phone, turning on the flashlight. "Will you be okay waiting here for me? It'll be less than five minutes and you'll be able to hear me the whole time."

She hesitates. Henry has followed us up the driveway, staying on his property as I settle Evie down.

"Go ahead and show her how to do yours first. I can wait." His voice is quiet.

Evie's eyes widen a tiny bit; this is definitely her preferred course of action. I give Henry half a brownie point for the offer. "Sounds good," I say. "Why don't you see if your breaker box is in the utility room? It'll be in the wall and look kind of like a switchboard."

He doesn't answer but I hear his footsteps move farther up his driveway.

I let Evie guide us into the house with my phone light then show her the breaker box against the wall of the small hall closet where the washer and dryer will go someday. We'll be doing laundry at the Dubs for a long time unless something amazing comes up for sale on Craigslist.

"See how some of these switches are flipped one way and some are flipped the other? They should all be that way, which means they're on." I flip one to show her. "You want to try?"

She nods and flips the rest, smiling as lights come on behind us and down the hall.

"Good job, Ev. Now why don't you put your pajamas on while I help Mr. Henry, then we'll watch a movie when I come back?"

"Okay, Mama." She whirls in the direction of her bedroom. "Sorry again that I broke everything."

"It's okay. We can talk tomorrow about what you learned from this, but for tonight, we'll fix the problem and then relax. Deal?"

"Deal!"

"I'll be back in a couple of minutes."

Henry is waiting for me near the door to his utility room attached to his carport and gestures me in ahead of him. As soon as I step in, something warm and dark streaks past me, and I jump back with a strangled cry.

"Sorry," he says. "That's Cat. He must have been hanging out in here."

"You have a cat named *Cat*? I would have pegged you for a literary reference. A Tolstoy or at least a moody Poe."

"I'm more into the Greeks," he says.

I shine my light on him, hoping there's enough for him to see my irritation. "Fine. Euripides."

His eyes widen.

"What?" I snap. "You're surprised I know my Greek dramatists? Your cat made a dramatic exit, didn't he?" We'd done a whole unit on the origins of theater in drama my senior year. I remember stuff like that.

"No, not surprised." But he sounds faintly guilty.

I let it go and shine the light into the utility room, spotting the breaker box. I tug the cover open and give him the same short lesson I gave Evie. I peer out his door to his house as he flips them, nodding when the kitchen light comes on.

"Looks like that worked." I'm about to add an apology for tripping the circuit in the first place, but he speaks first.

"Thanks for helping."

"No problem."

"For what it's worth, I do think your yard has reached levels that won't please the neighbors."

Is he for real? He says it like he's doing me a favor. "I'll take that under advisement."

"You're welcome. I can walk you back to your place. Not much moon tonight, so a second light will help."

"Actually, I'm not going in yet," I say, making a sudden decision. Instead, I cross his yard diagonally to reach the Santa face.

"What are you doing?" he asks from beneath the protection of his carport.

"I suddenly want this done tonight." I know he takes my meaning. Every time he looks out of his side windows from now until New Year's, he's going to see a Santa made out of lights.

There's a long silence as I scoop up one of the unused light strands and pretend to check its placement in our display.

Then barely loud enough for me to be sure I heard him, he mutters, "Bah, humbug," and disappears into his house.

I almost feel bad about my antics when I wake up on Monday. Henry's judgy "won't please the neighbors" had gotten so far underneath my skin that I'd let Evie do whatever she liked decoration-wise in the yard while I'd finished painting her room yesterday.

I probably would feel bad if Evie hadn't declared it the "best day ever" as she joyfully looped even more strings of lights around everything she could reach.

But she had, and since we'd never been able to do Christmas up big as renters, I wasn't about to shut her down. I have a full week of work and won't be home to do more lights before dark, but I can do lights around the window interiors after work. We have bins and bins of them from Bill, and since their house is two thousand square feet bigger than ours, chances are good I won't be able to use them all. I'm definitely going to try though.

I climb out of bed, smiling as I go to wake Evie and get her ready for school. No, I definitely don't feel bad. The huge grin on her face when we flipped on the lights—working correctly this time—had been totally worth it.

She chatters about the next phase of her decorating plans on the short walk to school, and as I walk to work, I figure out how to subtly revise her chaotic aesthetic and bring some cohesion to the Christmas explosion in our yard.

Our yard. Man, that feels good to say.

Mondays tend to be slow in the store since most people tackle their projects over the weekend. I spend a couple hours reconciling the books and taking care of the two customers we get. By midmorning, I'm wondering what busywork project to tackle next when the bell over the door chimes to announce Lily Greene.

She's always a delight, but I'm happier than usual to see her. I have questions.

"Good morning, Miss Lily. What brings you in today?"

She smiles at me, her lined skin a healthy peach color that belies her eighty-plus years. I make a mental note to invest in a sun hat. "I need plant food. Two of my fiddle-leaf figs aren't thriving like they should. Their sun is good, so I'll try some vitamins next."

"Sounds good," I say, leading her toward the gardening section. It's only a courtesy since Miss Lily no doubt knows the store better than I do. She's done business here as long as Bill has owned it, according to him. "How's the family?"

Miss Lily and her husband have lived in Creekville for twice as long as I've been alive. He retired as dean of the law school in Charlottesville before his death, and Miss Lily worked right here in Creekville as a high school English teacher after her kids were grown. They left and raised their kids in more metropolitan areas, but two of her grandkids have settled in Creekville in the last couple years after marrying locals. Her oldest grandson married a local too, but they're on assignment with his FBI job.

"Everyone's healthy and happy," she says. "Izzy will be in sooner than later to get weatherproofing supplies for the goat huts, so keep an eye out for her. How's life for you, dear?"

I have to step carefully here. Miss Lily's questions aren't always what they appear to be on the surface. She had more than a small hand in encouraging all of her grandkids' marriages, and she's been content since the last one, Landon's, fell into place. I wonder what she'll do now without more grandkids to marry off. I have a bad feeling some of the unattached young people of Creekville may be in her crosshairs soon.

Best to let her know I'm too busy for matchmaking.

"Did you hear I got the house? Started moving in this weekend." I'd mentioned on her last visit that I'd made an offer.

"Well, congratulations, honey. Isn't that something? You're a homeowner." She beams, and I can feel her genuine delight. "What kind of shape is it in?"

"It's rough," I admit. "But it's more cosmetic than structural. It'll take time and pinched pennies, but I'll be able to shine it up."

"If anyone can, it's you. I haven't been able to stump you with a repair question in over a year."

I grin and tap the side of my head. "If I learn it once, it sticks."

"You're fortunate," Miss Lily says. "I know too many people who keep learning the same things over and over again."

I pull a bag of Happy Frog from the shelf. "This is a new fertilizer we're carrying. It's organic, and it works amazingly well. It *can* be smelly for a couple of days, but it shouldn't be a problem if you aerate the soil."

"That's different than my usual brand." Her glasses hang from a chain around her neck, and she places them on her nose to study the label. "Does it matter if it's organic if it's a decorative plant?"

"Great question. To me it matters how these products are manufactured, and this is more earth-friendly."

She smiles. "I do like the earth. I'll take it."

I carry it to the register for her. "We're seeing a growing interest in organic products, which is great."

Her eyes assess me, her expression thoughtful. "Would this expansion into organic lines coincide with your hiring date?"

"Close. I realized in one of my business classes that we probably had an untapped market for this kind of thing, so Bill let me test new product sales for a class project, and it worked out well." I love that it's also a positive change I can make. It's not my job to save the whole environment, but I can work on it garden by garden in Creekville.

"You're a sharp one, Paige Redmond. Bill did well to hire you."

I know her compliment brings a visible glow to my cheeks, and I don't care. It's always nice to be appreciated.

"How is Evie settling in at the house?"

"She loves it. Went crazy decorating it yesterday for Christmas."

Miss Lily laughs. "I believe it. That girl is a firecracker. Has she made friends with everyone on the street already?"

"There's barely been time for that, and to tell the truth, there aren't many kids on Orchard."

"That certainly didn't stop her from wrapping me around her little finger," Miss Lily says.

"True. She'll make sure we meet all the neighbors soon, no doubt. Speaking of which . . ." I try to drop in the segue in an off-hand way, but her eyes sharpen.

"Yes?"

"Do you know much about the house next to mine?"

"The big white one? That's the Ellis house," she says when I nod. "I believe George Ellis left it to his only grandson when he passed three years ago, but the grandson only moved in this past January. Henry. That's his name."

"Can confirm," I say, bagging her plant food in the canvas tote she'd brought with her. "Do you know much about him? And before you get any ideas, he's too old for me, and even if he weren't, I'm asking because he hated me on sight, and I'm wondering if you might know why."

"That's unfortunate," she says. "I can't imagine a man with functioning eyeballs hating you on sight."

"Miss Lily, you charmer."

"Just a truthteller." She winks before growing slightly more serious. "I don't know much about Henry. I know George and his wife, Marley, went to visit their daughter, Henry's mother, up in Richmond when he was young. They were there over Christmas, and, well . . ." She sighs. "Marley passed pretty suddenly. I was never clear on what happened, but I got the feeling it was an aneurysm. We had the services here. That would have been at least twenty-five years ago. The daughter, Marie, would come to visit once a year or so, but always by herself."

I frowned. Interesting.

"Anyway, Henry teaches at Jefferson. Anthropology, I believe. He keeps to himself. I ran into him at the market not so long ago, and he was kind. Sorry to hear you're having a rough go with him."

"It's not your fault. I'll figure it out."

"I assume you've already spoken with him?"

"Yes, ma'am, but I make him angry even when I'm apologizing."

"Are you apologizing to keep the peace or because you actually did something worth apologizing over?"

I give her a tight smile. "A little of both. I accidentally painted him."

She winces. "Ah. I can't see a man like Henry taking that well."

"He didn't," I confirm. "But he was mad from the moment he saw me on the sidewalk looking at the house last month, so maybe he's just wired grumpy."

Miss Lily collects her purchase and pats my hand. "Christmas is coming. I've yet to mark one where a miracle hasn't occurred. Between the holiday, your pretty face, and darling Evie, Henry doesn't stand a chance."

I laugh and wave as she leaves the store, but my smile fades as I consider her info. I got barely anything new from Miss Lily, and if she knows that little, it means there isn't much to know.

Still, the man didn't appear on the planet fully spawned from nothing. There has to be more to him, but I can't even do a social media search on him because I don't know his last name. Ellis was his mother's maiden name.

I puzzle over this through the afternoon, and when our part-timer, Gary, comes in to close, I make quick work of getting him set up for his shift. Then I call Lisa to see if she can get Evie from afterschool care because I'll be about twenty minutes late getting home.

The library beckons. We don't have internet at the house yet, and my data is nearly maxed for the month, so I'll make use of the public computers. And if I happen to stumble across the New Release shelf and end up bringing home an armful of books that I definitely have no time to read but will read anyway, OH WELL. Life is full of risks.

Maggie, my favorite librarian, waves at me from the circulation desk. She isn't that much older than me—maybe thirty? We've developed a friendship of sorts over the last two years because it makes sense to stay on the good side of the dealer for my and Evie's reading addiction.

"We got a book on seahorses, so I set it aside for Evie," Maggie says. "I can hold it until Wednesday."

"She'll love that," I answer. "I'll bring her in tomorrow to check it out."

I could bring it home, but using the library's self-checkout station is one of Evie's great joys in life. She'd been nearly euphoric when we'd gone to Walmart in Roanoke and she discovered the self-checkout lane there.

The branch has two computers open, so I settle down and log in. Then I go straight to the site I'd learned to use exhaustively when I was in school: Rate the Prof. I'd avoided a couple of professors with bad reputations that way, and I'm hoping Henry has made enough of an impression on his students to show up in this database.

I narrow the search to Jefferson University and type "Henry" into the search bar and frown. I should have asked Miss Lily for his last name. It returns two options, and thanks to one of Miss Lily's nuggets, I know I'm not looking for Henry Westland, professor of composition, but the other Henry listed, Henry Hill, professor of anthropology.

Henry Hill? Seriously? He sounds like a character in one of Evie's old picture books. I smirk as I imagine the story. *Henry Hill is such a pill to all the folks on Orchard.*

Oh, that has a nice bounce to it. *To live beside this Grinchy Scrooge is nothing short of torture.*

His students, it seems, would disagree. He only has a half-dozen ratings on the Professor Grades website, not surprising for less than two semesters at the school. But they all speak well of him. I read through them, noticing a couple of patterns. "Strict but crazy-smart. Funny sometimes." "High standards but great lectures. Stealth sense of humor."

Almost every review contains some version of this. I mull that for a moment or two, and I'm about to do more digging when I catch sight of the time on the screen. If I'm going to accidentally check out a stack of books, I'd better do it now to get home before Evie gets antsy.

Ten minutes later, I'm on my way with a heavy grocery bag of books because it's easy to choose ten that fast if you judge them by their covers. I'll do more investigating tomorrow when I bring Evie back with me. She can search out the next *Warrior Cats* series, and I'll check out Henry Hill the Pill's bio on the Jefferson website.

Although . . . if his students are to be believed, he may not be such a pill after all. It's possible that a wry, funny man is hiding beneath his grouchy exterior, and as I stop by the Dubs' to fetch Evie, I resolve to look for the good in him.

Or at least to be more patient. As Evie and I walk the block to our house, I decide patience is something I can offer. If listening to the non-stop chatter of a seven-year-old after a long day at work doesn't teach patience, I don't know what could.

I turn into our walkway, a feeling of peace nestling inside me as I glance over at Henry Hill's house. Now with proof that at least some people who know him haven't hated the experience, I choose to believe this will work out.

The belief—and calm—lasts exactly the twenty seconds it takes Evie and me to reach the front door, where I find a paper in a "you're in trouble" shade of yellow stuck to the door.

"Code Violation," Evie reads aloud.

I snatch the citation and read it. *Infraction: Neighbor complaint for Christmas decorations prior to Thanksgiving pursuant to City Code Article XIII Section A. Action taken: Written warning.*

I need exactly one guess to figure out which neighbor has a Scroogey enough heart to call us in.

That's it. Hill the Pill is going to pay.

Chapter Eleven

Henry

POUND. POUND. POUND.

Someone is taking out unrepressed rage on the door knocker. I'm fairly sure I know who is abusing the poor wren. Guess the city came out already.

The question is whether I want to deal with my neighbor tonight. In literally every interaction we've had so far, she's required some sort of handling. Surely there's a point at which I'm no longer obliged to be the handler?

Pound pound pound.

That forces the issue if I want any more peace and quiet tonight. I walk from the kitchen where I'm preparing a rather delicious-smelling pho and open the door.

"What is this?" She brandishes a yellow piece of paper at me.

"I give up. What is it?"

Her scowl deepens. She reminds me of a gargoyle on the cathedral in Orvieto. "A citation from the city indicating a neighbor complaint about my Christmas decorations. It's a warning to take them down until after Thanksgiving."

"Very efficient for a municipal government." Good for them. I'd made a big enough fuss when I called to make sure they took my complaint seriously. It's good to see it worked.

"What is your problem, *Henry*?" she demands. She punctuates this with a tiny fleck of spittle on the "P" and by making my name sound like a curse. "I know this was you. Don't try to deny it."

"I won't. The city code is clear." *If you dug around into the deepest links on the city's website.* "Christmas decorations are not to go up until after

Thanksgiving and should be removed before the second week of January. Sensible law, *Paige*."

"A city ordinance is hardly a law."

It surprises me that she knows this. Perhaps she breaks so many that she's clear on the distinctions between ordinance violations, misdemeanors, and felonies. "And yet it carries consequences for breaking it."

"Mama?"

Not until I hear her daughter's voice calling from their yard do I realize that she's not with her mother.

"Just a minute, honey." She's sweetened her voice, but her face says it's a strain. "Everything's fine. Why don't you go in and pick a book for us?"

"Okay," the girl's voice calls back, but she sounds unconvinced that things are fine.

Paige waits until her daughter retreats into the house, and then I have all of her unwanted and undivided attention again. She shakes the paper at me. "This is a warning, not a fine. It says I have seventy-two hours to address this before further action may be taken. I want to reassure you that I'll be taking action, all right. You've poked the bear, and that's a bad idea when you're its neighbor."

She storms off my porch, whirling when she reaches the ground. "I'm sure you already have a list of traits you dislike about me, but let me tip you off on the very worst one: I match energy, and when I don't like yours—which I do *not*—I double down." She waves the paper one more time. "Congrats on doing a very dumb thing. It's about to get aggressively jolly around here."

And then she's gone, disappearing into the shadows of her as-yet-unlit front porch. I hope it's on her obnoxiously long list of things she needs to fix to make that place respectable.

What a . . . well, I know from one of Leigh's recent rants in our office that I shouldn't call Paige "psycho" simply because we disagree. Leigh says it's anti-feminist and minimizes women by stoking the narrative that they're illogical, overly emotional creatures. I'm not anti-feminist. I'm just anti-Paige.

What a . . . weirdo.

I don't have my first class until 10:00 on Tuesdays, so I don't leave the house until 9:00. When I walk out to my car, I spot a torn piece of paper tucked into the windshield wiper.

Great. A note from Paige, I'm sure. And not even a passive-aggressive one. Just an aggressive-aggressive one. Perfect way to start a Tuesday.

But when I pluck the paper out and turn it over, I find childish-looking handwriting stating, "Check your porch." This has to be from the kid. If the handwriting hadn't given her away, the pink snowmen she's doodled in two of the corners would have.

I double back through the house and open the front door to find a crinkly, flat-ish foil blob on the doorstep. When I pick it up, the foil has the sweaty feel of something that was warm and gradually left to cool. Inside, I find a...

I squint at it, not quite sure what I'm seeing. Is that dough? I retreat to the kitchen and set the foil on the counter, straightening it a bit. Then it begins to coalesce. Er, somewhat.

I'm staring at a cold snowman pancake. I think? I definitely won't be tasting it to verify, but it has three round connected parts, large on one end, smaller at the other, and the smaller one looks like someone attempted to give the snowman a hat. I smell it, and it has a distinct trace of fried flour like good pancakes do.

Is this a peace offering or a trap? What am I to make of a mangled snowman deposited in foil at my front door? And furthermore, how am I meant to respond?

Unsure of anything except that I'm not eating a cold, crumpled pancake for breakfast, I refold the foil and drop it in the trash can.

The question preoccupies me all day, as I try to decode the mystery of its appearance. I know *who* it came from—I just can't decide *why* the little girl would give it to me. And I wonder if her mother knows she left it?

"You're quieter than usual today," Leigh notes in the early afternoon.

I blink at her, trying to switch gears from thinking through what kind of odorless household poisons the neighbor kid would have access to. "Pardon me, what was that?"

Leigh smiles. "You're quieter than usual, which is saying something because you're pretty quiet."

It's my curse around attractive women. It's a small subset of humans in general who find anthropology as interesting as I do, and even a smaller subset of them who are women my age who would be interested in dating me. It's a non-zero number but only barely.

I've never been particularly good at talking to them, and in fact, both of my serious romantic relationships began with the woman pursuing me for reasons I fail to understand even now. I was tongue-tied then, and I'm tongue-tied now.

"Am I?" This is my very smooth answer to her "quiet" observation.

"Very," she says. "Especially today. Everything okay?"

"Yes, fine." Belatedly, I realize I should probably smile as I say this, so I do. Now it's Leigh's turn to offer a surprised blink before she nods and turns back to her laptop.

Magic with the ladies. That's me.

I suppress a sigh and focus on my own computer, channeling all my attention into finding the right illustrations for my lecture on osteology tomorrow.

The rest of the afternoon passes uneventfully. They always do—or used to until I spotted Paige scoping out the shack next door a month ago. But as I drive home, the mystery of the pancake is still dogging me. I could go ask, I suppose, but I doubt they're home yet. Their house doesn't stir to life until around dinner time. Paige doesn't seem to drive, so the only indicator I have so far is lights in their windows blinking to life around 6:30 at night.

I've caught up with my grading, and my lessons for tomorrow are ready, so I decide to spend a couple of hours with Dr. Chu's latest, a controversial treatise on genome mapping and its interface with healthcare that sounds somewhat interesting.

That's exactly what I do for close to two hours, when my stomach begins to rumble around the same time that a knock sounds at my front door. I open it a moment later to find nothing but a shoebox, a note taped to the top.

Another delivery from next door, probably from the girl. I suspect the only thing I'm likely to get from her mom anytime soon is a ding-dong-ditch and a flaming sack of dog feces.

I bring the box inside and set it on the kitchen counter. It's light, and something slides around inside. I nudge the lid off with the end of a wooden spoon to make myself a harder target if anything jumps out.

Nothing happens.

I approach cautiously, but when I look inside, all I find is an ornament, a seahorse with a Santa hat, made in China. The handwritten-in-kid-print note reads, "Sorry you don't like Christmas. I hope this helps. It's my favorite ornament because seahorses are cool."

Well, damn.

I have been recast from an order-craving neighbor to a grinch. There's no question about it.

I slump against the counter and stare at the Santa-hatted seahorse. It's not the first time I've been a grinch. Christmas has been hard since I was six and we lost my grandmother because of my own stupidity. It's a hard thing to carry at any age, but that young? During Christmas? It's never been the same since.

I haven't been the same since.

The seahorse glitters at me from tiny rhinestone eyes, a reproach as clear as if it could speak.

My problems are with the holiday. Not the lights. Not even the tacky plywood cutouts. And definitely not with the gift-leaving girl next door.

I have to find a way to make this right, but I make so few apologies, I'm not good at them. I make a point of committing as few mistakes as possible so I'm not in the position of having to apologize much.

I close my hand around the seahorse.

An apology is definitely due. I'm going to have to figure out how to give one to the daughter before her mother can take my head off, because that will definitely be her instinct the next time she sees me coming.

Chapter Twelve

Paige

"HE IS THE LITERAL worst, Bill. Ebenezer Scrooge the Grinch," I conclude my rant on Hill the Pill's antics the next morning.

"Sounds like it," he says with a laugh. "So what are you going to do?"

"Add more lights, for starters."

Bill laughs. "Normally, Lisa would pat you on the back and offer to help while I tried to persuade both of you not to escalate a neighbor war, but in this case, you'd both be right. I hear the media talk about the war against Christmas, but until this Hill guy, you couldn't have proved it by me. You probable better make it clear that he can resign himself to an all-out Christmas next door or . . ."

"Move," I say, when Bill can't seem to find something dire enough to finish his sentence with. "He doesn't need that big old house by himself. I'm going to Christmas him right into moving away."

"That's the spirit." He pauses. "Not exactly the spirit of Christmas, but I think this is a case where Santa would approve."

"Thanks, Bill. Want to help me figure out all the different places I can use those boxes of lights in my back shed? If we have Gary work Sunday, we can start on it after church."

"You bet, kiddo."

I head up to the front to consider the merchandise displays. It's not just my petty bone that's appeased by going even wilder with the decorations; the expression on Evie's face every time a new decoration goes up or a new strand of lights is connected would be payoff enough. Hill the Pill's total annoyance is a bonus.

I've nearly finalized my plans for the store window swap I'll do next Wednesday after we close early for Thanksgiving. I want something fresh and irresistible waiting for people on the morning of Black Friday.

It's not quite the event here as it is in bigger cities, but there will definitely be more people bustling in and out of Main Street stores, and they'll be expecting to see something special in the Handy's Hardware windows. I've trained them to expect it, and I make a point of exceeding their expectations with every new display.

The door opens and Wayne Gervis steps in, a man who could be an old forty or a young sixty. No one knows. In Bill's words, "He's looked that age for twenty-five years. I just don't know what that age is."

Since Wayne is Creekville's only code enforcement officer in addition to being one-half of our parks department as well as our de facto animal control officer on account of liking critters more than people, I suspect I know why he's here.

"Need something, Wayne?" I ask. "Something break?" He often comes in for supplies to fix up paint or patch sidewalks and other maintenance that falls under the purview of the city.

He slips his "City of Creekville" cap off and scratches his forehead before resettling the hat. "You happen to notice I stopped by your place yesterday?"

"You mean because you left me a big old yellow paper on the door?"

He sighs. "Yeah, because of that. I'm sorry, Paige. Your neighbor was real insistent, but I like what you're doing with the place. The lights make it nicer and the paintings kind of cover some of the ug—"

He saves himself with a cough.

"I understand, Wayne. I don't hold it against you. But tell me, do I really need to have that stuff down in seventy-two hours?"

The corner of his mouth twitches. "Thing is, I'm the only person on code enforcement, and it's just one of my jobs. I got kind of a full plate right now, trying to winterize . . . things."

I stifle a smile as I realize where he's going with this.

"Anywho," he continues, "wanted to let you know not to worry if I don't make it round before Friday. Lots of things, you know. To winterize. Then it's the weekend, of course. Don't work on the weekend. And I'm sorry to say, I'm probably going to be pretty busy on Monday and Tuesday. Especially Wednesday, because that's a half-day for city employees."

"With things?"

"Lots of 'em," he confirms. "So many things."

I paste on a mock serious expression. "I understand, Wayne. Can't ask you to come check out my compliance with so many other things that need doing first."

"Exactly. I'll try and get there week after next."

"But then I won't be out of compliance."

"Damn shame," Bill says.

"Reckon it is," Wayne agrees. "Anyway, have a nice evening."

Bill watches him go, grinning. "How about we get a head start on Saturday morning?"

"Sounds good to me. I need to give Tabitha a call today to pick her brain for some extra special touches." She'd been the queen of pranks during her years as a summer camp counselor, and while she's a big shot celebrity now, she proved a couple of years ago that she still had skills.

Bill shakes his head. "Poor guy. He won't know what hit him."

When an unfamiliar sound wakes me before my 7:00 alarm the next morning, I blink awake and stare at the window, gray light leaking through the panes, trying to figure out what I'm hearing. Then it hits me—it's the rumble of the garbage truck.

Shoot! Arshneel had told me garbage days were on Tuesday, but I forgot.

Dang it, dang it, dang it. Our trash can was overflowing with move-in debris, not to mention early-stage renovation trash. Since Hill the Pill can see my garbage cans from his carport, I don't want to reinforce his low opinion of my ability to adult.

The truck sounds close, maybe a couple of houses away, so I fly out of bed and head straight out the back door in my oversize Albemarle T-shirt, shorty plaid pajama bottoms, and socks, thankful that our temperatures in Creekville are still in the low sixties.

Still, I smother a yelp when the door shuts behind me. Those sixties are in the afternoon, and right now, the temps feel way meaner than that. Ten degrees meaner, at least.

I get the first trash can to the curb okay. I race for the other trash can and muscle it down my driveway, but it's much harder to wrangle because the bottom is full of heavy old things that we keep stumbling across in cupboards and drawers. This includes a rusty hammer, a dictionary predating me, an avocado green analog phone with cracked buttons, and a few empty photo frames.

I'm only halfway down the driveway when the truck reaches my curb, its claw coming out to grab and shake the first can loose. I try to make eye contact with the driver, but he won't look at me. He has to see me pushing this ridiculous trash can, doesn't he? But as the claw descends with the empty can, he's already looking ahead to Hill the Pill's house, where, of course, his cans wait neatly by the curb.

In a last-ditch effort, I run around to the front of the can and start dragging it. It's moving, but not fast enough. Between my adrenaline pounding in my ears, the whine of the truck's engine, and having my back turned to the road, I jump and curse when someone appears in front of me.

Not just someone—Hill the Pill. He lifts one side of the garbage can and nods toward the curb. I lift the other, and we rush it over just as the air brakes release for the truck to rumble forward, but the driver glances over, sighs like he's disappointed I made it, and brakes again.

We step out of the way as the arm lofts the can in the air and the junk of someone else's life tumbles into the truck. I don't take an easy breath until the empty can is back on the road and the truck has rolled on to Henry's house.

"Thanks," I say turning toward him. I'm surprised he bothered to help and even more surprised when I register his appearance. He's wearing running shoes, dark gray joggers, and a tank top with a dog's head and a logo reading "5K for K-9s."

It's not a tight tank top, but sweat has molded it to his chest, and more glistens on his bare shoulders. Whoa.

Henry Hill is YOKED.

He's also not wearing his glasses, and while I experience no Clark Kent/Superman confusion, this is definitely a different look, especially with his sweaty hair curling at the ends. This is a guy I would definitely look at twice if he jogged past me on the street.

I do not want to live with the knowledge that under his stuffy V-necks and khakis, my nerdy neighbor is a *snack*.

I clear my throat. "Thank you. I'll put a note in my calendar that this is trash day."

"No problem," he says.

"You were running?" What a stupid question. No, he was training with anti-Christmas guerilla forces. But I can't help it. Those shoulders are throwing me. I mean, they're *glistening*. Even weirder, he's not looking at me like I'm a bug he's trying to shoo.

"I run most mornings. Wakes me up better than coffee."

Leave it to Mr. Brown to be *nicer* first thing in the morning. I stifle a pre-coffee yawn, and he gives me a curt nod and turns up the driveway to his house.

"Thanks again," I call.

He raises a hand but doesn't look back, disappearing from view. I'm turning to drag my empty trash can back when his front door suddenly opens.

"Tell your daughter thank you," he says.

"Evie? For what?"

He hesitates. "She'll know." Then he shuts the door.

What the what?

Chapter Thirteen

Henry

SNIPPY NEIGHBOR IS WORKING with some hidden assets.

Or they were hidden until a few minutes ago when she panic-wrestled her trash bin down her driveway. But now that she's flashed some long and shockingly sexy legs in her brief pajamas, I can't unsee it.

What is wrong with me? Am I so starved for the company of a woman that I'm now sexualizing the prickly neighbor?

I consider this as I make coffee in my French press.

No, I decide. Any heterosexual male would have had the same reaction. That was a fine-looking pair of legs. And with her hair mussed and sleepy eyes, she was . . .

If she was anyone else, she might be irresistible, but I know too well how sharp her edges get when she's fully awake.

Still, this is a new facet, and in the privacy of my own mind, I can be as shallow about it as I want to be. Therefore, I freely admit that she is . . . what had the student called the sculpted head of Nefertiti in his essay? Ah, yes. Prickly Neighbor is a smokeshow. Reductive for a rendering of one of the most powerful women in world history but appropriate here.

Although . . .

It's also reductive to my neighbor. I sigh. I may question her taste based on her lawn decorations, and I doubt her judgment for purchasing that house in a bad bargain, but based on the small gifts her child has left for me, she's doing a solid job of raising the girl. She's more than a great pair of legs and pretty eyes.

It's time to admit that until either of us moves—not likely something that will happen soon—I'm going to have to come to terms with her living next door for the foreseeable future. That being the case, it's also time I made an effort to learn a bit about her to better form my opinions.

My students would be shocked to learn that I'm on social media, but I am. I don't use them, really. I opened Facebook and Instagram accounts several years ago but it was driven by anthropological interests rather than social ones.

These networks represented an unprecedented shift in human communication, one which I wished to observe for myself rather than live through without noticing it. That's the constant danger for anthropologists: preoccupying ourselves with the cultures of ancient times or distant places so deeply that we miss the time and place we're living in.

I tried for a year, watching the way acquaintances interacted before concluding that society as a whole was trembling on a collapse the scale of which hasn't been seen since Rome fell. It was quite enough for me.

Every now and then, I'll log in to get a sense of the prevailing winds when a particular controversy erupts in government, for example, but I don't post, and I don't interact.

Today I'm inspired to observe again, particularly the accounts of one Paige Redmond, prickly neighbor.

I settle at the table with my coffee and phone and open Instagram. She's easy to find, but her profile is locked, and I won't be requesting it. On Facebook, I have barely more luck. Once again, I find her. Once again, her profile doesn't reveal much to non-friends. But there is slightly more information since I can look at previous profile pictures.

She doesn't seem to have updated it in a few years, but in one of her older ones, she holds two balloons that form the number sixteen, and in checking the date that it was posted, a bit of quick math reveals that Paige must be around twenty-six now.

I set my phone down and regret my reaction at the sight of her this morning. She's nine years younger than me, not too much older than my seniors. It's indecent.

I may be an easily annoyed man, but I do try to be a decent one. Therefore, next week on trash day, rather than risk a run-in with Paige's long, bare legs, I'll bring her trash can to the curb if it hasn't been done when I leave for my morning run. Because the way my mouth had gone suddenly dry at the sight of her this morning hadn't been decent at all.

"Hey, Henry," Leigh says as she breezes into our office after her morning lecture. "Make any more real estate mogul moves lately?"

"Ha," I say. Leigh startles, and I realize it came out sharper than I meant it to. I clear my throat. "No, failed mogul here. That deal fell through, and that was it for me. Now I have a neighbor."

She furrows her brow. "You sound annoyed."

I shrug. "It was nicer when I didn't."

"You're an interesting case, Henry," she says, settling into her desk. "I'd like to figure you out some time."

I don't really want to be her case. And I'd prefer it if she said she'd like to *go out*, not figure me out. I'm not sure how to respond, even though she wears an expectant expression, like she's waiting for me to say something. *Think, you knob.*

Nothing comes to mind.

She turns to her work, and I can tell I'm already forgotten. *Smooth as ever, Hill.*

You have to work really hard to be this bad at women.

I try not to squirm for the next two hours as we work. I even attempt a couple of conversation openers. "So how are your classes going this semester?"

"Same as usual," she says, her tone distracted and her eyes not budging from her screen. "It's always the same as usual."

I'm not sure how human sexuality can be boring, but I'll sound perverse if I ask, so I let it drop. A half hour later, I try a different approach. "Looking forward to the Thanksgiving break?"

This time she looks at me like she's trying to jog her brain into recognizing I'm there. "I don't know yet," she answers. "I'm supposed to go skiing, but it doesn't look like they'll get the snowfall they need at the resort."

"That sounds fun." I sound like a vapid sophomore.

She looks at me strangely. "Again, only if they get the snow."

"Right." She goes back to her work, and I don't blame her. I'm making the kind of small talk I hate.

After another twenty minutes of trying and failing to think of anything intelligent to say, I decide to give up and go home. At least there I can work without distraction. I scowl. Maybe. That depends on what the neighbors are up to.

Their yard is blessedly still when I pull in, and the afternoon passes quietly for a few more hours until the growing sound of babble comes from the sidewalk, passes my house, and turns up the walkway to the one next door.

After a few minutes, the noise emerges from the house again, the girl's voice punctuating whatever they're doing with excitement. It sounds less shrill than usual, so that's something, I suppose. But when I hear hammering, I can't ignore it. They're supposed to be taking stuff down, not putting up more.

This is exactly why I liked not having a neighbor. You don't have to politely ask them to stop doing things they're impolite to be doing in the first place.

I try to ignore it for several minutes, but every time I think it's stopped, it starts up again.

I move to see out the side window. Snippy Neighbor is standing on the porch railing, wrapping lights around the top of one of the support columns while her daughter feeds her more from what looks to be an endless reel.

It already has lights. Why more lights?

I could have held my peace if they were doing yard work or something to materially improve the exterior of the house. But this is not that. Nascent thoughts of truce evaporate.

I walk out of the house at a no-nonsense pace so Paige doesn't think we're on friendly terms after our trash can run-in. *Boundaries and expectations*, I recite to myself silently.

I stop halfway up their walk. "Excuse me."

Paige makes a squeaking sound and teeters backward before she grabs the column in a bear hug. Her momentum knocks her feet from beneath her, and she wraps them around the column too. She is now a koala. An extremely annoyed-looking koala.

I shove out the errant thought that I would like to be a porch post.

"Are you all right?" I hurry toward her in case she needs . . . I have no idea what. Catching?

"Fine," she says, and the word is ground so fine between her clenched teeth, it's a wonder it doesn't emerge as a puff of powder. Gingerly, she stretches one foot down until she's sure she's found the railing. Then she maneuvers around with some kind of shimmy motion, plants her other foot, and straightens, still standing on the railing, her hand against the column for support.

"Hi, Mr. Henry," Evie says, her face brightening now that her mom is fine.

"Hello." I shift my gaze to Paige. "Ms. Redmond, may I speak with you, please?"

"Evie, honey, can you walk over to Poppa Dub's house and ask for the stapler gun?"

"Sure, Mama."

"Thank you, sweetie." Evie scampers down the street while Paige climbs down, but only enough to sit on the rail. She rests there casually, like she's got all the time in the world. "What can I do for you, neighbor? Are you here to measure the height of my grass to make sure I'm in compliance with your rigid sense of right and wrong?"

This is going well. I give her a cool stare. "Are you putting up more lights?"

She leans forward, her eyes snapping. "So many more lights."

"But the city ordinan—"

"I know the city ordinance. The code guy very helpfully cited it on my warning."

"Then why are you still decorating?"

"Because it annoys you," she says. "You're entitled. I don't like it."

"How does this help?" I wave at the reel of lights so I have an excuse to look away from her. I'm not sure whether the cool late-afternoon air or her temper is putting the color in her cheeks, but it's distractingly pretty. "It won't make the ordinance any less relevant."

"Correct," she says. "But it might make you less relevant."

"What does that even mean?" I expected her to be annoyed while she took *down* her decorations, not while she put up *more*.

"I deal with men like you regularly," she says. "I don't know if it's because I've been in service industry jobs that I have to listen to so many condescending . . . know-it-alls"—her pause tells me this wasn't her first word choice—"but you can't get me fired from this house, so I'm going to give you a big, giant clue: I won't be pushed around on my property, and every time you try, I'll push back harder." She stabs a finger at the reel of lights to make her point.

"I have the law on my side," I remind her.

"No. You have a city ordinance on your side, an ordinance with no teeth. I can't be jailed for starting Christmas a week early. The code enforcement officer doesn't have time to actually do the enforcement before decorating can officially begin." Her lips twitch, like she knows something I don't. "And if you think I'm going to let my daughter watch a Scrooge bully me out of going all out for our first Christmas in our own home, tell me where to take out a billboard to clear that up right now. Because *no*."

I have never heard anyone say such a definitive no. There aren't any hard sounds in the word, yet she still makes it sound like she's spit out a curse full of jagged consonants. I step back and try not to flinch when I realize I've literally ceded ground, but her narrowed eyes show me she didn't miss it.

I've heard Scrooge before, but . . . "I'm not bullying you." I don't like that label at all.

"You're harassing me."

I take three more very quick steps backward. I've never been accused of harassment either. "I'm not. I'm attempting to keep the peace on our street. I warned you that it was quiet. I was trying to help you understand the culture of this neighborhood."

She hops down from the railing and stalks over to me, hands on her hips, somehow staring down at me even though I've got at least six inches on her. Her finger comes up and waggles disconcertingly close to my face.

"Look, Scrooge or Grinch or Captain HOA or whatever your supervillain alter ego is. You better get right with the Spirit of Christmas because I've heard that smack comes back to haunt you. At the very least, you better stay out of *our* Spirit of Christmas, because I will do anything to make my kid happy, including a completely unreasonable holiday display. But pushing me to Clark Griswold levels? That's you. I have more boxes of this stuff in my shed, and I'm not afraid to unpack them."

Now it's my turn to fight a twitch of my lips, but I can't help it. "Did you say 'smack' comes back to haunt me?"

She scowls. "You learn to watch your swears when you've got a kid listening."

"I see." And my slight amusement fades as I do. "I understand your wish to give her a memorable Christmas, but is it worth alienating all your neighbors to start before Thanksgiving?"

She lifts her chin. "You're the only one I see standing in my yard whining about it. In fact"—she reaches into her jeans pocket and pulls out her phone—"let's test your theory and see how much they care."

She opens Facebook and mumbles "Creekville community page," as she taps. She's quiet for a few seconds, her fingers busy, before she gives me a grim smile and puts the phone away. "I've just invited the whole town to check out the best light display in Creekville next weekend. You know, *after* it's legal."

It is a stunning escalation. "I lobbed a water balloon, and you're firing back with a tank."

"Bet."

I frown. "I don't want to bet."

She rolls her eyes. "Don't you spend time around college kids? 'Bet' means 'you better believe that's what I did.'" She takes a step toward me. "And I'll do it every time. You are *not* ruining this for Evie."

The snap in her eyes is almost alarming in its intensity, and I turn and walk back home, trying to keep my dignity intact after failing to come up with a suitable retort. But the truth is, her reaction has shaken me.

It won't ruin anyone's Christmas to wait a few days before littering their yard with tacky decorations. And I really am trying to do her a favor by helping her acclimate to the Orchard Street culture.

Am I overreacting?

There's probably nothing more effective than the faint smell of other people's chimney smoke, the arrival of dusk, and the cold tang of November in the air to inspire reminiscences. But as I think of the most stinging accusation from Paige—that I'm trying to ruin her daughter's Christmas—I find my memories drifting back to the handful of Christmases I can recall before it was ruined for me too.

I wander down the hall to my grandfather's study and the leather-bound photo albums he'd kept there. I pull one down and leaf through it, repeating this several times until I find the one that coincides with my childhood.

Settled in his leather armchair, I go through it slowly. We must have visited Creekville twice that year, once in the summer and once at Christmas. I'm missing one front tooth in the pictures; that would have been the summer after kindergarten and the Christmas of first grade.

My grandmother loved Christmas. Pictures of me sitting between her and my grandad show us wearing Christmas sweaters and smiling at the camera. There's another one of us making Christmas cookies, our faces pressed together and grinning as I hold up a gloppy icing mess that was possibly meant to be a stocking.

There are over a dozen pictures like this. Me sitting in a pile of discarded Christmas wrapping, playing with a Lego set. Carolers who had come to the front door. Grandad and me standing in a barely-there dusting of snow and laughing at our tiny snowball.

As far as Christmases past went, this was the last good one. The next year, my parents had bought a place in Richmond, eager to host their first Christmas. Grandma and Grandad had come that year, but only Grandad had returned to Creekville.

I'd never been able to come back here after that. I couldn't. It had taken twenty-eight years for me to feel ready, and there were some days when I bumped into a memory in this house that made me wonder if I'd still come back too soon.

I close the album and tuck it under my arm, carrying it out into the living room. Now that I've finally faced it, I know I'll want to go through it again, the memories of those childhood Christmases bittersweet but with far more of the sweet.

I set it on the coffee table, and my hand brushes against the ornament Evie left for me. I turn the little seahorse over, studying its glitter flourishes and the curve of its tail. She's only seven or eight, so the ornament can't be that old, but it still shows sign of wear in a couple places, as if she's spent a good deal of time running her fingers along its familiar ridges and curves.

It's loved the way all shabby things are—with uncritical eyes—and if I am a Grinch, this uncomfortable feeling in my chest must be my heart growing.

Maybe it's time to make peace with Christmas. To make sure my neighbors enjoy a peaceful Christmas Present. It may never be my favorite holiday—that would be El Colacho, a baby jumping festival in Spain—but there's no reason it can't be Evie's without a few simple adjustments from me.

I turn the ornament over one more time before setting it on the photo album, a small shrine to the best parts of Christmas. The Ghost of Christmas Past has done its work. Ironically, the word "ebenezer" refers to an altar built in remembrance, and as I remember the uncomplicated time before grief and guilt, I wonder if Marley Ellis didn't have a little something to do with all of this.

Chapter Fourteen

Paige

I COULD GO THE rest of my life without ever seeing Hill the Pill march up my walk again and be perfectly happy.

But here he comes in his V-neck sweater glory, his jaw set.

I turn up the volume on my phone, which controls the speaker set inside the window. It's a cheap Bluetooth thing, but it's gone from playing softly to blasting, and that's all I need it to do right this second.

As he gets closer, I sing along, and since I possibly know every Christmas song ever made, I don't miss a single word as I belt out, "Do They Know It's Christmas?" Most avowed Christmas haters loathe this song especially, so the only way it could be better is if it were playing, "You're a Mean One, Mr. Grinch."

I brighten. It's a good idea, and I pull it up in my playlist as Hill the Pill reaches the porch steps.

"Hello," he says.

Hello. He's so stiff and formal. I nod back, a tiny smile of satisfaction escaping me as Thurl Ravenscroft sings about being cuddly as a cactus.

Henry nods. "It's nice to walk up to my theme song."

I study him for a second, then press pause. "Did you just make a joke?"

"I know two," he says. "The other one's a knock-knock joke."

Another joke. What is going on here? "Can I help you with something? Do you need me to turn my music down?"

"If I asked you to, would you turn it up louder instead?"

"You're beginning to understand how this all works."

He shakes his head. "I'm not here about the music."

I'd been trying to affix a giant red bow over our front door when I spotted him. "The decorations?" I guess.

He shakes his head. "To make an apology, actually."

I sit straight down on the porch. With him standing on the walkway, it makes us almost eye level. "You're kidding me."

"I'm not. And I wanted to return this."

He's holding a plastic bag in one hand, but he holds his other one out, and I recognize the well-loved seahorse resting on his palm.

"Evie's favorite ornament."

He nods. "She left it for me the other day. Said she hoped it helped me like Christmas. It worked, so I thought I better give it back."

When I stay there, staring, he steps closer and sets it on the step next to me. "Tell her thank you. It helped."

I look from him to it and back again. "You can tell her yourself when she gets home from school today."

"If that's okay with you?"

"As long as I'm around, sure."

"I'll do that."

We both fall silent. It's fine for a second, but that stretches to three and starts to feel weird, then stretches five more and it's awkward as hell, so I speak to break the tension, except he does too.

"I guess I better—"

"I was hoping you might—"

We break off and stare at each other, and I feel a bubble of laughter threatening to escape me, a sure sign that we've reached peak awkwardness.

"I was hoping I could explain why I've been . . ." He trails off like he's looking for the right word.

"A pain in the—"

"Scrooge," he says at the same time.

"Like, which part? There's a lot of them."

He winces. "I know. And all the parts." He holds up the plastic bag, angling it so I can see that it's from Bixby's. "I brought a bribe in case you haven't had breakfast yet. There's an assortment of pastries and muffins since I don't know what you like. What do you say?"

I practically lick my chops. Bixby's is a rare treat, and it feels un-neighborly to say no. "I can be bought. But I have to warn you that there will be no reduction in Christmas craziness around here, not even if there's a chocolate croissant in there."

"Why would I get Bixby's and not get the best thing on the menu?"

"I don't know," I say. "Why would you hate Christmas?"

His lips twitch. "Touché, Prickly Neighbor."

"Just dishing it back, Hill the Pill."

"So croissant, conversation, and truce?"

I eye the bag. "I'll agree to the croissant and conversation. Truce depends on what you have to say."

"Fair enough." He glances around like he's wondering where my porch furniture is.

"Pull up some plank," I say, scooting over and waving to encompass the warped floorboards. "Sorry we're not set up for entertaining yet. It's going to be a while because some guy ran up the bidding on me, and I used up my cushion for stuff like renovations."

He drops his head and stares at the concrete. "He sounds like a real jerk."

"I thought so. But there's new evidence coming in, and I'm still deciding."

He nods and climbs the steps, settling on the porch with his feet on the top step, his legs together, knees bent. He looks like a very proper 1950s schoolgirl. He makes a few adjustments, shifting this way, then that, and it's so uncomfortable to watch that I feel the laugh threatening again. I absolutely can't laugh at him right now or I'll upset our new truce. But of course, knowing it's a bad time to laugh makes it harder not to, and my mouth quivers in the first sign of betrayal.

No, no, no. No laughing. Maybe I can excuse myself to fetch us coffee inside until the threatening laughter passes? I'm about to offer when Henry stands up again.

"Would you like to do this at my house? It's pretty comfortable over there."

"Yes." That's an easy yes too. I've been dying to see the inside of some of these Orchard Street houses. I'm not passing up a chance. I can hold my breath and do a slow count until the laugh passes while we walk next door. It works, and by the time we climb the porch, the urge has subsided.

Thank goodness. I may not like Henry Hill much, but it'll be better if we can be civil, and he doesn't seem like the kind of guy who's going to deal with one of my laughing jags if he thinks it's about him. They don't even make sense to me, so it's not like I could explain it.

As he waves me through the front door, I take in as much as I can without looking like a thief casing the joint. The traditional interior matches the outside vibe of the house, and I suspect this is all a holdover from when his grandparents lived here, not his own stamp.

The inside has a fall vibe, and it's not a bad thing, but it definitely feels like houses did when I was a kid. Warm beige walls, deep brown accents, not much print on the fabrics, but they're higher quality. The wood furniture is dark, but the built-ins are a medium honey oak color, and I have a feeling if I walked into his kitchen, I'd see the same.

All in all, it feels like a slightly outdated space that was decorated by someone with good taste, warm and cozy, where a lot of houses now tend toward cool and light.

"Dining table okay?" Henry asks.

"Sure." I follow him through the living room arched doorway that leads to a dining room, only instead of a long formal table, a round table for six sits beside the window overlooking the side of my house. And the giant Santa face made of lights. Not sorry.

A stack of books with a notebook on top suggests he works on this table too, and I can understand why noise distracts him. But why not just go to a room farther away in the house? If I hear a good opening in the conversation, I'll ask.

He waves me into a seat but turns slightly toward the kitchen. "Would you like some coffee or tea?"

I've already had a coffee infusion this morning, so I shake my head. "Water would be nice."

He nods and returns a minute later with a glass of water for me and a steaming mug of coffee for himself. He sets each cup down, his movements careful and precise, and pulls one item after another out of the Bixby's bag.

When he gets to the chocolate croissant, he extends it toward me. "I assume you would like this one?"

"Yes, please." I barely resist making grabby hands. "Bill and Lisa's daughter, Tabitha, turned me onto these, and I'm beginning to worry I might have a problem." Like that even getting one once a week is still $24 a month I can't afford for only pastry.

"Bill and Lisa?" he asks.

"You've probably seen them around my place a couple of times. They live on Mulberry."

"One street over," he says. "Is that who you sent Evie to? Are they her grandparents?"

I take a bite of my croissant as I consider how to explain. "That's not an easy yes or no. How about we trade information? You tell me what your deal is with Christmas, and I'll explain about them?"

He nods. "It's not a long story, and I'll spare you the dramatic details, but Christmas is hard. How old is your daughter? Around seven?" When I nod, he continues. "When I was her age, my grandmother died a few days before Christmas."

He falls quiet, a faraway look in his eyes, and remembering the scant details Miss Lily had shared, I say, "Was it sudden?"

A blink, a quiet sigh, then, "Yes. And it was my fault."

Oh, wow. I have no idea how to respond to that, especially since I don't know the circumstances. But since asking how someone died is about the rudest thing ever, I don't say anything.

"My parents have always told me it wasn't my fault, and intellectually, I understand that. But there's a seven-year-old boy somewhere inside me that doesn't, quite." He sighs and takes another sip of his coffee before setting his mug down. "Anyway, I guess I've been a Scrooge ever since. Or maybe a grinch? Scrooge was the money-grubber, wasn't he?"

"He was. Wouldn't let poor Bob Cratchit off work for the holiday."

He gives me a small smile. "That's not me. I teach anthropology at Jefferson. It's not exactly a get-rich-quick plan."

"It's better than mine, which is managing a small-town hardware store."

"But do you like it?"

"I kind of love it," I admit.

"Me too." Another sip of coffee. I get the sense that he does it as a way to buy time to frame his words to come out exactly like he wants them to. "But you're right in another way about Scrooge. I went through some of my grandparents' old photo albums last night, and it was like hanging out with Christmas past. Perhaps I've been a humbug about it long enough. After getting Evie's present, I wonder if it would be appropriate to give her one in return?"

I consider this. I'm insanely protective about Evie and men, doing little-to-no dating since she was born because I'm busy, but mostly because I'm careful about who gets to be in her life. But my instinct says that if Henry gets her something inappropriate, he'll err on the side of not knowing what a kid her age likes, not something that crosses a line.

"That would be fine," I say. "Can I ask what you have in mind?"

"Brine shrimp."

My eyebrows go up. "She likes fish sticks, but I don't know if she'll go for shrimp."

He smiles again, and this may be the first time that I've seen a flash of genuine warmth in his expression. For a split second, he reminds me more of a guy I'd hang out with than a stiff neighbor I'm trying to figure out how to negotiate a peace with.

"Brine shrimp are more like a pet, which is another reason I wanted to check with you. They're called Sea Monkeys, which I know isn't a seahorse, but I thought Evie might enjoy them. They come in a kit with a small tank—very small—and she can start them as eggs and watch them grow. They don't require much maintenance."

It's so thoughtful on so many levels that I am forced to reassess Hill the Pill completely in this moment. It does sound like something Evie would go bananas for, but the fact that he's checking with me is an extra level of consideration.

"Who are you?" The words are out of my mouth before I even think about them, and he squints and gives the tiniest head jerk, like the question has come from nowhere. Because it has.

"What do you mean?"

"I mean . . ." I don't know what I want to explain, so I don't. "Never mind. Evie will love the brine shrimp. Thank you for thinking of her." I sip my water to keep any more incredulous words from coming out of my mouth.

"All right." He pauses, scratches his chin for a moment, then says, "I also wondered if you'd like some help with the decorations."

I choke and splutter on the water, slapping my hand over my mouth, but not before a bit of the spray lands on his cheek. I watch, mortified, as he calmly wipes it away. This dude has gone from being rattled by the dumbest things to being rattled by nothing, not even a woman accidentally spitting on him.

"Sorry," I manage when I'm done coughing. "I thought you asked if you could help with the decorations at my house."

"I did."

"Then yes."

Now he looks surprised. "I expected to have to talk you into it."

"Normally, you would, but if I don't get help, Bill will insist on doing it, and he barely retired as Clark Griswold. So yes, I'd rather get it done before he shows up and goes to work when he should be taking it easy."

"Clark Griswold? Is he in Creekville?"

My mouth drops open. "*National Lampoon's Christmas Vacation?*"

"Haven't seen it."

I close my eyes. "That's painful. That is *painful* to me. We'll need to fix that soon."

"All right." But he doesn't sound too certain about this.

I take my last bite of croissant and stand up, brushing my crumbs into the wax bag. "Come on, then."

"For what?"

"For decorating."

He stands and reaches for our cups. "And you'll explain about Bill and Lisa?"

"Absolutely. I'll tell you all about them while you're crawling around on my roof, hammering nails in."

"I . . . but—"

I'm already at the door. "Get a move on, Griswold. Time to work."

Chapter Fifteen

Henry

ONE WOULD THINK I'D understood exactly what I was getting myself into when I offered to help Paige. But one would be so very wrong. Apparently, she was simply waiting on a second pair of hands to really take things over the top.

"You scared of heights?" she asks, heading toward her shed without checking that I'll follow. But I do.

"No."

"Good." She swings open the shed door. Several seconds of disturbing noises follow. Scrapes of things being dragged across concrete, a muffled curse, something metal clattering to the ground, and finally, Paige emerging with an extension ladder. "You're on roof duty."

"Because you're afraid of heights?" I guess. What else would explain her sending an amateur up to the roof?

"Nope. But I'm giving you a job a sea monkey could do while I fix the wiring on the external outlet I need."

"Oh."

She smirks at me. "Unless you want to trade."

"Definitely not."

She nods. "Then let's go."

Soon she has the ladder leaning against the front porch and me standing at the foot of it, holding a handful of plastic clips in a shape I haven't seen before.

"You're going to attach these lights at six-inch intervals." She holds up a strand of lights with larger bulbs.

"That's the kind everyone used on their houses when I was a kid. How old are these?" I ask.

"Pretty new," she says. "They're a retro look but more energy efficient. Anyway, you can eyeball the intervals. Just go along the front of the eaves. Hold the strand against the wood, then clip it. I'll put in the first one so you can see what I need."

"So I won't be actually on top of the roof?"

She smiles. "No. Even I haven't really done that, but I'm sure I can figure it out. For today, you'll stay on the ladder. Now watch."

I do. She climbs it quickly, reaching the lowest corner of the eave and slipping the wound string of lights from her shoulder, neatly clipping it against the wood. But I barely process how she does it, because I've seen marble sculptures rendered far less impressively than her butt in those jeans. Wow.

I blink and glance down to refocus. I have *got* to start getting out more. With women.

"Henry?"

I look up into her questioning face.

"Did that make sense?"

"I've got it." I do not. But I'll have to trust that when I take her place on the ladder, I can look at what she's done and figure it out. I don't have a high degree of faith that I will, but it's better than admitting I was paying attention to . . . the wrong thing.

She's down the ladder in a flash, and I make the disturbing discovery that the only thing that improves the view of her ass . . . ets climbing, is her coming back down.

Once off the ladder, she extends her hand to me, and I hold mine out for her to deposit a dozen clips. "Just keep going. Holler when you need more."

"I will. But where will you be?"

"Right here, getting these bushes lit."

"Perfect. Then you can tell me about Bill and Lisa."

As soon as she's satisfied that I'm in place at the top, she starts in on her explanation. "Bill and Lisa basically adopted us two years ago. Before that, we lived in an apartment across the hall from my brother, Noah. And before that, I was making poor choices because I became an orphan at eighteen and didn't feel like dealing with it. So there's the story."

She says all this as she alternately messes around with a web of Christmas lights and bear-hugs a shrub.

"Sounds like there's probably a good deal more details between that beginning, middle, and end." I'm not going to force anyone to talk about hard things. I certainly don't. But I'll listen. I do that fairly well.

"You're right," she says.

She doesn't add anything to this, and I think that may be the end of it as she focuses on her hedge wrestling, but she surprises me a few minutes later. "You didn't ask me how my parents died or about Evie's father."

I've placed the third clip, and now I have to get down to move the ladder, so I do, stopping when I reach the ground next to her.

"I don't love it when people ask me prying questions. Why would I do that to you?"

"Most people do."

I shrug and move the ladder over, pausing with my foot on the first rung. "I'm not most people." I climb up again.

I've positioned another clip when she calls up, "Do you want to know?"

"Yes."

Long pause, then, "Okay. I'll tell you."

I wait as I get the next section of lights anchored. I'm not hopeless. I'm just not handy. If Paige were doing this, I suspect she'd be picking up speed as she went. I won't, but what I lack in speed, I'll make up for in dogged consistency.

"My parents were killed in an accident in March of my senior year."

"I can't imagine." I hadn't lost people who'd been part of my everyday life. Not my parents.

"It sucked. I didn't handle the anger well, and I took off."

Her voice is hard and flat. I've seen her irritated plenty of times, but this is an anger that I can feel even eight feet above her on the ladder. I don't know what to say, so I say nothing. Perhaps that's the right thing because she picks up the story.

"Bad decision, bad decision, months pass, more bad decisions, more months. Anyway, I'm not proud of it, but I ended up pregnant. I came home to Noah, who put me back together and helped me with Evie from the day I showed up."

"Sounds like a good guy."

"The best," she says. "Which is why, when he started dating Grace, Bill's daughter, I knew I had to do whatever I could to get out of his way. She works

for NASA, and she couldn't do that here. She'd come back to take care of
Bill when he was sick, but when he got better, NASA hired her back, and she
would have gone, and Noah would have let her go to stay and take care of us.
So I made sure they got together. And everything worked out."

I move the ladder and climb again, expecting her to pick up the thread of
the story, but after a longer silence than usual, I realize she's done telling it.
But I'm not done listening. I want to hear the section that explains how she
ends up as my neighbor.

She's probably gambling I'll let it drop, but that won't happen. I'm not an
anthropologist by accident. I'm deeply interested in why people do what they
do. I'm fascinated at both a cultural level and an individual one. In general,
I prefer studying both with the distance of a scientist, but I'm invested in
Paige's story, and I want to know about this last piece.

"Paige?" I look down between my extended arms, watching her as I attach
the next clip. "You skipped the part that's your superhero origin story."

"There's no part like that."

"Then at least tell me the part where you end up with this house."

She gives such a deep sigh, I can hear it all the way up by the roof, but
she starts talking again. "I knew Noah wouldn't leave as long as he thought I
needed him. He'd take care of us in sneaky ways. Buy Evie new clothes or toys
and tell me they were thrifted. Switch our leases with the apartment manager
without telling me so that I was paying his one bedroom rent, and he was
paying for my two-bedroom."

"I like him," I say, without thinking about it.

"Everyone does." I can hear the smile in her voice.

"How did you convince him you were independent?"

"Grace, Bill's daughter, was running the store for him. They hired me to
work part-time over the holidays. I did so well, they hired me full-time so
Grace wouldn't feel bad about leaving. Bill was comfortable with me running
the store."

This is the first time I've heard a note of pride in her voice, and my fingers
tighten around the string of lights. It's a reflex I don't quite understand.

"We got to know each other pretty well in the months that Noah and Grace
dated, and Bill and Lisa fell in love with Evie. Most people do. So when I went
to them for ideas of how to convince Noah that he could move to Charleston
with Grace, they had a few suggestions. I knew my job wasn't going to be
enough to put him at ease, but we brainstormed and came up with a plan."

The rhythm of the story is rising. "I feel like I'm watching a TV show where the good guys are sweeping off the table to plunk down a diagram, and everything is about to turn around."

I hear a snort of laughter, some rustling, then Paige appears on the lawn beside the ladder. "I don't believe you watch TV."

She's got me there. "I don't."

Tapping on her lips, she studies me for a moment. "Documentaries. Or public radio." Something in my expression makes her laugh. "I knew it."

"All right." I give her a slight scowl. "I'm very predictable. Finish the story."

"We spent a couple of weeks figuring everything out, but on Christmas, I surprised Noah with his 'go live your life' package. A list of teaching openings in Charleston. A move to Creekville for Evie and me, right into the apartment above Bill and Lisa's garage for the cost of utilities. That left me enough for daycare for Evie so I could go to school. And I got a bunch of grants and things. I saved, thrifted, and sacrificed. I graduated. I got a promotion and a raise. I bought a house. I moved in and proceeded to torture you."

I climb down the ladder again, this time stopping to stand in front of her. I cross my arms and give her a narrowed-eye look that would tell any student who has ever had me that Dr. Hill is quite serious. "Do you know what I do for a living?"

"Teach at the college."

"But do you know what I teach?"

A slightly guilty look flashes over her face. "Yes."

It startles me out of my serious look. "How did you know that?"

"I googled you when you were being an as—"

"Understood," I cut her off. I go back to my serious look. "Studying anthropology means that I've examined the origins of countless myths and legends."

Her eyebrow goes up, a look of puzzlement on her face.

"You," I say, unfolding an arm to point at her briefly, "are a legend." I can hear it in all the details she didn't share. She has rare grit, and I hope people tell her so. It's the least I can do after being such an as—well, a Scrooge.

A range of expressions plays across her face. Surprise, gratification, and possibly . . . was that a hint of trepidation before she crosses her arms and gives me a level look?

"That's nice of you to say."

I allow the smallest smirk. "I'm rarely nice."

She gives me a nod of acknowledgement. "That's nice of you to say," she repeats, "but I want to be clear here: I'm not going to date you."

"You . . . what?" That came out of nowhere.

"I'm not going to date you. You're old enough to be my . . ."

My eyebrows shoot up.

"Uncle," she finishes, clearly not what she was going to say first. "But I accept your truce." Then a sunny grin breaks out on her face. "And I'd love to be friends."

I smile back. "Despite being rejected for a date I never wanted, and in spite of having been aged at least twenty years in your mind, friends sounds good."

"Great. Now go finish the lights up there."

I turn to the ladder but pause. "How old do you think I am, anyway?" I don't have any gray hairs. Not even *thinning* hair.

"I'm not going to answer on the grounds that I'll incriminate myself and you might not give Evie the sea monkeys I really want. I mean, she really wants."

"Thirty-five," I tell her. "So maybe your youngest uncle."

"I don't have any uncles," she says. "Maybe that's why it was a bad guess. But you're almost ten years older than me."

"You're twenty-six?"

"Fifty-two if we're counting life experience."

Her mind is so quick. It frustrated me the first few times we clashed because I came out feeling foolish on the other side. "You're almost funny, you know, kid."

She pokes my chest. "Evie is the kid." She pokes it again. "And I *am* funny. Go do the lights."

I climb up the ladder and pause at the top. "You're not my type, anyway."

"You don't like girls? That tracks."

I stare down at her and spot a mischievous grin. "Not that it matters, but no, I don't like girls. I like grown *women*."

It's her turn to scowl. For once after a match, Scrooge is tied with the girl next door.

I could get used to this.

Chapter Sixteen

Paige

Being friends with Henry Hill is much nicer than not.

There's no way I'm toning down the Christmas craziness. What Evie wants this Christmas, Evie will get. Next year is soon enough to start teaching her principles of design. This year is about the celebration in all its gaudy green and red glory. Country Christmas? Sure. Three different versions of Santa? Why not? LEDs *and* incandescent lights? In jewel tones and primary colors? Oh, and white ones wherever Evie likes them? Bring it on.

To his credit, Henry doesn't say another word about it. Instead, he waves each time he sees us. Tuesday, he knocks on the door while I'm heating Hot Pockets.

"Is Evie here?" he asks, holding up a bag.

"Hey, Henry. She is." I glance behind me. We're not fit for visitors yet, but I don't want to break our fragile peace by not inviting him in. I step back and gesture for him to enter. He'll either have the grace to recognize we're a work in progress or he won't. I can't worry about it either way. "Let me get her."

She's sprawled on the floor coloring in her rainbow room, a truly happy space and the only one that is mostly finished. It's stunning to see the before and after pictures. "Evie, honey, Mr. Henry is here. He brought you something." Her forehead wrinkles, and I reassure her. "He mentioned you'd been leaving him gifts. I think he wants to say thank you."

That's enough for her. She scrambles to her feet, her crayons abandoned as she runs out to see Henry, skidding to a stop a few feet away.

"Hi," she says, eyeing the bag in his hand. It's possible she's learned that crinkly plastic bags produce delicious high-fat, high-carb treats from me in my role as Mother of the Year.

"Hi," he says, still awkward. It's kind of cute now that I've learned to ignore his bark. "I brought you this." He pulls out her seahorse and hands it to her.

Her eyes brighten and she reaches for it before changing her mind and trying not to let her face fall. "I gave it to you as a sorry gift for ruining your house."

"It's not ruined. It's good as new," he says. "And I really like this ornament. But it seems kind of sad at my house, and I think it'll be happier here."

"You do?" She looks at the seahorse with poorly disguised longing, and my heart squeezes the tiniest bit that she'd give it to him as an apology when she loves it so much. Maybe we do eat Hot Pockets and too many treats from plastic bags, but maybe I'm getting the big stuff right.

"I do. In fact, I was so worried it was lonely, I thought it would like some friends."

"Go get your ornament," I say, and she rushes over to scoop it up, then stays, curious about what's coming next.

Henry reaches into the bag and pulls out a brightly colored box about the size of a kid's shoebox. "It's a sea monkey kit," he explains. "You can grow them and . . . stuff?"

He looks toward me for help. I don't know why he's worried because Evie is squealing. I give him points for not wincing.

"Ohmygosh," she says with all the considerable excitement she can muster. She accepts the box and immediately begins reading it aloud. "Hatch and grow your own pets that really come alive." Her eyes go big and round. "Mr. Henry, these are real, alive sea monkeys?"

"Brine shrimp," he says. "But some people think they look like sea monkeys, so that's what they call them."

She plunks right down on the floor and opens the box, exclaiming at each thing she removes. "Food! And EGGS! Baby sea monkey eggs! Can I do them right now, Mama? There's even a little tank."

"After dinner, Evie. But then yes. You can start your aquarium."

"Please can I do them now? Dinner is just Hot Pockets anyway."

I resist flinching but I can't do anything about my cheeks going warm. I generally don't like to advertise how often that's what we have for dinner. "There's broccoli on the side," I say weakly.

Henry nods in understanding.

"We don't have broccoli," Evie says, still not looking up. "There's no greens in the fridge. I checked because I didn't want any for dinner."

There is no way that my cheeks aren't bright red. I cough. "I'm sure there's something good in there. Anyway," I say, talking over Evie when she sounds like she's about to narc on me again, "thanks for the gift, Henry. That was very thoughtful."

"Yes, thank you for the sea monkeys, Mr. Henry." Evie pauses from studying the pictures on the box long enough to beam up at him.

"I'd invite you to stay, but . . ." I sweep my hand around the living room to indicate how not ready it is for company. It's tidy. Ish. But it's not the kind of space I want to invite friends to hang in. I give my head a small shake. *Friends.* Who'd have thought?

"I'll be going," he says. "I've got dinner of my own to make."

"You should come and see my sea monkeys tomorrow," Evie says. "I bet they'll already be so big."

I smile and walk him to the door. "I'll manage her expectations. Thanks for bringing those over. They were a hit, obviously."

"Of course." He gives me a nod and disappears out into the night.

I force Evie to leave her tank long enough to eat dinner, which she scarfs down in two minutes flat, and she's right back to the tank again. "Can I google stuff, Mama?"

"Sure, honey." I log into my laptop and make sure it's in safe mode, and she happily searches for videos and facts about sea monkeys, all of which she shares with me as I sand down the built-in bookshelves on either side of the fireplace at the end of the living room. It's an awkward placement because it forces the orientation of the living room to be long and skinny instead of wide, but I've got ideas. First among them is getting the pine ready for a coat of white paint.

A knock at the door startles both of us a half hour later. "Busy tonight," I mutter, but as I approach the door, I spot Henry through the broken shutters.

I open the door with a surprised, "Hey."

He's holding two foil-covered plates. "I like to cook, but usually I have to freeze my extras. Thought maybe you'd like them instead."

I stare at him, honestly speechless as I accept the food. He has not once been what I expect him to be, first in a bad way, and now in a good one. "Thank you."

"No big deal. Just some stir-fry. Won't hurt my feelings if you don't like it."

Then he hurries down the stairs, stops on the bottom steps, and comes back up.

"Actually, I don't think I fully understood the position I might be putting you in when I bid against you for this place. I'm sorry. I don't know how to make it up to you, but I thought perhaps dinner sometimes until you get an oven that works?"

I press my lips together, trying to figure out how to take this. First things first, I guess. "The oven works. Stove too. I just don't use them much."

"Oh." He looks lost.

"Hill . . ." I look from him to the plate and back again. "Is this charity or an apology? Because I will only accept one of those things."

"Definitely an apology. I can't go back in time and think harder about the consequences of bidding against you, so I'm not sure what else to do."

I peel up one side of the foil and take a whiff. "This is a start."

"It is?" His tone is wary but also slightly hopeful.

"It is."

"All right. I cook often." Then he nods and hurries down the steps again toward his house.

He's such an odd dude, but I smile as I close the door.

I sit down and eat a delicious chicken and vegetable dish over lo mein noodles. They have a lemon-garlic taste, and even Evie picks out the pieces of chicken and declares them yummy.

The next day, I teach Evie the fundamental lesson that you return a plate like that washed and full of goodies, piling them with brownies and sugar cookies we bake in Lisa's kitchen before depositing them on his porch with a thank you note.

That night, I go to take my garbage cans out only to discover they're at the curb. I'm sure I can chalk that up to him.

On Saturday, I'll work closing, and Evie and I spend the morning in the yard. I'm adding lights wherever I can fit them, and Evie is turning sticks into witches stuck together with tinsel.

"This one is a nice witch." She holds up a stick figure tied with cheap green curling ribbon. "Can I go give it to Mr. Henry?"

I glance over at his house. We haven't seen him in a day or two, but it should be okay. "Sure, honey."

She runs over and knocks on his door. A moment later he answers, and I hear her explanation that she's made him a good witch. I hope he knows to take it, and I give a small sigh of relief when he does, solemnly examining it like he's inspecting the workmanship of a master.

I can't quite make out his low response, but he disappears into his house and Evie plops herself down on his top step.

"Come on back, Eves," I call. "Let's give Mr. Henry some space."

"He said I could make a village here," she calls back and waves.

I'm about to question what this means when Henry himself emerges again, this time with a stack of papers and a mug of coffee. He takes a seat at the café table on the porch, settling his papers in front of him. I walk over, curious. In our two weeks of residence, Henry has not yet been a front porch sitter.

Something is different about him as I walk over, but I can't figure it out until I'm standing in front of the steps by Evie and have a better view of him. He's wearing jeans. It makes me slightly uncomfortable, like if your high school principal showed up to work in sweats. Wilder still, he's not wearing a V-neck. Instead, he's wearing a thermal in dark green, and honestly, it should be as boring as his sweaters, but instead, I'm having a flashback to the morning of the Great Trash Can Rescue.

His glasses are missing too. So now what I have is an almost-hot neighbor sitting on his porch and watching my little girl play with stick witches. Thank goodness he's clean cut to the point of boredom or it might be an issue. If this man ever grows scruff . . .

"What's going on, friends?" I ask.

Henry smiles at me. "Christmas witches, I think."

"Yep," Evie confirms. "They're going to brew a potion that makes presents!"

"Oh, the endless present potion. Nice. What will they make it from?" Henry asks.

She holds up two different leaves and a roly-poly curled into a ball. "This so far. Have to hunt for more ingredients."

"Good plan," I tell her. "But bring your stuff back over, and only hunt where I can see you."

"I don't mind," Henry says. "She can stay over here if she wants. I've been grading midterms all day, and it's nice sitting out here to do it in the fresh air."

I'd probably rather grade in the fresh air than in my house all day too, but I don't want to push our newfound truce. "Okay, but only until I have to leave for work."

"Sounds good, Mama." She picks up one of her stick witches. "Mr. Henry, I need your stick witch. He has to help with the spell."

"Here you go." He picks it up from the table and brings it over. "But it's just on loan. I'll need him back when the spell is done."

My heart melts a little. He's sure getting the hang of Evie pretty quickly. She accepts the stick, and I realize I'm staring at his backside as he returns to his papers. Jeans do it way more favors than his chinos do. Nice, professor. Very nice.

"Mama?" Evie's voice interrupts me, and as I blink and shift my attention toward her, I swear I spot the faintest smirk on Henry's face, but when I dart a look at him, his eyes are fixed on his grading. "Is this a good spell? Holy moly, roly-poly, a gift for me, when I stir, one, two, three!"

"That sounds like an excellent spell. I love your little brain."

She claps a hand on top of her head. "It's not little."

"Not as giant as mine yet."

"I'll grow."

"But your brain only grows if you stuff it with information."

"So listen in school?" She sighs. "How come everything is always listen in school?"

I laugh. "Because it's the right answer, unless it's—"

"Read books," she interrupts. "I know."

But it's not sassy, because she loves both school and books.

"How will you know if your spell works?" Henry asks.

"Um, Mr. Henry, it's not my spell. It's the Christmas witch's spell."

"That's what I meant." He looks as serious as usual. "How will you know?"

"It already did," she says patiently. "See?" She holds her hand out, palm flat, nothing in it.

"Oh." He presses his lips together, like he's trying to figure out where to go next. "That's a very nice . . ."

"Seahorse," she answers. "A golden one. And it's alive. Isn't it pretty?"

"Yes, shiny."

"I need more witches." Then she wanders into Henry's yard.

"You really don't mind?" I ask as we watch her.

"Do I strike you as someone who says things he doesn't mean?" His lips twitch, and I smile in return.

"You definitely do not. Fine, then. I'll just be over in the yard setting up the spotlights."

He swallows visibly. "The spotlights?"

"Yeah. If I've already told the whole town we've got the display starting the Friday after Thanksgiving, I better deliver, don't you think?"

"You're still going to do that, hmm?" He looks like he'd love to add more, but he doesn't.

"I am. I mentioned it to Evie and now she can't wait. Which is why I have to be careful what I say around her. I don't break my promises, and I accidentally mentioned that part of my payback aloud when I was . . . annoyed."

He shakes his head. "Right, the doubling down. If you ever want to double down on those brownies or cookies again, feel free."

I smile and head back to my yard, monitoring Evie as she explores at Henry's. She already has three large leaves in her hand, and I'll have to remember to check her pockets for rocks before her jeans go in the hamper.

Sunday goes much the same. When we appear outside, so does Henry, settling onto his porch with a smaller stack of papers. Evie helps until she's distracted, then she wheedles permission to go see her Dubs. I tell her she can stay for an hour and text Lisa to make sure Evie sticks to it, though I'll probably have to retrieve her for lunch anyway. I don't want her taking up their whole day when we'll be over there for Sunday dinner too.

Sure enough, I have to fetch her home for lunch, but when we head back out for more decorating, Henry reappears as well. This time, Evie drags the empty refrigerator box into his driveway, flattens it, and turns it into a stage where she practices her four lines for her class Thanksgiving pageant.

I like that Henry doesn't come over to help. He doesn't know how to do the setup I'm doing, and I hate it when men try to help at things they think they should be good at but aren't. It happens all the time when a customer asks me a question in the hardware store and some nearby man jumps in with the wrong answer. Henry seems to be fine with the fact that he's not handy.

He disappears with a goodbye in the late afternoon, and I retreat to the sidewalk to look at our house as a whole. I've managed to place everything from the tens of thousands of lights to the cartoony wooden cutouts in a way that tells a story, drawing the viewer's eye from the starting point of Santa's journey at the North Pole at "stage left" in the yard, to the end of the story where a young child is delighting in the pile of presents under a painted tree that I draped with lights.

Bill's handpainted scenery isn't the kind of thing one can buy in a store. He's spent time and love on these over the years. Do they suit my taste? No. But eventually, I'll figure out how to make it my own. For now, doing the Handy's Hardware windows scratches that artistic itch.

Sunday dinner is always early, around 4:00. Tonight, Lisa serves a delicious roast, and I'm thankful she goes out of her way to spoil us with the things I can't afford. We firm up plans for Thanksgiving, and it's time to tell Evie the surprise I've been holding onto.

"Guess who's coming home for Thanksgiving?" I ask her. "Tabitha!"

"Oooh, Auntie Tab." She smiles. She thinks it's fun knowing someone on TV, especially since Tabitha is Creekville's only celebrity who isn't a Civil War hero.

"And Grace," I add, "which means—"

"Unc!" she shouts and jumps up to do a happy dance.

"Yes," I tell her. "Uncle Noah is coming."

"And they'll sleep at our new house like I always used to sleep at his?"

"Not this time, Eves. We don't have a room ready for them yet, but they can come over as much as they want, and you can come here to visit as much as you want." I shoot a quick glance at my bonus parents to make sure that's okay. They're both smiling.

"Yay, yay, yay! I can't wait to show them my sea monkeys!"

"Speaking of which, it's time to head home and check on them." I don't know if I'll ever get used to saying "home" and meaning our own little house, but so far, I love it every time.

"Awww," she says. "But I want to stay."

I look at her, surprised. "I thought you'd want to check on your tank."

"I do, but I can do that later. If I leave the Dubs, I can't come back all the way until tomorrow."

This makes Bill laugh and sweep her up into a spin hug. "How about if you let her stay until just before bedtime, and I'll bring her back. We've got a football game to watch anyway."

I agree to this plan because I'll never feel like Evie has enough family in her life, and I want to give her all of it I can. "One condition: no whining about tooth brushing at bedtime. Promise?"

"Promise!" Then she trots off with Bill to watch the game.

"Why don't you go get some quiet time?" Lisa asks. I know she's not trying to get rid of me; downtime as a single mom is a rare thing, and she's offering up two hours of it.

"Thanks, Lisa." I leave her with a hug, and I'll make sure Bill gets his when he drops off Evie.

"Say hi to the handsome professor for me," she says, walking me to the door.

"Lisa!" I turn and gape at her. "It's not like that."

"Maybe it should be." And she shuts the door on me with a laugh.

Chapter Seventeen

Henry

I STEP OUTSIDE, INTENDING to go to Paige's house, when she materializes out of the dusk on the sidewalk.

"Hey," she calls. "Beautiful night."

There's a nip in the air that speaks of autumn and adventure without the biting cold that sometimes creeps in deep into the wet winter months.

"Hello," I say in return. "I was heading to your house to see if you'd like to come over to dinner." I peer past her. "Where's Evie? I made pizza on a pizza stone. Thought she might like it. I doctored ours up a bit."

"She's with the Dubs. We have Sunday dinner with them every week, and I told her she could stay until bedtime."

"You remind me of the Balkans." I'm not sure what to say next.

"The Balkans? Like in Europe? Croatia and whatever else is around there?"

"Yes." It sounds asinine coming out of nowhere, so I try to explain. "Joint family is common there. Parts of India too. It's when extended family all help with the raising of children. That's what you and the Winters family remind me of. It's . . . nice."

I flounder for a word to sum up what it feels like to watch their arrangement. "The children in those cultures are notably happy and well-adjusted compared to other child-rearing models. And adults are less overwhelmed." I have no idea if turning this into a monologue is making this better or worse.

"Sorry Evie's joint family is keeping custody until bedtime. Still," she adds, "pizza is a pretty serious word. I need to investigate your claims of 'doctoring' and also figure out why you're cooking it on rocks."

I give her a small smile. "It's a pizza stone. It makes for a crispier crust. You're certainly welcome to try it. I have dessert too."

She sighs. "I don't care if you're only tricking me so you can lock me in a cage and fatten me up before you bake me. Dessert bribes will work every time."

"I'm not trying to bribe you." Why is it that I so often get twisted around when I'm with this woman? I always manage to say the wrong thing in the wrong way with her.

"Kidding, Henry." She's already moving up my walkway. "I want to try your pizza and eat some dessert, but I'm trying to make it seem like I'm doing you a favor."

I relax a fraction. "I see. In that case, I would appreciate it if you could come in and do some quality control."

"If I must," she says, brushing past me. She smells like . . . vanilla? The bakery kind, not the imitation kind.

Inside, I wave her to the table, which I've set, and return from the kitchen bearing a pizza and a salad.

"I'll try the pizza, but I truly don't have room for vegetables."

I put the plate down in front of her and take my seat. "Did you have vegetables with your Sunday dinner?"

"Potatoes."

"Any vegetables with color?" I'm sensing a not-so-hidden pattern in her eating.

"Corn," she announces triumphantly.

"That's a grain. Anything else?"

She says nothing.

"Mmhmm. You don't have to eat the salad. I'm not your dad. But I'm also definitely not giving you the panna cotta I bought for dessert if you don't."

"But you just said you're not my dad."

"Correct. I'm trying to be a good neighbor. A good neighbor asks after your health. An even better one *looks* after your health."

She grabs her fork, stabs a large forkful of salad, chews it up, and sets her fork down. "Happy?"

"I don't have an opinion on it," I say. "But I'm pretty sure your liver is thanking me."

She rolls her eyes. "What kind of pizza is this, anyway? That amount of green is sus, but it smells divine."

"Sus?" She has a unique talent for using words every ten minutes that make me feel older than dirt.

"Suspect. What is it?"

"Basil pesto, broccolini, and baby spinach," I say. "Thin crust baked to the perfect texture. Tell me what you think."

She takes a bite. Her eyes widen, showing a gray rim around her iris I haven't noticed before.

"I've gotten used to eating pizza Evie's way, which means cheese, and on an adventurous day, cheese and pepperoni, but oh, man. This is amazing."

"Thank you."

She laughs, and it startles me.

"What?" I ask.

"You," she says after another bite and a happy sigh. "No false modesty. You just expected me to say it was good."

"I've made this before. I know it's good, so I didn't expect you to say it, but your assessment doesn't surprise me." When she only laughs again, a smile flickers at the edges of my mouth. "All right, I appreciate you saying so."

"Better," she says.

We talk easily for the next few minutes as we eat, and I ask questions about her store. What kind of customers come in? How do they act? What do they buy?

"Why all the interest?" she asks when I want to know the average age of the customer. "Are you a secret Handy's Hardware investor I should know about?"

This pulls another small smile out of me, and I know it probably looks sheepish. "Occupational hazard. I'm fascinated by all kinds of microcultures."

"You're an odd dude."

"Not the first time I've heard it." Not by a long shot. People don't often say it with their words, but they say it with their expressions. I rather like that she's put it out there so baldly. "Did you leave room for dessert?"

She grimaces. "I tried but someone made me eat my greens."

"Out of neighborly concern," I remind her. It sounded almost fatherly, the way she said it, and I don't care for her viewing me as on par with Evie's Poppa Dub—especially when I'm closer to Paige's age than his.

"Can we take a breather?" she asks. "Maybe pace ourselves before we tackle the panna cotta?"

"I suppose." I'm not entirely sure what a breather constitutes. If it means sitting around making small talk while we digest, well . . . perhaps I'll change my answer.

"Would you be willing to show me around the house?" she asks. "I've wondered what the rest of it looks like."

"Oh." I'm surprised she wants to see it. I don't often find people to be as interested in my spaces as I am in theirs, but for me, the more I learn about a person's environment, the more keys I have to decoding their morphotype. "Yes. Let me clear this, and then I'll give you a tour."

She gets to her feet and helps, taking her own plate. I probably shouldn't let her, but I suppose when someone is a friend, you do that. Clearing other people's places is for formal guests, and already Paige and Evie both feel more familiar than that.

When we've washed and set the dishes in the rack to dry, I wave to indicate the room around us and say in a professor voice, "This is the kitchen."

"You don't say."

"Indeed. It's the center of the middleclass American suburban home where families gather to interact informally and to share news of their day as part of a dinner time bonding ritual."

"Fascinating," she says, playing along. "Do go on."

I lead her through the rest of the first floor, making up cultural "facts" on the fly. "This is the bathroom, an odd word given how many of these sanitation chambers lack not only a bath, but even a shower, another common apparatus for washing. In Britain, these rooms are simply referred to as the toilet, which seems more fitting given that one of these indeed may always be found in the misnamed 'bath' room."

I pass the stairs to the second floor, indicating with a wave that above us are the sleeping chambers, which are underutilized in the sleep-starved modern society. I wouldn't mind showing them to her, but it would mean showing her my own room, which feels awkward, frankly.

The only time grown women see my personal bedroom, it's . . . not for a tour. The idea of her peering into it is odd in a way I can't explain, so I simply brush past it, showing her my grandfather's office and ending in the living room.

I conclude my lecture on the use of shelf space for the display of "mementos that always reveal far more about their collectors than they generally intend."

"Most illuminating," she says, "and yet not. I don't see much of your fingerprint in any of these spaces. Why is that?"

"My contribution was that completely asinine faux lecture."

She grins. "I enjoyed it. You sounded like a documentary narrator trying to keep a serious voice in a film about monkeys when they're flinging their poop."

I blink rapidly. "I don't know what to say to that."

"It means you have about the driest sense of humor I've ever heard."

I smile. Most people don't realize I've cracked a joke half the time. Actually, half is probably a low estimate. "Thank you."

We're smiling at each other now, and then somehow, in a way someone has surely explained with science in a dusty dissertation, the mood changes in the space of a couple of heartbeats. Our eyes catch and stay there, and my smile melts away, leaving us simply staring. It's intimate. It would be like that with any human. As a species, most of us are surprisingly bad at prolonged eye contact.

Paige's smile fades too, into an inquisitive expression. Each time I look at her eyes, I see something new. A new color, or tonight, the traces of all the laughing she does carved delicately into the skin at their corners.

I have the strangest impulse to touch them, to see if I can even feel lines so faint. Almost without thinking, my hand drifts up to follow through on the urge, and her skin is soft against my fingertips. Soft and warm. I trace it along her cheekbone, mesmerized, but Paige steps back and the spell breaks.

I slide my hand in my pocket instead. What was I thinking? My fingertips tingle. They've always been sensitive, but this is bizarre.

Experiments have shown that a couple can fall in love within four minutes by silently staring into each other's eyes after answering a series of increasingly personal questions. We're three minutes and fifty-five seconds and several questions short of the danger zone, and I scramble to think of something else to say to keep it that way. "Dessert?"

She looks startled—as well she might when I bark the single word at her.

"That sounds good. I think I can handle it now. The panna cotta," she adds, like there might be some confusion.

Honestly, there is in the aftermath of the moment we just had. At least for me. What was that? I excuse myself to the kitchen, replaying those few seconds as I plate the cream-thickened custard. It was the strangest sense of connection, of everything standing still except for the sounds of our breath.

I just want to know so it doesn't happen again. It didn't mean anything, but it could seem important if it keeps happening. Neither of us has room for that kind of complication, I suspect. The last thing I want is to be the cliché of a professor dating someone practically young enough to be doing her undergrad, even if she's already done with school. Those men are ridiculous, and I won't be one.

Not that I want to date her, anyway. We've managed to get comfortable with each other quickly—far more quickly than I do with most people—and there's no need to read more into it than two people making a point of being civil.

When I emerge from the kitchen, she's settled into the easy chair in the front room. I hand her a plate and set mine on the coffee table. "Seems like a good night for a glass of wine."

"Sounds good, neighbor. You should enjoy one, but I'm sober, so . . ."

Oh. "Sparkling water?"

She smiles. "Perfect."

I retreat, wondering if she's trying to diffuse the strangeness too, reminding us of our connection to each other with that "neighbor."

I return with a glass of sweet white Bordeaux for me and a LaCroix for her, but I pause when she reaches for it, wrinkling my forehead. "Tell me the truth, are you drinking this because you aren't legally old enough to drink wine?"

"Very funny," she says, taking the can.

And it's not, exactly, but it does ease the . . . tension isn't the right word. It pairs too easily with "sexual," and that's not where my mind is at. It eases the oddness.

She tries a bite of the panna cotta, and her face lights up. "Where did you learn to cook like this?"

"That's a no-bake dessert. And I didn't make it."

She gives me a look.

I smile. "I guess you mean the other dishes. I did a study abroad for a semester in Umbria, Italy, and I grew interested in it there. The signora who hosted me was happy to teach me. I've tried to keep up with it since. I watch cooking shows and tutorials and read cookbooks."

She tilts her head, savoring another bite as she studies me. "Do you do anything casually?"

"Not if I'm interested in it." Anything worth knowing is worth knowing deeply.

"What about dating?"

Now it's my turn to shoot up an eyebrow. It appears we have not moved past our earlier moment.

"Oh, I didn't mean it like that," she says, seeing my expression. "I mean do you ever date casually? You've been in Creekville long enough to have been out on a few dates, right?"

I don't get the sense that she's trying to work this around to herself, but I'm not sure what she's getting at. "I haven't dated since I've moved here, no."

"Tragic love story? Broken heart?" Her voice is too cheerful for two sad phrases. "Oooh, I know—pining for someone unattainable."

That guess startles me so much that it makes her laugh.

"That's it! You're pining for someone. Unrequited love. I'm very good at other people's love lives." She leans forward, her eyes sparkling. "Tell me all about it, and I'll help you solve it."

"There's no unrequited love." I sound grouchy about it, which makes me feel grouchy about it.

She smiles wider. "But someone you're interested in? Someone you haven't taken out yet?"

I give her a stern look, but her expression doesn't waver. "I suppose there is someone."

"I knew it," she crows. "Who?"

Twin reactions of relief and slight deflation ripple through me. She clearly has no interest in me for herself, which is excellent, but does she have to make it so obvious? I frown slightly. I don't enjoy being a paradox. Not a foolish one, anyway.

"Come on, you can tell me. I can help you figure out how to land her."

"Land her? Is she a fish?"

"I don't know," she says. "You won't tell me anything."

"We're veering close to a hellish Abbott and Costello routine."

"Who?"

I'm about to answer her when I spot her smirk. "Ha. Funny."

She shrugs as if to say, *Obviously.*

"There's a woman at work. Leigh."

She holds up her hands in the international sign for "A . . . ?" "A custodian? Another professor? A secretary? The *dean*? I need details."

"Another professor. We share an office."

She leans so far forward, I'm not sure how she hasn't tumbled from her seat. "Oooh, this sounds good. Tell me about her."

"She teaches psychology."

"Is she pretty?"

I shoot her a quelling look. "Does that matter?"

"It doesn't *not* matter." She snorts when I glower. "Don't deny it. Is she?"

A long pause, but she shows no signs of getting bored. "Yes. She's pretty."

"Yes! Now we're getting somewhere. When are you taking her out?"

"It's not that simple."

"It's exactly that simple," she argues. "Why haven't you gone on a date yet?"

"We share an office. It would be awkward if we don't mesh."

"Is that what kids these days call it?"

"Paige . . ."

She grins. "How long have you been sharing an office? Shouldn't you know by now if you click?"

"Just this semester so far. She's new."

"So almost three full months. That's plenty of time to know if you vibe. Do you get along?"

"Yes."

"No problems with sharing the space? No constant irritation from things she says or does? That's promising," she notes when I shake my head. "Has she complained about any of your habits to you?"

"She hasn't." I'm slightly offended she asked, but Paige continues on.

"Then ask her out." She sits back like it's that easy.

I stifle a sigh and sip my wine.

"But what?"

If I don't tell her the whole truth, she won't let this go. Her stubbornness is on display through my side window, winking his Santa eye at me every two seconds. "She doesn't really see me like that."

"Like what?"

"Like someone to date. This is embarrassing. Can we change the subject?"

"Definitely not," she says. "Do you know Lily Greene?"

The gracious woman in the fine foods market. "I've met her."

"She's the most skilled matchmaker in Creekville and long may she reign, but I want to be just like her when I grow up, and I'm pretty good at it too. I had way more to do with my brother getting married than he realizes."

"Sounds like a good story you should tell me right now."

"So we don't have to talk about your unrequited love? No chance. I can help you figure this out."

"No. I can't tolerate the idea of making it"—more—"awkward in the office if this went poorly. I wouldn't want her to be uncomfortable sharing a space if she declines."

Paige sits back and gives me a look of surprise mixed with approval. "That's thoughtful."

"Don't sound so surprised."

"Why wouldn't I be? You handled me entirely wrong."

"Fair," I grunt.

"How long will you be sharing an office?"

"She'll get her own in January."

"I'm going to mull." And then she settles into the armchair, eating bites of her panna cotta, her expression far away.

I finish my wine, and I like that our silence is comfortable. I always feel like people are waiting for me to speak, and I don't like talking just to talk.

"I've got it," she says so suddenly that I jump. "We make you look dateable. And then when she can't stop thinking of you as dateable, you ask her out."

"Make me look dateable?" I've never uttered a stupider sentence.

"Yeah. A makeover! We'll make you look so good."

"Do I look bad now? And who is we?"

"Evie and me, of course. I know you only ever see me in jeans and tees, but I promise, I have an excellent sense of style, and she inherited it. We'll work magic."

I notice she didn't answer whether I look bad or not, and I fight the impulse to ask again like I'm a junior high girl before her first dance. Worse, I have an even stronger impulse to hear Paige say I look good. Time for evasive maneuvers. "Fine. Make me dateable."

Because if this evening has shown me anything, it's that I desperately need a distraction.

Chapter Eighteen

Paige

I JUMP UP AND turn toward my house. "Headlights in my driveway. Bill must have brought Evie home."

I head for the door, and Henry follows. Sure enough, Evie runs around the front of the pickup but veers toward us when I call her name from the porch.

"Hey, Mama!" She barrels into my waiting arms at the bottom of the steps like she does every time she sees me, whether it's been an hour or a full workday.

"Hey, rainbow unicorn. How was the game?"

"Commanders lost," Bill says, climbing from the truck.

Lisa comes around from the other side. "Evie was adamant that we come see her room. Hope that's okay."

"Of course." I turn to smile at Henry. "Thanks for feeding me. I'm going to have to hibernate until Thursday now, but it was worth it."

He's still up on the porch and smiles. "My pleasure."

It's the kind of thing people say all the time. Fast food drive-thrus, for example. Bank tellers. Flight attendants. All the people. Everyone. And yet...

Something about the strange vibe of the night makes his words land differently, and they get me right in the lower belly where watching Bogart kiss Bacall in *To Have and Have Not* always gets me.

I wave goodbye, and Evie and I start across the yard, but we don't make it even to his driveway before she stops.

"Come on, Mr. Henry," she calls.

He stops halfway through his doorway and turns. "Pardon?"

"To see my rainbow room. I'm showing it to everyone."

I give him a reassuring look. "Henry was just telling me he has some work to do." Evie would invite the whole world to do everything because there isn't a single introverted cell in her body.

He steps back out. "It can wait a few minutes."

Uh, what?

But yep, he's shut the door behind him and is coming down the stairs.

"Go take the Dubs inside," I tell Evie. "We'll be right there."

She skips ahead and opens the door, chattering about all the things she's already added to her room—a witch's corner, a secret portal in her closet that's invisible to grownups, and the list goes on as the door closes behind them.

"Should I have not said yes?" Henry asks.

"No, that's fine, but I don't want you to feel obligated. Evie and I are working on boundaries because she has none."

"I don't feel obligated. I want to see how the pink from my sweater looks on the wall. Maybe I'll use it in my office." His mouth curls at the corner, and without thinking about it, I give his chest a light shove.

He takes a step back, and I freeze. Why did I manhandle his pecs like that? "Oops. Sorry. We're not really play-shoving neighbors."

"Please don't do that again." His voice is polite and even, and I'm about to apologize again when he adds, "Not unless you warn me first, so I can brace, and you can see that I'm strong and manly and can't be pushed around by a small female."

"I'm going to push you again for using the words 'manly' and 'small' since I am not small but average, and I won't be mischaracterized just because you decided to overachieve on height."

"Very well." He nods, his face still serious. He crosses his arms. "I'm ready."

I snort and give him another play shove. He doesn't move.

"Fine. That was pretty manly."

"Thank you." Not a single thing changes about his tone or expression, but somehow I can sense that he's laughing inside.

"You're an odd guy, Henry."

"That's facts," he says, and this catches me so off guard that I gape. A tiny smile appears. "I do pay attention to the slang of the youth. All part of being a cultural anthropologist. I just know it's very"—he pauses and looks as if he's thinking—"cringey when I do."

I shudder. "Promise never to do that again."

Another nod. "No cap."

"Stop it," I beg. "Come see the rainbow room and don't say any more words." I can still sense the silent laughter as he follows me into the house.

"—and that's the secret portal," Evie announces as we join her in her room. Lisa and Bill are sitting on her bed and Henry stays in the doorway, glancing around at everything. His eyes are . . . well, a week ago, I would have said judgy, but I can read him slightly better now, and I suspect they're just curious. He's taking it in, cataloguing, matching it up with what he knows about the "average American girl child."

"That wall is going to be for pictures." Evie points to the wall without doors or windows.

"What kind of pictures?" Lisa asks. I know how her brain works. She's digging for a gift idea.

"All the memories I'm going to have," Evie explains. "Like with friends or when everyone comes home on Tuesday to see my play."

"The class play she was rehearsing," I explain to Henry. "She's a pumpkin."

"The *best* pumpkin," Evie adds, while I mouth, *The only pumpkin.* "You're coming too, right, Mr. Henry?"

"I don't think—"

"Evie, honey." I interrupt to save him from having to let her down. "Henry has to work, but you're very sweet to have thought of him."

"I don't think I have to work," Henry says. "I'd be happy to come. It's been a while since I've seen a good Thanksgiving play."

All three adults stare at him, and he blushes. "If that's okay."

"It's great," Evie says.

We all look at each other and nod.

"It's great," I tell him.

"Thanks for letting me see the room, Evie. The pink is nice. I better go. I need to . . ."

"Do that thing," I supply.

"Yes, that thing. Nice to have met you all." He gives us a polite nod and leaves.

Lisa looks at me with her eyebrows raised, but I only give her a tiny headshake.

"What are you talking about?" Evie asks.

"Your room. What other plans do you have for it?" I ask.

She frowns. "No, I mean you and Nana Dub had a whole conversation but not in words."

I can't help but laugh. "You're too smart for your own good, kiddo."

"So you're not going to tell me?" she presses.

"I'm not going to tell you."

She sighs. "Fine. Now I'll show you all my stick witches."

She's off and running again while her Dubs listen indulgently, and I'm left pondering the puzzle of Henry. The more pieces I get, the less sense he makes.

Why, then, do I want more pieces?

Monday night is full of lots of hugging and hellos when Noah and Grace drive in from Charleston, and Evie is fixed to my brother's side with Gorilla Glue, thrilled to have her uncle back. I promise to give them a look at our new place after Evie's play the next day.

Tabitha and Sawyer's flight is delayed out of New York the next morning, so it's a smaller but still overwhelming gaggle of adults sitting on the third row for Evie's show. I'd left a note on Henry's windshield promising him he truly did not have to come, leaving my number in case he wanted to text me that he needed to cancel.

But no text comes in, and as the lights dim in the noisy school gym, he slides into the seat I saved him at the end of the row.

There are only two second-grade classes at the elementary school, but the gym swells with every relative those sixty kids have ever known, plus at least one sometimes grumpy neighbor.

It makes me slightly cranky. I'm so worried about him having a good time that I can't enjoy it myself, although I do give Evie my full attention for all four of her lines. Most of the kids are in the chorus on risers below the stage, singing songs about gratitude and . . . I can't make out the words of one, but I think Henry might be right when he leans over and asks, "Is this a song about giblets?"

The cheers are loud, the laughs are louder, and the applause at the end is rousing. Through it all, Henry looks bemused, but he stands for the ovation with everyone else when the lights come up. The kids pour from the wings and out of the risers to get their congratulations.

"Tell Evie she did a great job," Henry says as the applause starts to die down.

"You're not staying? Evie will want to see you."

"I'm going to slip out and check on"—he pauses, looking for an excuse—"some things."

A panic answer, but I get it, and I smile. "Sounds good. Thanks for coming."

"I'm glad I did. See you at home." Then, as if only registering his words after he hears them, he shakes his head and adds, "I mean not at *our* home. At your home." And then he *cringes*. It is *glorious*. "While I'm at my home. I'll see you at your house from my house. Never mind," he growls, when I can't fight a smile. He heads to the exit like the second graders are chasing him out.

Lisa takes off after him, and I watch in confusion as she flags him down, barely registering Evie when she makes it to us and Noah swoops her up in a hug. Whatever Lisa and Henry talk about, it's short. He appears to listen intently, says something, listens again, then nods. Lisa pats his arm, he leaves, and she comes back to us.

"Henry will be joining us for Thanksgiving," she announces.

This is both a surprise and not a surprise. This will be our third Thanksgiving with the Dubs, and they're pretty fluid, always with a couple of strays or singletons from church brought into the mix. It's an "everybody's welcome at all times" kind of vibe.

"Sounds good," I say. But I'm surprised he accepted. Whatever he thought it would be like to have Evie and me as neighbors, we must have exceeded his worst-case scenario. I'll make sure he knows he's not obligated to dinner. Or school plays. Or decorating. Or anything else.

We walk Noah and Grace to our place a few minutes later.

"I can't believe you stuck her with all this stuff, Dad," Grace says, stopping to stare at the Christmas explosion in our yard. "You can tell him no, Paige. Otherwise, it won't stop."

"She likes it," Bill protests.

"She does not like it," Grace says, rolling her eyes.

"You do too, don't you, Paige?"

They both turn to me, which is the worst. Grace is right, but I wouldn't hurt Bill's feelings for anything. "I'm so grateful for it," I say. And I am. I know Bill gave it all to me because he cares.

"See?" he says triumphantly to Grace.

"I *do* see," she retorts. "I see that Paige is too nice to admit it's a headache. Did you notice she didn't say she loves it?"

Bill's face falls. "Is that true, Paige?"

"No, Bill. I'm so glad we have it. Truly."

"Well, good," he says, his smile returning. "Let's get on with this tour."

Evie drags Noah straight to her room to tell him all about it, and I give Grace a tour of the place, describing my renovation plans.

She nods at every point, understanding probably better than I do how much work it will take. She helped build my old apartment, after all, and helped her best friend remodel her fixer-upper a couple of years ago. Her friend had repaid the favor by setting Grace up with Noah.

"I can see what you like about this place." She pats one of the plaster walls. "It's the definition of good bones. But even with supplies at cost, it's going to be expensive and take forever."

"I know." I'll make my first mortgage payment in two weeks, and while I'll have the money for it, I won't be able to save nearly as much as I hoped. It'll take forever to get a car at this rate, and forget Evie having any unplanned growth spurts, much less any unplanned emergencies. I'll have to build a reserve first to handle those things, and I want that to be at least a thousand dollars before I even start my car fund.

None of this would have happened if Henry hadn't tried to outbid me, but I can't hold it against him. I know he'd make a different choice now, and I know every time he comes over, he gets that the slow pace of repairs is his fault. I'm petty enough to take a tiny bit of satisfaction from that, but I know him well enough now not to hold the bidding against him anymore.

But I don't want to talk about my stressful finances with anyone else right now, so I smile at Grace. "I know it's going to be slow, but it'll be so worth it."

"So tell me about those shelves over there." She nods at them, taking the cue to drop the subject.

After a fun visit, we get a group text that Tabitha and Sawyer have landed and will be home shortly, so everyone heads back to the Winters house—except for me. "I'll catch up," I tell them. "Just have to do something real quick."

Once they've turned the corner, I hurry over to Henry's house and knock.

"Hello," he says.

"You're not even surprised when it's me anymore."

"You and Evie are literally the only people who ever knock."

"Oh." That's kind of sad. I wonder if it bothers him, but I can't tell from his neutral tone. "I wanted to tell you that you definitely don't have to come to Thanksgiving. I can tell them that you decided you had other plans."

He gives a slow nod. "Would you prefer that I not come?"

"No," I say so quickly that he starts. "I mean, yes, it would be great if you came, but I don't want you to feel pressured. The Winters clan is overwhelming. Evie is the tip of the iceberg."

"Then if you don't mind, I'll accept."

"For science?" I ask, a grin creeping up on me.

"For science," he agrees, the corner of his lips twitching. "What should I bring?"

For a second, I lose my train of thought. It's a victory every time I win that almost-smile. "The wine," I say. "I know you're an outstanding cook, but so are all of them, and there will be more food than everyone can eat. But trust me, you're going to want the wine."

"Very well. Would it be out of place if I brought an appetizer?"

"You really want to participate in this American social ritual, don't you?"

"Yes. Better science and all."

"Bring an appetizer. Evie and I will be over there early to hang out with my brother, but if you come around 2:30, that should be plenty of time to enjoy appetizers before the main event."

He nods.

I tilt my head. "You really don't talk much."

He leans against the doorway, arms folded. "That's not what my students say."

Why is this kind of . . . sexy? I never had any handsome professors. Maybe this is a belated crush-on-teacher thing happening? But no. This isn't a crush. He's a moderately entertaining neighbor who is better looking than I first realized, that's all.

Still, I dredge up a helpful buffer topic. "By the way, I've been thinking about Project: Makeover, and—"

"Pardon?" He looks utterly confused.

"You know, Bag-a-Babe? Your office mate?" He flinches at the terms as hard as I meant for him to, and it makes me laugh. He's so easy to tease. "I told you, we're going to do a makeover on you. When does the semester end?"

"Second week of December."

I reach up and touch his jaw without thinking. I regret it the second I do, but I feel trapped—committed, really—to forging ahead, because snatching my hand back will make this even more of a thing. "How long does it take for you to grow a scruff?"

I run my finger lightly along the sharp angle of his jaw, like I'm the scruff inspector. *Why am I being such a weirdo?!* I just have to act like this is no big deal, so I make sure my face wears the same expression as when I'm trying to measure the perfect lumber cut for a customer.

He reaches up and takes my hand, pulling it down, but softly, turning it over to study my palm. I'm self-conscious about them; I wear gloves when I work, but they still show calluses. He runs the pad of his thumb over them, a touch lighter than a breeze, but it tickles my whole body the way it does when a soft wind catches the long tendrils at the nape of my neck.

I slide my hand from his and tuck it in my back pocket, casually, like that's what I meant to do with it all along.

He looks at me like he's forgotten what we're talking about.

"Scruff?" I remind him.

He rubs his hand along his smooth jaw. "Probably five days, give or take."

"About as long as it takes my leg hair." And then I have to fight hard not to squeeze my eyes shut because why did I just say that? No one—especially not my neighbor—needs to know how long it takes to grow my leg hair.

His face now looks like he's switched from anthropologist to biologist, and I'm a bug under his microscope. A weird bug.

I forge ahead. "Do you do a university Christmas party?"

"By college, yes."

"And when?"

"After grades are due, so the Friday before Christmas."

"Okay, so you need to start working on your scruff about two weeks before that. I'll tell you when it's the right length and then you just maintain it from there."

"I . . .what?"

"You have to start making some changes now, gradual ones that she'll notice. Is this party formal or casual?"

"Business dressy, I think." He looks uncertain. "Is that a type of dress code? I was planning on my nicest slacks and Oxford."

This guy. Who even calls button-down shirts Oxfords anymore? Henry Hill, PhD, apparently. "You will definitely not be wearing those. Your assignment in the next two weeks is to buy a pair of gray trousers, not chinos, in a medium to light shade, and a black button-down shirt." I run my gaze over him, imagining the body I glimpsed in his running clothes freed from the bondage of frumpiness. Or I do until my cheeks grow warm at the picture in my mind's eye.

This is getting ridiculous.

I retreat down the stairs, then add over my shoulder, "I'll also need to investigate your shoe situation before then."

"You're very strange," he calls after me.

I give him a thumbs up because . . . I don't know why. Because I agree, and I don't want to slow down long enough to acknowledge that he's right. *Thumbs up, yes, I'm a total weirdo. At least right now.*

And then I speed walk across my yard and make my escape.

Chapter Nineteen

Henry

I WALK OVER TO Mulberry Street and scan the house numbers until I find the Winters residence halfway down. The driveway is full, so it's for the best I live close enough to walk.

I didn't see Paige at all yesterday; the only evidence she was even home was the house lights flipping on after 8:00. She's been keeping the Christmas lights off, whether to avoid fuse problems or for other reasons, I'm not sure.

That's a relief. I may have come to find the Redmonds less annoying—kind of enjoy them, even—but I still hate their gaudy yard. It truly doesn't fit on Orchard, and the less I have to live next to the neon North Pole, the happier I'll be, even if today is the last day of aesthetic peace and quiet.

I walk to the front door. There are only seven adults and Evie, but I can hear the hum of conversation, punctuated by high laughs and . . . was that a grunt? I haven't even knocked, and this is already a much different Thanksgiving than I normally share with my parents.

They'd invited me to join them as usual for their country club Thanksgiving feast, but even before Mrs. Winters had invited me over, I'd already turned my parents down. That's partially why I'd driven up a couple of weekends ago: to spend time with them so they wouldn't mind me skipping Thanksgiving.

But I'm tired of country club holidays; the only conversations I can have there are small talk because the only familiar faces there are people I've met at previous Thanksgivings. We could do this for the rest of our lives, all the same people, and we still wouldn't progress past surface chatter.

I shift the platter I brought, take a deep breath, and knock.

The door flies open to reveal a grinning Evie. "Hey, Mr. Henry. My sea monkeys are swimming all over everywhere. Will you come see them soon?"

"Um, sure, if it's okay with your mom."

"It will be," she says with a confidence I'm learning is specific to seven-year-olds. "Anyway, glad you're here," she continues. "I wanted to come get you, but Mom said give you some peace, for gosh's sake."

I fight to keep my smile at friendly instead of a full grin; I don't want her to think I'm laughing at her.

"I'm sorry to keep you waiting."

"It's fine. Mama!" she calls and runs off.

Paige appears around a doorway and looks confused to find me standing by myself in an open door with a plate of food and some wine tucked under my arm. Probably not as confused as I am though. I've seen Paige in every variation of jeans, Dickies, and overalls with T-shirts and flannel imaginable, and that one memorable morning, in her pajamas. Her short pajamas. But this is not that Paige.

She's in a soft-looking sweater and tight pants and boots. And she's wearing makeup. Not a ton, but her eyes are brighter, and her lips look slightly different. I hate to use the word moist, but yes. That. And a little pinker?

Paige is at minimum pretty on her worst day, and this is *not* her worst day.

"Hey, Henry. Come on in. You've met everyone but Tabitha and her husband. I'll introduce you."

She leads me toward the back of the house and the kitchen. It's bustling with women. Mrs. Winters relieves me of my offerings.

"That's an appetizer if you're ready for those," I say as she slides the plate from my hands.

"Perfect." She sets it on the counter and peels back the foil.

"Cranberry brie bites," I say, feeling self-conscious. I'm not sure why. Is brie pretentious at a meal hosted by a family who owns a hardware store? Will it look like I tried too hard?

The only woman I haven't met yet swoops in to pluck one up and sample it, and my eyes widen as I realize I have failed to put together an important fact: the Tabitha that Paige has casually mentioned is Tabitha Winters, major celebrity chef.

"So good," she pronounces.

My cheeks heat far past the temperature I cooked these at. "It's your recipe."

She pauses, chews a couple more times, and shakes her head. "No. Similar but not exact. You added something. Thyme?"

I nod.

They could have hosted the quarterback of their favorite NFL team, whoever is at the top of the music charts, and the most famous supermodel in the world at the same time and not have left me as starstruck as meeting this woman does.

"You're *that* Tabitha Winters," I say. Stupidly. Because clearly she and everyone else in the house are aware of this. "I didn't put that together somehow."

"Uh-oh," Grace says. "You've found a fan. Poor guy."

"In real life, I'm Tabitha Reed now. My husband, Sawyer, is watching the game with my dad in the den if you want to join them."

"Tabitha, this is my neighbor, Henry Hill," Paige tells her. "And now I know why he's such a good cook. He's been stealing your best recipes."

I shake my head. "Only following them, not stealing."

"Stealing and improving," she says. "You'll have to tell me about other tweaks you've made. Come and meet Sawyer. Cooking my recipes is how he won me back."

"Won you back?" I ask.

"We'll tell you the story over cranberry brie bites."

I turn to catch Paige's eye, not sure if I'm supposed to stick with her or roam, but she smiles and jerks her head in the direction of a room leaking sounds of a football game and several loud male groans.

Tabitha makes the introductions, and once the men establish that I don't follow football, Noah and Mr. Winters turn back to the TV and Sawyer gets up and suggests we go outside.

We find Paige sitting on a glider, watching Evie gallop around the backyard.

"She's riding a unicorn," she explains.

I nod. Sure. Why not?

We eat and chat. Or Sawyer and Paige do, really. It's nothing deep, but it feels like more than small talk. These are the conversations of people who are entirely comfortable with each other, and before long, they're asking me questions. How do I like it here, what does an anthropologist do, exactly, is

Evie the best or what, and from Evie herself, why do I think Santa picked the North Pole when he could have picked a beach to live?

I answer all of these to everyone's satisfaction, I think. At least, Evie seems to accept my theory as an anthropologist that Santa chose a region that is largely uninhabited by humans so he can do his work without interruption, unlike the beach, where lots of people go to visit.

Bill calls us in to eat, and once we're settled around their table, I'm almost relaxed. I don't feel that way around new people often, but with the Winters family, I don't feel like one of them, exactly, but I also don't feel like an outsider.

By the time the dishes get passed around the table, I'm even kind of comfortable—until a question from Tabitha sends things off the rails.

"So is it awkward dating a neighbor?" she asks us. "Like, did you have to agree on a fallout plan if things don't work out?"

Paige chokes on her water, and Grace starts laughing.

"Tab, they aren't dating."

"They aren't?" Tabitha looks from me to Paige, then over to her mother. "I thought you said they hang out all the time, and he cooks her dinner. And didn't he go to Evie's play? And now he's here."

Noah's eyebrows snap together, and Paige shakes her head. "Just neighbors," she says. She throws a look I can only describe as pleading in Lisa's direction, and I add a silent boost to it. *Yes, Lisa, change the subject. Please.*

"They're not dating, Tabitha. Leave them alone. By the way, Paige, I've been meaning to tell you that your lipstick is really pretty."

"Thanks," Paige says, her coughing fit under control. She looks back to normal except she won't make eye contact with me.

"But I don't get how that's not—" Tabitha starts, but her mother cuts her off.

"I learned the most interesting thing about lipstick from Presley at the salon the other day," Lisa continues while Paige saws at a piece of turkey so tender it falls apart at a touch. "She said that the way you can choose your best neutral lip color is to find a shade that matches your" —she pauses and glances at Evie, then says—"areoles."

This time Noah spits out his water, at least three forks clatter to their plates, Bill shakes his head, and Sawyer's fork freezes halfway to his mouth.

Evie's voice slices through the moment with, "What's an areola, Mama?"

This is not the change of subject Paige and I were hoping for. I think I can confidently assume that on her behalf.

All three of the other men turn to look at their wives speculatively, and I drop my eyes to my plate. I will not be participating in this conversation. Nope.

Tabitha clears her throat, and I don't know her well enough to guess whether she's about to save the situation or blow it up more. "That's interesting, Mom. The network makeup artist says the best way is to try a bunch and pick the one that looks good. Like a normal person."

Sawyer nods. "Although I'd be willing to help you try this other method."

"All right," Grace says, "that's enough." She shoots me an apologetic look. "I'm pretty sure this is payback for driving up the bidding on Paige."

"Then why am I suffering?" Paige complains.

"Are y'all done now?" Grace asks, darting glances at the three main offenders.

Lisa gives me a small smile. "I believe I am."

"Fair enough," I say. "I deserved it."

"Tab? Sawyer?" Grace fixes them both with a hard stare. Tabitha might be the oldest sister, but it feels like Grace is the one who runs the show.

"Only for Paige's benefit," Tabitha says.

"I was serious," Sawyer says.

"Shut up, Sawyer." Grace's tone is mild, and Sawyer grins.

"I did *not* deserve it, so thanks, everyone," Paige mutters.

I'm not sure what to think or how to react, but I do have to fight the urge to both laugh and study Paige's lip color more closely. I punt by glancing to Bill's end of the table. "Would you pass the beets?" I ask. I hate beets, but it's the only thing sitting right in front of him.

Paige decides we need a change in conversation too. "I'm helping Henry with a love project."

"Excuse me?" says Noah, looking perturbed.

"He wants to date the goddess he shares an office with, and I'm helping him," she says.

Noah relaxes.

"So there you go." She sweeps a pointed glance around the table. "Not dating. In fact, I'm helping him date someone else."

"Interesting," Tabitha says. "What's the plan? Shock and awe?"

Paige shakes her head. "I can't tell you too much or he'll get nervous, but this will be a gradual glow up."

Grace nods. "Sneak attack. Nice."

"I'm right here," I say.

Tabitha glances at me. "What does that have to do with anything?"

Sawyer shakes his head. "Give up and give in, man. Your girl was one of them as soon as they met."

"Not his girl," Paige says.

She doesn't have to say it like she's insulted by the idea.

"So Henry has the Office Goddess. You got anything interesting going on in the romance department, Paige?" That's Tabitha. I don't think I like her, but also, I'm very interested in Paige's answer. If there's anyone paying her visits at her house, I haven't seen any evidence of it. It's good to know who might be hanging out next door. For reasons of . . . it's just good to be aware, safety-wise? Yes. It's good to be aware of my surroundings for safety reasons.

"The UPS driver keeps spending his lunch breaks in the store," Bill says.

"Ooh, Mike?" Grace asks. "He's cute. Something going on there, Paige?"

Paige shakes her head. "No. We went to lunch once, and he tipped poorly."

Noah winces. "Dead man walking."

I remember Paige referencing waiting tables. It's easy to see why it would be a dealbreaker for her.

The conversation drifts into smoother waters after that. No, "drifts" is the wrong word. It speeds all over the place like a cigarette boat, but I keep up. Barely. In my head, anyway. I listen and don't try to jump in. I learn more that way.

After everyone has had second and even third helpings, Bill declares it's time for the men to clear the table and clean up.

"Not you," Lisa tells me. "You're a guest."

I catch Noah's eye and try to communicate my fear of being left alone with these women.

"Sorry, Lisa, but Henry ate, so he has to help clear the mess too."

"I don't mind," I assure her, rising and reaching for the nearest plates. "I'm tidy by nature." I try not to wince at the sound of my own words. I know I can be formal—even stiff. It's my tendency, and I don't worry too much about fighting it. But "tidy by nature"? For my next trick, I should pull out knitting needles and whip up a tea cozy.

Not that I knit.

But I would kind of like to learn . . .

The clearing and cleaning is about twenty minutes of joking and light wrestling, the brothers-in-law occasionally capturing each other in head locks or snapping each other with towels. They act as if they've grown up in this family, not married into it in the last two years, and I envy it. I was always a quiet kid, and after my grandmother, I got quieter.

When we join the women in the living room, Sawyer and Noah tuck themselves in with their wives on the sofa. Bill and Lisa have taken the armchairs. Paige and Evie chose the love seat, but even Evie's boundless energy was no match for the post-turkey tryptophan, and she's sound asleep with her head in Paige's lap.

I smile at the picture they make. "She's out cold."

Paige returns the smile, and for a half a second, our eyes meet and hold, but I blink and drop my gaze. I think that love study was done on people who stared into each other's eyes for four consecutive minutes, but I don't want to risk it being cumulative.

"She goes hard and crashes hard," Paige says. "And honestly, I probably need to get home." She glances outside. "I have to get up before dawn to make sure the store is ready for Black Friday."

"Bill," Lisa says, swatting his arm. "Why did you schedule her so early?"

"He didn't," Paige says. "I scheduled myself. He's done it for enough years. But if it's okay with you, Evie wants to sleep over here, and then Noah and Grace will bring her back and watch her at my house when she wakes up tomorrow."

"Of course, honey," Lisa says. "But you can't leave yet. There's still dessert."

Paige glances at me. "It's up to you," she says, barely fighting a yawn. "I wouldn't want to pull you away early, and I'm not going to leave you here to fend for yourself against them."

"No, that's fine. I'm on the verge of a turkey coma too." In truth, the only space left to sit is on the sofa with the Winters girls and their husbands, and that feels even more awkward than lipstick-matching talk.

Well, *almost* as awkward.

"Then it's decided." Paige slips from beneath Evie and makes sure she's settled comfortably before she straightens. "We'll head out."

"Together," Tabitha notes.

"Knock it off, Tab," Grace says, and Sawyer pinches his wife.

"Yes, together, Tab. That's what happens sometimes when two people live next door to each other and are ready to go to their own, separate houses."

Paige delivers the retort without any heat, and yet, I feel the slightest twinge when she says the word "separate." It's never struck me as a lonely word until now.

"At least take a pie home with you," Lisa says, climbing to her feet. "Each," she adds. "We've got so many."

"You're welcome," Tabitha singsongs.

"Show-off," Grace says, then she pinches her sister, who seems to find it less cute than when her husband does it.

"I'm definitely taking home a pie made by Tabitha Winters, Queen of *Dinner Reborn*, and I'm definitely not sharing," I say with a stern look at Paige.

She snorts. "I'll have to settle for eating my own whole pie by myself, I guess."

After several minutes of goodbyes and leave-taking, we walk back to our place, side-by-side, our hands full of pie, reviewing the best dish of the meal, which turns out to be all of them—except for the beets, although Paige even liked those.

I pause at the foot of my front walk. "I'm glad Lisa invited me. Thanks for letting me tag along."

"No problem," she says turning to face me. "Remember how much you enjoyed it tomorrow when the lights blaze to life and stay up for six weeks."

I grimace. "I'll try."

"And definitely remember next week when I'm working on Project: Office Goddess."

"That is not what it's called."

"Oh, it is," she says, giving my foot a light kick.

"No kicking."

Her eyes narrow. "Or what?" She gives another lazy kick aimed at my shins, but I catch her foot between my calves.

I don't press hard, but it'll be hard for her to get away unless I want her to. "Or consequences."

She goes very still, shifting her pie to one hand and resting it against her hip. She reaches out and grasps a handful of my sweater in front and gives it a slight tug. "It'd be a shame if I had to ruin another of your sweaters, Henry."

We're eighteen inches apart, and neither of us can lean back without us both losing balance. We're standing with our feet on the ground, but for the space of a breath, I feel all the tension of a highwire act.

Ultimately, I blink first and take a step back, releasing her trapped foot.

She takes a couple of seconds longer to let go of my sweater, finally releasing it, then smoothing down the section she bunched.

I swear I can almost feel the texture of her palm through my sweater and the shirt beneath it. It's as odd as the tingling fingertips were.

"Don't shave starting next Sunday," she says like she didn't experience the same electrical dysregulation between her hand and my chest. "And prepare yourself for imminent love. She won't be able to resist you by the time I'm done with you."

With that, she waves and continues on to her house.

Why does it feel quieter when Paige leaves now than when we left a house full of six noisy adults?

She's a decade younger than you, my common sense reminds me as I rub where she'd smoothed my sweater. *Let it go.*

I don't ask myself what "it" is.

Chapter Twenty

Henry

LET IT GO.

You want three words designed to tempt fate even when you don't believe in fate? Those are the three you need.

I've barely gotten home from my run—an extra-long one to pay for the midnight slice of Tabitha's pecan pie I can't bring myself to regret—when there's a knock at my door. I open it to find Noah on my doorstep, holding Evie's hand.

"Hello," I say, uncertain why Paige's brother is knocking on my door at 7:30 on a Friday morning. Or ever. They're smiling, so there must not be anything wrong.

"We're pulling a surprise!" Evie announces.

"That," Noah says, grinning at her. "We're giving Paige an early Christmas present, and by we, I mean us, Grace, Tabitha, Sawyer, Lisa, and a couple of other friends. Grace is running the project while Bill is at work keeping Paige busy until her shift ends at 3:00. We've got a short time for a big job, and we wondered if you're free today."

I'm not following. "An early Christmas present? A job?"

"Paige knew what she was getting into with this fixer-upper, but we want to give her a boost. Grace and Tab wanted to redo her bedroom while she's working, but I know my sister, and she's going to want the living room done first for her and Evie to hang out in. So Evie here shared her mom's Pinterest board, and we ordered everything she needs to do the makeover. Now it's just going to take some manpower."

"And girl power," Evie reminds him.

"Especially girl power," he agrees. "If you're free, do you want to come pitch in? I can promise there will be no discussion of "—he looks down at Evie— "of lipstick." He seems to consider this. "Well, as long as you don't look like you're still thrown by it. If you do, it's probably all they'll talk about."

My lips twitch. "Why is that unsurprising?"

"You've advanced to the intermediate level of Winters Family Studies, I see."

My smile breaks free. "Is being an unwilling victim part of the coursework?"

"It's essential. So you're in?"

I look down. "I suppose I'm already dressed for it. Let me feed my cat, and I'll be over."

"You have a cat?" Evie asks. "Can I see it?"

"He doesn't come out," I tell her. "He lurks, and I think he's feral. I put food out for him, and we stay out of each other's spaces."

"He'll come out for me," she says confidently.

Noah exchanges amused glances with me. "I don't doubt it. But right now, we need to get to work, Evie. Ready?"

"Ready!" she says. "Come over soon, Mr. Henry, okay?"

And I do, finding the small living room full of cheerful chaos. Grace is overseeing Noah on the flooring, and there's another couple there I don't recognize. Grace introduces me to her best friend, Brooke, and her husband, Ian, who is Lily Greene's grandson.

"I met her in the market the other day," I told him. "She's very nice."

Ian looks amused. "Did she ask you a bunch of questions about yourself?"

"Yes."

He smiles even wider. "No doubt it was stuff she already knew about you. Well, you truly belong in Creekville if you've had the full Gran experience. Welcome to the crew."

"I'm just here to work," I say awkwardly. I'm not marrying in.

He gives me a strange look. "That's what I said."

I nod my head, feeling even more foolish. "Right."

We work all day, Lisa disappearing with Evie from time to time when Evie gets too bored. Noah asks Tabitha to snap lots of pictures for her during the process.

"She likes to see the change," he says. "I don't know if she'll feel the same when it's us doing the work, but I figured we better take them in case."

It's a small living room and a big crew, but even with a short lunch, I'm still not sure it's all going to come together. An hour before she's due home, the walls have been repainted and the carpeting torn out and new bamboo flooring installed, but the old furniture has been crowded into the extra back room, and her front room is now a big empty box.

Brooke and Noah have barely started removing the old front door to replace it with one that Lisa picked up at an estate sale. I can see why they're doing it: at some point in the past, the previous owners had replaced the original door with a builder-grade stock door. It's serviceable but has no character.

"Bill's been working on this," Lisa says, smiling as the old door comes off its hinges. "He's really good at restoration."

The new—old?—door has a glass window for the top half, etched with an art deco design that feels appropriate on a house from that era. He's painted it a soft, mossy green color that hints at the direction Paige will eventually go with the exterior of the house.

A few minutes before 3:00, Brooke straightens from oiling a hinge and pronounces the door done.

"So now we wait," Noah says. "Bill says he's sending her home right at 3:00."

I've been glad to help to compensate in a small way for driving up the price on her. I have a feeling that's why Noah extended the invitation. But this next part, where all the people who love Paige present this as a gift feels like it would be wrong to intrude on.

While they all scurry with last-minute touches—sweeping up flooring dust, adding houseplants to the built-in shelves, straightening the Roman shades Ian spent most of the day installing—I slip out and return home, tired, sweaty, paint-stained, but pleased.

Every major world religion has a form of penance, and every major system of justice has a path for restitution for a reason; it definitely makes you feel better. Hopefully, today's efforts have repaid some of the time and money I cost Paige.

Her lawn is still the worst, and I'm dreading when the Christmas lights come on tonight for the season, but . . .

I hope we made her happy today.

Chapter Twenty-One

Paige

I STAND ON MY walkway, delighted. "What in the world?"

Bill practically pushed me out the door at 3:00 exactly. "I don't want to get in trouble with Lisa by keeping you, so don't dawdle. Get home and go hang out with your brother. Maybe if you do, we can get some time with Grace tonight."

I hadn't questioned his motives at the time, but now, I suspect there was more to his marching orders. Because this house is not the same house I left.

Someone has replaced my front door with an amazing art deco-style door, complete with an etched window, and painted it a green that will perfectly complement the exterior trim color I'm planning.

"Guys," I say, even though there's no one to hear me. Lisa and Bill really are the best, and once again, I take a moment to send up heartfelt thanks for their goodness. This is more than generosity: this is the gift of people who *know* me, who have taken the time to give me exactly what I need.

I'm sure Grace and Noah will be waiting inside with the full story, so I hurry up the front walk, meaning to rush in and thank them. Except I have to stop when I get to the door to admire how pretty it is. The precision of the etching, the unbelievable luxury of having old glass. Its luster is subtle but distinct from modern safety glass. I'll have to warn Evie to be extra cautious about slamming this door.

Maybe it's because I'm absorbed in the door that I don't notice the muffled commotion behind it, but as soon as I open it, shouts of "Surprise!" nearly scare the daylights out of me.

"Aaah!" It's a yelp. A puppy yelp. An embarrassing yelp. But it makes Evie laugh, so I don't regret it, and as I step into my transformed living room, I can't process what I'm seeing. The deep beige walls are now a delicate gray setting off the white bookshelves. Leafy houseplants brighten them, and the soot on the fireplace bricks is gone.

Bamboo flooring in the perfect shade of walnut has replaced the tired carpeting, and Roman shades cover the windows.

"We did a makeover!" Evie shouts.

"I can see that. I'm stunned."

"Good stunned?" Grace asks.

"Definitely."

Noah comes over to give me a hug. "I'm going to be honest, we didn't do it for you. We did it for Evie."

I sniff into his shoulder, unable to fight a huge smile. "Dork." That's how he's always gotten away with doing things for me that I'm too proud to say yes to. The idea that Evie would even care about me getting the modern transitional living room aesthetic of my dreams . . . it makes me chuckle, and then . . .

"Uh oh, floodgates are open," Noah says as he feels me shaking.

"Laughing fit?" Lisa guesses.

I straighten, and I'm definitely laughing. This isn't one of those times that it stresses me out because no one in this room will mind. I wish I could explain why these laughs overtake me sometimes, but these people don't need an explanation. They're family.

"She's been doing this for about a year," Lisa says. "She feels big stuff, and it comes out like this sometimes."

They all look slightly bewildered but they smile indulgently.

"The furniture is in your bonus room," Grace says. "We know you want to restore it. We just wanted to clear it out so you could get the full effect. We'll move it back in before we go."

I'm still laughing, looking at the empty living room and thinking how hilarious it would be if I'd come home to this without anyone to yell, "Surprise!" I'd have thought I'd gotten robbed by burglars who did some light renovating before they made off with shabby furniture. This makes me laugh harder.

"Your neighbor came over too," Noah says.

"Yeah, Mr. Henry helped a ton," Evie says. "But I guess he left."

The thought of Henry working with this group of crazies all day makes me lose it worst of all, and by now I'm having a hard time breathing, and my sides hurt. But the fact that they hurt only makes me laugh more.

Noah shakes his head, smiling. "I think what she's trying to say is thank you," he tells the rest of them. "Now we'll go move your furniture, and you can enjoy the new space."

By the time they've moved in the dining table, chairs, sofa, coffee table, and easy chair, I've pulled myself together, my chest and sides hurting, but my heart full in the best way.

"Sorry about my fit," I say. "Lisa is right about the big stuff. It just comes out like that, but I swear it's happy laughing. Thank you. I can't believe you did all this, and I love it."

"Yeah, well, none of us are getting you anything else for Christmas, so enjoy it," Noah says.

"Perfect." I grin at him. "You're the best when you're not being the worst."

"Unc's never the worst, Mama," Evie says.

"You don't know him like I know him," I say, winking at her.

"I'm taking Evie's side," Grace says.

We joke some more, and I give everyone a million more thanks before they leave. They're going to hang out at Brooke and Ian's place tonight, but they promise Evie to come see our Christmas Light Spectacular the next night.

When I close the door behind them and lean against it, I narrow my eyes at Evie. "I can't believe you kept that a secret from me. If you're getting good at keeping secrets, I'm in trouble."

"I didn't know," she said. "I found out when Unc brought me back this morning."

There's less than two hours until sunset, so we spend the time taking a walk over to Main Street and admiring the holiday displays in the windows. Evie's begging to see mine at Handy's, but I tell her we have to save the best for last. We check out the bakery, stationery, salon, dress boutique, and yarn shop windows, each doing something new and lovely.

We stop in the pet store so Evie can admire the fish. She doesn't know it yet, but I've been saving to get her a fifty-gallon tank with some tetras for Christmas, and Santa will be supplying her with her most favorite fish tank castle in the store.

At last, after we've explored all the other shop windows, I lead her up the street to Handy's, making her walk backward so she can't peek. Then I turn her around.

Her eyes glow and her grin is huge.

"I know the story, Mama!"

I've drilled this into her ever since I started doing the store's windows two years ago. Every display must tell a story with the merchandise that will tempt people to come in and buy it because they can see themselves in the story, or because they want to be in the story.

For example, spring is an appeal straight to the ladies, with brightly colored watering cans, floral print gloves, and charming sun hats, all worked into a scene filled with mischievous bunnies—garden statues—poking their heads around cute picket fences and shiny galvanized pails bristling with the gardening tools. We sold out of everything in the window in two weeks, including bunny statues.

Bill had only shaken his head. "First time I've ever seen people putting rabbits in their garden on purpose."

Christmas is *the* time to shine, to use all my creativity to make magic with the homely merchandise in Handy's.

I crouch beside Evie. "Tell me the story."

"Someone whited out the world and Santa and the elves have to save it!"

"Very good, honey. That's exactly the story I wanted to tell." Almost everything in the window is white with a few important exceptions. What should be a normal-looking living room decked out for the holidays is instead all white. A white Christmas tree, white presents, white walls, white rug, a sleeping white dog. And it's flat white too. No sparkle, shimmer, or shine.

In the middle of the "living room," a red ladder is set up, the shape of it reminiscent of a Christmas tree. It's a cheerful pop of color, and I've laid a shelf across each rung, so that looking into the window, the ladder resembles the letter "A" but if you drew the crossline four times instead of once. Each side of the shelf boasts something for the project it becomes apparent is underway: paint cans on one, a pile of artfully arranged painter's tape on another, and so on.

Then, off to the left, three elves huddle at work in a corner while a life-sized Santa in the most gorgeous red suit looks on in approval. So far, they've only painted a small corner of the living room, but everywhere "their" brushes have touched, warm colors bring the stark room to life.

"Everyone who sees this window today will think, 'Hm. Interesting. But Handy's had a better window last year.' But guess what happens when they see it tomorrow?"

"What?" Evie asks, her excitement making me smile even more.

"Magically, those elves will have gotten to work all night, and tomorrow, even more of that room will be painted. And even more the day after that. Until guess what happens on the night of Christmas Town?"

Her eyes are huge. "The whole room will be painted, and the story will be done?"

"Exactly! It'll take everyone a few days to realize what's happening, but instead of coming to see the window once, they'll want to come see it every day, and every day there will be new supplies on the ladder for them to consider buying."

She throws her arms around my neck. "You're the smartest mama!"

"And you are the very best girl."

I hug her, so happy in this moment that having Evie pressed against me is the only thing keeping my heart from exploding out of my chest. I'm not sure what I've done to deserve this kid, my job, or the friends and family who performed a minor miracle in my living room today, but I'm so incredibly grateful for all of it.

When Evie strains ever-so-slightly away from me, done with the hug, I let her go and stand. "Should we go home and turn on the lights for night one of the Christmas Spectacular?"

"Let's do it!" she shouts.

"You stay on the sidewalk," I say when we get there. "I'll flip the switch on the count of three." I've wired them to be controlled with the porch light, which took a lot of YouTube tutorials, swearing when Evie wasn't around, and the equivalent of a 401K in extension cords. I open the door and reach inside to the switch. "Count us down, Evie!"

"Three, two, ONE!"

I flip the switch and the lawn blazes to life. No surface has been spared a light, a cutout, a bow, or an oversized ornament. They wind from the roof down to the ground, around every piece of greenery, hanging from trees and trailing down their trunks. It looks like a second grader decorated it, and it's because a second grader was quite literally the art director. I would loathe every bulb if it weren't for the pure joy shining out of Evie's face, brighter than every string of lights combined.

I hurry down the walkway to join her, and we stand beaming at what we've wrought.

"I love it so much!" She claps and jumps, then begins pointing out her favorite parts.

Henry's porch light winks on, and a minute later he joins us. He's wearing joggers and a long-sleeved T-shirt, the athletic kind, black, plain, and yet riveting in the way it outlines his chest.

Seriously, how did I not notice his chest and shoulders from the get-go? I have *got* to make sure he doesn't hide them under sweaters anymore. For Office Goddess, I mean. If she has even half a hormone in her body, she'll pay attention.

"Isn't it amazing, Mr. Henry?" Evie's breathless question snaps me to attention.

Henry smiles at Evie, then the house. "It's really something."

Evie runs over to one of the painted backdrops to fix a light that's flipped the wrong direction.

"What do you think?" I ask, wondering if he'll tell the truth.

He runs his eyes over the entire scene, moving slowly from left to right.

"I hate it so much," he says, and the sincerity in his voice makes me laugh. Not the overwhelmed, can't stop kind of laugh. Just an honest-to-goodness feel-it-all-the-way-through-my-chest laugh.

"Thanks for helping with the inside anyway," I say. "I can't believe you guys did that."

"It was your brother's idea. Happy to help out a little."

"Seven hours isn't a little."

He shrugs. "I'm caught up on grading."

We fall into silence, watching Evie dart around the Christmas madness. A couple of cars drive by and slow down, taking in the spectacle. An older couple walking a corgi stop to study it.

"This your place?" the man asks.

"It is," I say.

"We live up the street at 379. Walt and Connie."

"Nice to meet you," I say. "I guess I'm your newest neighbor."

Connie clears her throat. "You and your husband have certainly gone all out with the decorating."

Henry shakes his head and points to his house. "I'm a neighbor too."

"Ah. So you live next to . . . this." She looks at the yard, the flashing lights, the bright paint, the sparkle.

I'm not sure how hard she's trying to be diplomatic, but it's not hard enough.

"Festive, isn't it?" Henry says, his voice cool.

"It's certainly that," she says.

Another car slows as it passes, then stops. The back window rolls down and a child near Evie's age sticks out his head.

"It's Santa, Mom," he says at nearly a shout, and Evie, hearing him, straightens and waves.

"So cool, right?" she calls back.

He waves and hangs out of the window as the car begins moving again, his eyes transfixed by the display.

"So cool," I repeat to Connie with a polite smile. Even a small town like Creekville has snobs; I've dealt with her type often enough in Handy's.

"Yes, well." She looks at her husband as if expecting him to do something.

He clears his throat. "It's a different look than we usually have on this street."

"I'm aware." I say this with the same polite smile. I want to say, "It's not my fault. I hate it too." I want to say, "I'm with you, but I did it for my kid." But I also want to say, "I moved in two weeks ago, so why is this our first meeting?" People who only show up to complain are not my people. I'm paid to put up with it at work. I'm not doing it here.

There's a long silence. I'm not going to break it. I know Henry won't. Finally, the man gives us a nod and they continue their walk up the street.

"I don't think they like it," Henry says in the understatement of the year.

"You did warn me," I say.

"For what it's worth, there's no ordinance determining how many lights or decorations you can have. Trust me. I'd know."

This makes me laugh, but I feel the slightly manic edge lurking in it. "They'll survive for the holidays. I'm not changing it." I nod at Evie, who is sitting in front of one of the painted panels, talking to the elves.

"Understood," he says.

There's another lull, but it's pregnant, waiting for one of us to spill words into it. Mine would be something like, "Come over and hang out with us and just be in our space."

This worries me. I don't want Henry to be part of our routine, so why is that instinct so strong? Am I having some kind of daddy issues that are drawing me to him? I frown. No. I have an actual father figure in Bill. Besides, the more time I spend around Henry, the more I realize he's an old soul, but he's not actually that old of a human.

Still too old for me though.

I must gravitate to him because Mike the UPS Guy is the only date I've been on in the last two years, and the holidays have gotten me thinking about couples. I've been surrounded by them all week with Noah and Grace plus Tabitha and Sawyer in town.

"So back to school on Monday, right?"

He nods.

"We need to plan more strategies for Lulu—"

"Leigh."

"Her. Do you usually say hello when she comes in?"

"Of course."

I think for a second. "Don't tomorrow. Pretend to be distracted. She'll notice when you don't do what she expects."

"That's rude."

"It isn't. She'll say hello to you. Take a second to focus on her, like your mind was far away, and then you say hello. Be sincere and friendly but go right back to your work. You don't want her to think you're mad at her. Just really into whatever you're doing."

"This sounds silly."

"Trust me, Henry. I understand women. I understand what gets their attention and what they want in a man."

"Someone unshaven with bad manners?"

"Ha. No. Someone rugged with a slight air of mystery."

"And ignoring her will cultivate the mystery?"

"Do you have to study courtship and mating rituals in anthropology?"

"Uh, yes. Sometimes."

I pat his arm, content that I've found the right motivation. "Think of this as an American courtship ritual."

Henry sighs. "Very well. Are there other steps to this plan?"

"Yes, but I don't want to overwhelm you. You'll do this a step at a time, a gradual makeover so that she's paying more and more attention to you but she's not sure why. If you do it all at once, you come off as trying too hard."

"It doesn't sound any less ridiculous."

"Trust me, Henry. Do you want a shot with Lulu?"

"Leigh."

"Then listen to me."

He sighs but doesn't argue anymore, and we watch Evie for a bit, waving back at passing cars and enjoying the heck out of her first Christmas Spectacular. Henry shifts beside me, like he can't find a comfortable position to stand in. I consider introducing another topic of conversation, but the romance coaching has shifted the vibe between us, created a distance, and it's best to leave it that way.

When the silence has tipped into truly awkward, he slides his hands in his pockets. "Anyway, Merry Christmas," he says. "I better go do some grading."

"You said you're caught up."

His expression is easy to read with the help of the bajillion bulbs in my yard: a fleeting deer-in-the-Christmas-lights look. "I meant planning."

"Sounds good." Then I squint. "Henry? What is . . ." I reach up and touch his jaw. I've felt it when it was smooth under my fingers, but now there's a faint scruff.

He's definitely got a distinct five o'clock shadow, and I snatch my hand back when the scrape of the bristles shoots a current up my arm. My fingertips are overly sensitive. Maybe not usually. But they are right now.

"I haven't had facial hair in a long time. I wasn't sure how fast it would grow, so I thought I better start it now for your plan."

Right. My win-over-Office-Goddess-with-a-makeover plan. Office Goddess who Henry blushes when he talks about. Office Goddess who is more educated and definitely more childless than I am. Office Goddess who, without a doubt, has far fewer complications to offer. Almost anyone would.

"Good job." I keep my voice neutral. "You're an A-plus student."

"Thanks," he says. "Anyway, better get ready for classes on Monday."

"Good luck," I mumble when he's too far away to hear me. Because that man is going to walk into a classroom full of students who are suddenly hot for teacher.

Whew. Glad he's clearly off-limits for me. I still have no time for a relationship, and if I did, I'm not even sure what kind of guy I want. But I do know that even though I underestimated Henry's hotness—possibly by a lot—what I don't need is a much older, emotionally closed off, reforming grinch.

Chapter Twenty-Two

Paige

A FEW CARS HAD driven past on Friday night to see the lights. But Saturday? Saturday is crazy.

By the time I fill in more of the window display after closing, it's almost 9:00 when I get home, and even though Evie is hanging with Noah and the Dubs, she made sure the Christmas Spectacular was in full effect, the lights blazing a welcome home.

The street is a steady stream of cars, and it's clear our place is the main attraction. Whatever adults of good taste and sense may think of our display, they're driving cars full of kids who clearly love it, all of them slowing or even stopping in front of our house.

I let myself in through the back door, and I'm about ready to change into pajamas and crash when my phone vibrates with a text from Henry.

HENRY: Is it too late for you and Evie to come get hot cocoa?
PAIGE: Evie is with Noah.
HENRY: Do you want hot cocoa?

Yes. But no. I'm tired, for one. But for two, I'm not sure it's a great idea to see Henry and his confusing scruff. But I bet he makes a good cocoa.

PAIGE: Be right over.

I take a minute to change. I've been in my work clothes too long and they probably smell like paint and sweat. I swap them out for soft leggings, and I'm reaching for a T-shirt when I hesitate and grab a sweater instead. Not like it's sexy or anything. It's a soft wool blend V-neck I found thrifting, and it happens to make my eyes look more blue.

I slip it on and walk over to Henry's, this time going from my back door to his.

He opens it at my knock with a look of mild surprise. "Something wrong with my front door?"

"There's too many cars going past, and I'm peopled out today." I walk past him into the living room. "Where did they all even come from?"

Henry blinks at me. "Didn't you put it on the town Facebook page?"

I frown, then groan. "Yeah, when you were being difficult. I forgot about that."

"I wasn't being—" He breaks off at a look from me.

"Anyway," I say, settling myself into the sofa and tucking up my knees, "I was promised cocoa."

"Coming right up."

He's back in less than a minute with two mugs, one of which he hands to me before settling on the other end of the sofa.

I take a sip and give a happy hum. "This is really good."

He shrugs.

I take another sip and watch him over the rim of my mug. "Anyone ever tell you that small talk isn't your strong suit?"

His lip twitches. "I hardly need to be told that."

"So you know."

"I know."

"Why don't you like small talk?"

"Takes too much energy."

That is such a quintessentially Henry answer that I laugh. "How many miles do you run each week? Ten? Twenty? *Thirty*?" He nods. "Thirty miles a week but small talk takes too much energy."

"Different kind of energy."

I drink more cocoa, noticing again how silences feel okay with Henry. He never tries to fill them like they make him nervous, and with him, I often don't feel the need to either.

"I get that," I say after thinking about it. "Some days are physically demanding in the store. Lots of bending and lifting and hauling. And some days are so busy with customers that all I do is answer questions and help them all day. Guess which ones make me more tired?"

He smiles. "I don't have to guess."

"Then I'm going to sit here and not say anything."

"I'd like to see you try."

I give him a half-hearted glare and settle farther into the sofa, sipping the cocoa, enjoying the flavor, listening to the silence.

The silence . . . "You don't have any Christmas music on."

"I definitely do not."

"This is more of your war against Christmas?" I tease him.

"No war against Christmas. It's just not my thing."

"Head's up, you might want to make it your thing, because Evie's already talking about taking you to Christmas Town. She was so excited when she realized you moved in after Christmas last year. It'll be your first one, won't it?"

"My first . . . wait. What is Christmas Town?"

I stop with my mug halfway to my mouth and stare at him, jaw slightly dropped.

"What?" he says, mildly annoyed. "This is clearly something you think I should know."

"I mean, yes. Definitely. It's what Creekville is known for. People have been getting ready for this since October. Noah proposed to Grace at Christmas Town two years ago."

"None of that tells me what it is."

I set my mug on the coffee table and lean forward. "It's a town-wide tradition. The Friday before Christmas Eve, the town square is turned into Christmas Town. And it's full of booths from local clubs and shops selling holiday stuff. Good food, cool toys, and gifts. It starts with a parade right at sunset. High school band, the Cub Scouts, all of it. The mayor rides in the first car, then she gets to this platform at the front of the square and waits for Santa. He's last in a sleigh, with real reindeer and everything, and then he—"

Henry doesn't look right. His face has gone blank, and he's staring off into the distance. Wherever his mind is, it's not here.

"Henry?"

He doesn't answer me. Maybe he has a fear of parades the way some people fear clowns?

"Henry," I say, this time scooting toward him on the couch, ready to snap my fingers in front of his face or check his pulse or something.

He turns to look at me. "Sounds nice. I guess it's pretty late. I shouldn't keep you any longer."

He starts to push himself off the sofa, but I reach up to catch the soft sleeve of his shirt. "Henry." He sits down. "Why don't you tell me why you hate Christmas?" I ask gently. "Like the *real* reason. I feel like there's way more to the story than I've heard so far."

"I don't hate it." He says it with the force of habit, like he's learned that this is the socially acceptable line, so he repeats it, but he doesn't believe it.

"You do. I'd like to understand why."

"It's nothing. Forget it."

There's never been more of a "something" than the way he just said "nothing." I get the feeling there are very few people he talks to about important things. I have Noah as a sounding board whenever I need him, and I'm more and more comfortable going to any of the Winters women about things. Sometimes all people need is a listening ear. I have a feeling Henry hasn't found one of those in a long time, but if I push right now, he'll close off more.

I don't like it. I like the relaxed version of Henry I've gotten to know, the one who cracks sly and unexpected jokes, who quietly shows up to meet a need I didn't know was there, like an invitation to hot cocoa at the end of a long day. I want to repay the favor. That's what friends do.

"You're an interesting guy, Henry. Complicated."

He shakes his head as I scoot back to my corner. "People always think that because I'm quiet, but I'm not that much of a mystery."

You definitely are, I think but don't say. "You have more layers to you than I expected after that first day in front of my house."

He smiles slightly at that. "More layers than 'grumpy curmudgeon'?"

"Yes. You're not old enough to be a curmudgeon. You need at least thirty more years. But they're really interesting layers." I lean against the arm of the couch and consider him. The jokes. The intuition when someone around him needs something. Those were two of the unexpected layers. But there are still more. Fitness buff hiding a rocking body. Shy guy who's crushing on the school hottie. Conscientious teacher who isn't dialing it in.

"You should let more people see you," I tell him. "That's going to be a big part of Project: Makeover. Letting Lulu—"

"Leigh," he corrects me.

"Whatever. Letting Office Goddess see more of you."

"Is there some type of formula to follow? I don't try to act any one way. I'm just me."

I cock my head. "You think so? Do you talk to her as easily as you do to me? Joke around? Help her with stuff?"

"Not exactly. It doesn't feel normal with her. It feels normal with you."

This makes my stomach flutter, which causes me to frown and forge ahead. "This is what you need to let Lulu see."

"Leigh."

"Right. Let her see this side of you."

His eyes lock with mine. Several long moments pass, but I won't look away. I want him to get it. The eye contact breaks when he slouches in his seat. "I'm different with some people than others."

"You can be more intentional about it."

"How, Paige?" He sounds tired and skeptical.

"Let's try it right now. You keep up your guard even when you think you aren't. You have to practice letting it down."

He's resting his head against the back of the sofa, staring up at the ceiling, and he sounds amused when he answers. "Is this where you drag my deep dark secrets out of me?"

"Basically," I say.

"Go ahead."

I stretch out a foot and nudge his thigh. "You can start by telling me your tragic Christmas backstory. Tell me what happened to your grandmother and why you feel like it's your fault."

He's silent for a long time. So long, I'm beginning to think he won't answer until he gives a heavy sigh, and that flutter in my stomach returns. He's going to share with me, and whatever it is, I have a feeling I'm one of the few people to ever hear the story. This is important, and I don't want to blow it.

He turns toward me, tucking himself into his corner the way I've tucked myself into mine. I'm sitting this way because I'm already that comfortable in his home. I bet he's doing it because he feels safer this way, his back protected, and my heart squeezes for him.

"We used to come visit my grandparents here all the time. I loved this house." He glances around. "My mom was their only child, and I'm the only grandchild. They spoiled me when I was here. My grandmother and I baked, and my grandfather and I would take long walks, and he would tell me about the history of Creekville."

He scrubs his hand through his hair, and when he removes it, a few tufts stick up. I want to reach over and smooth them down, but I don't want to derail his story.

"I was very young. That's probably why I don't remember this Christmas Town thing."

"Maybe, but next year is the twenty-fifth anniversary of the tradition."

"So it's almost as old as you, but didn't start until I was eleven. That's strange to think about."

I don't like this train of thought. "So you came as a baby, but not when you were older."

"No. My parents bought our first house, so my grandparents came to spend our first Christmas in it with us. It was in a small town outside of Richmond, and they also did a big Christmas thing. Santa on a sleigh and throwing candy. Reindeer pulling it."

He falls quiet, back in time again. We're at the root of the Christmas problem. I feel it. This time, I tuck my toes under his leg, a way of letting him know I'm here and listening without breaking into his thoughts with words.

After a while, he picks up the story. "I think that was the first year I understood what Christmas and Santa were. I was so excited for the parade." He smiles. "I must have made my mom sing me the same three Christmas songs a thousand times that week, including 'Rudolph.' But." He stops.

I scoot forward and wrap my arms around my knees, keeping my toes tucked under his warm thigh, and wait.

"I can't listen to that song now. Or any of them."

"What happened?" I ask quietly.

"The tragic backstory." There's no smile as he says it. Just a flatness. "I wanted a good spot to see Santa. My gram was game, so we went down an hour early. Then we played games until it was time.

"The parade started, and it was all stuff I didn't want to see. City officials. A horse club. Cheerleaders. I wanted Santa and his reindeer. I'd lean way out trying to look down the road to see if I could spot them."

A knot forms in my stomach, maybe a premonition of what's going to come as I picture an impatient little boy, eager for his first sighting of Santa. I press my face into my knees, still listening, but wishing I could go back and undo whatever is about to hurt Henry.

"Finally, the band stops, and I can hear bells. 'Sleigh bells,' Gram tells me. But the parade stops and starts every time the sleigh pauses to throw candy.

It's taking forever. And then finally, I can see the reindeer. He has two pulling him."

He's slipped into present tense, like he's in that moment, right now.

"What I hadn't told anyone was that we made a craft at school. 'Reindeer food.' It's oats and colored sugar. Stuff like that. The instructions said we were supposed to sprinkle it on our lawn on Christmas Eve."

"Evie's class made that in first grade. I remember it."

"I wanted to give it to the reindeer myself when they stopped by us. Finally, the sleigh gets to us, but I freeze, because the reindeer look huge up close. I'm trying to work up the guts to go feed them, and I don't even notice Santa throw candy my way. Gram turns to pick it up for me, and I can tell that Santa is about to move on, and I have to feed them now or never."

Oh no. Oh no, oh no, oh no. A terrible sixth sense tells me exactly where this is going. I press my face tight against my knees.

"I pull the food out of my pocket, and I run forward right when Santa snaps the reins. The sleigh lurches forward, someone screams, I look up and see these huge animals coming at me, and I know right then that something very bad is going to happen. I freeze. I can't even yell. Then Gram shoves me hard, and I go flying to the other side and land right past them, my hands all scraped up. I bang my chin really hard. I still have a scar from the stitches."

It's quiet for a few seconds except for the faint rasp of his finger running over his chin beneath the scruff. I can't look up to see it myself. I can't.

"Gram pushed me out of the way, but it terrified the reindeer. It was chaos, and I was lying there bawling, my hands over my head, crying for my mom. And Gram." A long pause. "I didn't see it, but she tripped. I guess she would have been okay, but one of the reindeer reared and struck her in the head. Her temple. They rushed her to the hospital. She was in a coma for two days, and then she was gone."

I feel him waiting for a response from me, but I keep my face pressed against my knees.

This poor man, this dear, lovely human, hates Christmas because . . .

I try to force the words from my mind, but they march through it anyway.

Because his grandma got run over by a reindeer.

Oh my—

I can't even—

I try. I try so hard. It's the worst Christmas story I have ever heard. I feel so hard for the young child Henry was, but still, no matter where I try to redirect my thoughts, a laugh is clawing its way out of me. I would give anything to keep it in, but . . .

His grandma got run over by a reindeer.

There is no way to unremember that. To unhear it.

To keep the laugh back.

My body begins to shake, and I know he can feel it through the sofa cushions and my feet tucked beneath him.

Oh please, please let him think I'm crying. Please.

Because it is unforgivable to laugh right now. But I can't stop.

"Paige?" Henry's voice is tentative. A pause, and then he touches my shoulder. "Hey, are you okay?"

What do I do? The worse this gets, the worse it gets. "Can I use your restroom?"

"Of course. Down the hall past the stairs."

I keep my chin tucked as I hurry past him to the bathroom, praying he still thinks I'm crying. I lock the bathroom door, lean against it, fight for a big breath, and . . .

Whew.

His grandma got run over by a reindeer.

I hear the corny song in my head, and immediately start laughing again. I shove my face into a towel as the laughter pours out of me and just let it come, laughing until my sides hurt, laughing until it's uncomfortable to breathe.

I've had to explain to people over the years that my parents died in a car accident, and I have to conclude that the only thing worse than having to tell someone your loved one died tragically is telling them your loved one died comically.

Every time I think I'm about to pull myself together, I imagine myself having to tell people my parents got run over by reindeer, and I lose it again.

I have no idea how long it takes before the laughter finally dies down to occasional shudders, but probably close to ten minutes. I'm surprised but thankful Henry hasn't come to check on me. I splash cold water on my face and dab it dry, forcing myself to repeat the phrase "Grandma got run over by a reindeer" five times quietly to make sure I won't laugh.

When I'm sure I've got it together, I return to the living room. Henry is where I left him, staring into the distance again.

"Are you all right?" he asks when I sit on the sofa.

"Yes, thank you."

He nods and falls silent. It's not our usual, comfortable silence.

After several awkward seconds I ask, "What about you? Are you okay?"

He doesn't answer for a bit. Then he says, "We're friends, aren't we?"

"I'm as surprised as you are, but yes. We're friends."

"Would you like to hear an interesting feature of this old house?"

"Sure." His tone is weird. Distant. Overly polite.

"The duct work is strange." He gets up and walks toward the front door. "Sound carries all over the house."

My stomach sinks. I know where this is going. "Henry, I—"

"I never noticed it because I've never invited anyone over before." That's a gut punch. "But it turns out that you can hear things happening far away in the house, for example, all the way down the hall. And it might be muffled, but there's no mistaking it." He opens the front door. "It's good to know. I'll have to look into correcting that before someone else embarrasses themself."

I stand. His desire for me to leave is crystal clear. But I don't want to leave, not this way. "Henry, I'm so sorry. I know it's not funny, but—"

The "but" makes him flinch, and I wish I could take it back.

"Have a good night, Paige."

It comes out sounding exactly like "Leave now."

I want to explain, but I don't know how to. And worse, even thinking about it causes the tickle of laughter to start again in my chest. I nod and slip past him out the front door.

When I turn to apologize one more time, the door closes, so quietly, so precisely, that it's somehow worse than a slam.

I cross to my yard and go in through the back door. I know how to repair a lot of things thanks to my job at Handy's, but not this.

How do you fix something you break that badly?

Chapter Twenty-Three

Henry

I WAKE UP SUNDAY feeling no better about that whole scene with Paige.

I know Paige tries to find the light side of everything, but that? I did not expect.

Her reaction is exactly why I don't tell anyone. Let them think I'm a grinch or a Scrooge or just an ass in general. I'm used to it. I became a quiet kid after my grandmother passed, my anxieties taking over, but ultimately, that became a good thing. I became an observer instead of a participant, and that led me to my career.

People may think anthropology is boring and dusty, but I genuinely love it. I would study and learn all these things even if I didn't get paid. So say what they might, I overcame that guilt to do something good because of it.

It hurt to have Paige sitting there, laughing. It's humiliating to think I was trying to comfort her when the only tears she was crying were tears of laughter.

At me.

As my students would say, it sucked.

Midmorning, around the time she and Evie get back from church, there's a soft knock at my door. I ignore it. Later, when I hear Paige and Evie working on something in their holiday hellscape, I don't come out like I usually do to watch or even help. I move to the office where I won't hear them.

It's not until it's dark and the irritating parade of headlights from Christmas light gawkers starts flashing through my windows every minute or so that I leave the house, heading out for a walk to clear my head. That's when I find a package on my doorstep.

It's a manila envelope filled with paper snowflakes and a folded note.

Dear Henry,

I'm so sorry for the way I acted last night. I never should have laughed at something that has made you so sad for so long. I feel like the worst because I am the worst, and I hope you can forgive me.

I will be keeping up a regular supply of bribes in hopes that you'll see how sorry I really am. I also hope they help you feel like Christmas isn't the worst. You have every reason to feel like it is, but I see it much differently since having Evie. Maybe her influence will help too?

Merry Christmas, Henry.

Evie has added a note in her careful seven-year-old printing:

Toodles taught me how to make these snowflakes. I know we don't get White Christmases too much, but if you hang these in your windows, this will help! They will also decorate your house. It's kinda plain for Christmas.

"Toodles" is what Evie calls her Aunt Grace. There must be at least three dozen intricately hand-cut snowflakes but putting them in the window will send Paige the wrong message. Hanging them up will say we're back to normal or getting there. But that isn't true.

I slide them into an unused drawer in the kitchen and head out on my walk.

I return an hour later, my head no clearer, but I've had one insight: after wandering a good bit of the town, there's no question that Paige has the brightest display in Creekville. Cars are still coming through, slowing to a crawl in front of her place as I turn up my walk.

No doubt this didn't happen last year, and I wish it wasn't happening this year. I loathe the intrusion; I'm sure the other neighbors aren't thrilled either.

I go to bed grumpy and toss and turn all night, my poor sleep made worse when I dream three times in a row that I'm wrapping the same strand of lights around the sycamore in my front yard without ever finishing. I just wrap it, round and round the trunk, and nothing happens. I don't run out of lights, and they never turn on.

I head into work feeling out of sorts. I even overslept for the first time in years, leaving myself no time to shave off the idiotic scruff Paige wheedled me into growing.

I make it to my class on time, but it's certainly not my best day, and I fumble during the lecture in ways I haven't since my TA days.

When Leigh walks into our small office after lunch, I don't notice. I'm too busy staring blankly at my computer, reliving the sound of Paige's muffled laughter coming through the vents.

"Hey, Hill," Leigh says after a couple minutes. "You lost in space over there or what?"

"Hello." I look up from my screen. "When did you come in?"

She looks amused. "About five minutes ago. You've been thinking hard. Noodling over something brilliant?"

I scrub my hands over my face, distracted by the feel of the stubble. It's sharp. I don't like it. I can't wait to finish my afternoon class so I can get home and shave it off. "No. Sorry. I slept poorly last night. I'm off my game today."

"Hmmm. I have to say, if that's why you've got that shadow going" —she indicates her chin—"insomnia might be working for you."

Perhaps I'll keep it a few more days.

This is where I should keep the conversation going, but I'm honestly too tired. I'll try tomorrow, but for today, I'm in survival mode. I give Leigh a nod and turn back to my laptop, forcing myself through my slide deck one more time to verify it's at least comprehensible before my next lecture.

"I said, are you happy to be getting to the end of the term?"

I look at Leigh again and realize she's repeating the question. "End of term? I suppose. It means grading a huge stack of papers though."

"You can always give them a multiple-choice test and run the Scantrons. It's a lot easier."

I shrug. "I need to assess how well they understand the interrelatedness of the ideas we've covered, not how well they guess."

A small smile plays around her lips. "I'm the same, Dr. Hill. I give them an essay exam, not a multiple-choice test."

It's custom on some campuses or even within particular departments for colleagues, even ones who have known each other for years, to address each other as "Professor" or "Doctor." I've come to suspect Leigh only calls me Dr. Hill when she thinks I'm being formal. It's her way of taking a dig at me.

"Very good, Dr. Riggins," I reply. "That's sound pedagogy."

"I know that," she says dryly, not realizing I'm teasing her back. It's Basic Pedagogy 101.

"I know you know that," I say, finding a smile so she gets it was a joke.

"Well-played, Henry." She stares at me for a second longer before turning to her work with another smile.

As I finish my class prep, I realize I have inadvertently used Paige's strategy to attract Leigh's attention. And given the fact that Leigh noticed my grooming and engaged with me more than usual, I have to acknowledge that Paige was, in fact, correct.

Interesting.

My second class goes well enough, perhaps because the post-lunch crowd is always a bit sleepy themselves, but I head straight to my car when I finish teaching. I won't nap when I get home as it will only disrupt my sleep tonight, but I do want to be in the comfort of my own house for the spacing out that's plagued me all day.

I must pass Paige's house to turn into my driveway, and though I try to ignore it, I can't help noticing that something about it is different. I pull into my carport, frowning, not sure what it is.

Cat has left a tribute—a dead lizard—and next to it is another offering from next door. I kick the lizard away to deal with later and scoop up the small box decorated with childish drawings of candy canes on the cardboard.

Inside, I find a candy cane made out of red and white pipe cleaners with a small actual candy cane, like the kind that comes in a long strip. A note on folded notebook paper with ragged edges reads, "Mom says Christmas is not your favorite. I got three candy canes at daycare, but I saved this one for you because it's not broken."

If it was as simple as liking the holiday as much as I like Evie, I'd already be wearing a Santa hat. But it's not.

I set the box on the kitchen counter. I'll at least use it to stir my hot chocolate later.

Their yard display catches my eye through the side window and I stop. I realize what's changed. One of the big wooden cutouts is missing.

The one with Santa being pulled by his reindeer.

I stare at the space it used to be for several long moments before I turn my back on the window and continue to the couch.

Nice try, Paige. But it isn't enough. Perhaps nothing is when the first person you've opened up to turns your pain into a joke, a funny story someone told her once.

I go back to the kitchen and put the candy cane with the snowflakes and shut the drawer tight.

Chapter Twenty-Four

Paige

NOTHING IS WORKING.

I've tried everything I can think of to get through to Henry. He doesn't answer texts or knocks. The gifts we leave disappear inside, but there's nothing further. No acknowledgment. Nothing.

I'd hoped that even if he couldn't forgive me, at least he'd enjoy the gifts from Evie. I explained that he didn't like Christmas, and it was hard for him because he had sad memories. Her first instinct had been to run over and comfort him, but I convinced her that he needed some space.

I hadn't expected him to freeze her out too. It breaks my heart to see how hopeful she is each morning as she carefully sets her gifts on his doorstep, how disappointed she is when I have to tell her each day when I pick her up from daycare that we haven't heard from him yet. But her heart is so tender that after five days without a word from him, she only says, "He must have a big sad." And she begins plotting what to leave for him next.

It's a long week. We're busier than usual at the store, which is good. It helps keep my mind off increasing worries while I'm at work. But outside of work, they pile up just the same.

Henry has magical avoidance powers, and I don't see him coming or going. I don't catch glimpses of him inside his windows—not that I'm trying to creep on him. But it makes his house feel like a big, dark cloud hovering next to mine, and I wish I knew how to fix things.

By Thursday morning, I'm tired like I used to be when I'd come home after working a double at the diner in Granger. I'd collect Evie from Noah across the hall and listen to her chatter about her day as she splashed in the tub while I tried very hard not to fall asleep sitting on the floor next to her.

Thursday apparently doesn't believe I've been punished enough yet, because it plays out like the Monday-est Monday. Evie wakes up complaining of a stomachache, but I'm sure she has a strong case of "I don't want to take my spelling test," so I walk her to school anyway.

I'm working by myself until our part-timer, Gary, a retired plumber, comes in after lunch because Bill and Lisa went to Charlottesville to celebrate his two-year anniversary of being in remission by getting his annual PET scan and spending the day in the city. This is fine until just after 10:00, when the school calls and my stomach sinks.

"Ms. Redmond, Evie threw up in class and she's running a fever. When can you come get her?"

If I can't get hold of Gary—and I usually can't—then I can't get Evie. That's the answer. There is no one to watch the store if I leave. There is no one to watch Evie if I bring her home. The daycare won't take her if she's sick, and her emergency contacts are having a long overdue day to themselves an hour away.

But she also can't stay at school.

I miss Noah intensely in that moment, but that's pointless too. Even if he were here, he couldn't leave his classroom at school to go get her.

"Ms. Redmond?" The secretary sounds concerned.

"Um, hey, yes. I'll be there in twenty minutes or less." Because I have to be. Because there are no other choices.

As soon as we hang up, I try Gary's number. As usual, it goes to voicemail, which also as usual, is full. I try twice more before accepting that I have no options here.

I hang up the phone and cut the volume on the music, then make an announcement to the customers over the store's PA.

"Attention, shoppers. This is Paige, the store manager. I'm so sorry about this, but I'm going to have to close the store right now for about an hour. If you'd like to bring your purchases to the counter, I can ring you up. If you're still shopping, I can hold anything you like at the register until I return. I'm very sorry about this, folks. But I will need to clear the store in ten minutes or less."

The customer nearest me, an older gentleman, comes to the register with his jug of antifreeze, and I ring him up. Two more customers simply leave. Another sets her shopping basket on the counter and says she'll be back.

I ring up another customer for plant food, but the woman behind her steps up to the counter, emptyhanded.

"Hi," she says. "You don't know me, but I'm Elizabeth Curlew."

"You work in the yarn shop and buy things to fix the loom sometimes."

"Yes, that's me," she says with a smile. "Can I help with anything? I can keep the store open for people to browse until you get back if you want. It's my day off. And this register isn't too different from ours. If all I have to do is scan the barcode, I could probably even ring up customers for you."

A knot forms in my throat. It's humiliating that I can be as perfect and proactive and innovative in the store as possible and still not be able to do this job the way it should be done. "No, thanks." My voice is tight, the shame leaking through, and I hope she doesn't hear it. "I'll be fine, and I'll be back shortly. Just something I have to tend to."

She nods and gives me a kind smile before leaving. I do a fast circuit to make sure I haven't missed anyone, close and lock up, and set off at a jog for Evie's school. The whole time, I'm trying to figure out what to do with her, and by the time I've reached the office, I've come up with exactly one idea. It's not a good one, but there are no other options.

"Hey, Mama," Evie says to me, her voice soft and weak from her chair in the small front reception area.

Her cheeks are fever-bright, and I feel like the worst mom ever for not believing her when she complained of being sick.

I rush over to her and gather her in a hug, pressing her too-warm body against me. "You feel pretty rotten, huh, baby girl?"

She nods against my chest.

I squeeze my eyes shut. I wish I had a car. I'm going to have to make her walk nearly a mile back to the store, and there's nothing I can do about it. I'll try piggy-backing her for as long as I can and turn it into a fun adventure.

"She can't come back until she's been fever- and vomit-free for twenty-four hours," the clerk tells me, not unkindly, when I sign the early dismissal form.

"I know, Sharon. Thank you for calling me."

"I should warn you that there's a flu going around. We've got over twenty kids out with it today. She'll be all right but keep her hydrated and make sure she gets lots of rest."

I smile my thanks and draw a deep breath before I turn around with a smile on my face. "Let's go, Eves. You're not going to believe the sick day setup I have for you."

Outside of school, I cajole her into climbing onto my back, and she simply rests her head on my shoulder as I try to entertain her with observations about everything we pass. "Few people know this, but that lamppost was installed there by George Washington when he visited Creekville on his way to Thomas Jefferson's house to play racquetball."

Evie gives a single puff, like that's all the energy she has for a laugh. "That's electric, Mama."

"Hmm, you're right. I must be thinking of a different lamppost." That wins an actual laugh from her, but a weak one.

I keep up my nonsense facts for as long as I can, but I can only go about ten minutes before she's too heavy to carry. She's a sturdy kid at sixty pounds, and I'm feeling all of them. She has to walk the last two blocks to the store, and by the time we reach it, she's exhausted.

"Come to the back room, and I'll get you all set up," I tell her.

One of the things I encouraged Bill to stock a couple of years ago was air mattresses around the holidays for people who had family come and visit. I settle Evie into the office chair and make a nest for her as best I can. I inflate an air mattress and resettle her, then grab a sleeping bag from the camping section for her to use as a pillow.

"I'm going to run and grab you some medicine to help your fever come down, but I'm going to leave my phone with you so you can watch whatever you want. I wish I could take you home to rest, but there's no one to watch the store, so you get to be princess of the back room today." When I hand her my phone—a rare privilege—she doesn't take it.

Instead, she rolls to her side and closes her eyes. "It's okay, Mama. I'm just sleepy."

My heart clenches hard. I hate watching Evie suffer, and guilt presses in on me. "I'll be back before you know it."

I hurry around the corner to City Drug, where Ethan Farley, the pharmacist, smiles at me from behind the counter at the rear of the store. Sometimes we flirt, but just for fun. He knows way too much about how many UTIs I've had for me to ever date him.

"Hey, Paige," he calls. "Love the window."

He's got three customers waiting and no one on the front register. I don't want to leave Evie for a minute longer than I have to, so I fly down the cold and flu aisle and grab the fever reducer I need.

"Ethan, Evie's sick and no one's watching her. Can I pay later?"

"Absolutely. Go."

I sprint out of the store and back to Evie, mumbling an apology to a customer who is reading the "Closed" sign as I fumble with the lock.

"I brought you meds, Eves," I say, stepping into the back room. She's asleep. I debate whether it's better to let her sleep or to dose her to bring the fever down. I'll check her temp and decide. I pull the first aid kit out of the office and run the temporal lobe thermometer across her forehead. It reads 101, and she stirs but doesn't wake. It's not great, but it's low enough for me to be okay with letting her sleep.

I turn off the back room lights and leave the office light on, the door cracked so she won't wake up in darkness, then unlock the front door and see to business. There's a steady flow of customers, but I still have time to poke my head back and peek in on Evie, who is asleep each time.

When Gary comes in at 1:00, I explain the situation.

"Evie's sleeping in the back room?" His eyebrows snap together in a deep furrow above his nose. "Why didn't you call me? I'd have come in sooner."

"I did. No answer."

He pulls his phone from his pocket. "Dang it. I suppose I ought to check it more often if I want it to do me any good. Sorry, Paige. Go on and get that little girl home. I can handle the store."

"Thanks, Gary, but I'll be in the back. It wore her out walking here, and I'm going to let her sleep as long as she needs to before we head home. I'll catch up on office work, so if you need me, just call back there."

"Won't need you," he says. "Stay with Evie."

"Thank you, Gary. I really appreciate it."

Ten minutes later, he pokes his head through the back door. "I called my daughter. She's here to run you and Evie home," he informs me gruffly.

Another inconvenient knot forms in my throat. I feel so useless, but I won't turn down the ride. Not for Evie. I swallow past the shame and smile. "Thank you, Gary. You didn't have to do that."

His eyes fall to Evie's still form. Even in sleep, the discomfort is clear on her face. "Yeah, I did. And Shelly understands. Her kids are teenagers, but sometimes they've got to be babied too."

He disappears and Shelly steps in, her face crinkling with worry when she sees Evie. "Let's get you two home," she says. "That baby doesn't need to be sleeping on a concrete floor."

"She's on an air mattress," I say, my cheeks burning. I hate the judgment in her tone, but I can't argue with her. Even though I've done the very best I can do, she's right. I hate it. I hate that we've been on our own for not quite a month, and I'm already failing.

I wake Evie long enough to get her to stand so I can scoop her up and carry her to Shelly's car, monkey style, her legs wrapped around my waist, her hot face tucked against my neck. I lay her in the back seat, where she falls asleep again, and I listen to Shelly's home remedies on the short drive to my house.

Less than a mile, and I couldn't even do that by myself.

When she pulls into my driveway, I give her a tight smile and get Evie out before managing a thank you and escaping into the house.

I get some medicine into her and settle her into bed, waiting until I hear the deep, even rhythm of her breathing before I leave the room. I'll find some things to do while I watch over her.

I start by filling a water bottle and setting it beside her bed along with clean pajamas and underwear for when she inevitably sweats through her school clothes. I get a small bedroom garbage can to use as her puke bowl and hunt up crackers to try to coax her into eating when she wakes up.

Then I retrieve the mail from the box beside the door, gather my laptop, earbuds, and a couple of pillows from my bed and settle into the corner of her room to work through the bills.

Mostly there's junk mail, but the gas bill is in the stack. It shouldn't be too bad since November is pro-rated, but when I open it and read the balance due, I stifle a gasp. The stove, furnace, and water tank run on gas, and the washer and dryer will too when we eventually get some. I haven't used the stove much, and with the two of us, we haven't used that much water either, especially since we don't have a dishwasher or washing machine. But we do use the furnace, and the bill is almost seventy-five dollars higher than I expected.

That's nearly half the amount I plan to set aside every month to save for a car, and after today, it's feeling more necessary than ever.

I stare at it in disbelief. How could it have gotten this high? I've only run the heater when the house is still too chilly with layered socks and sweatshirts on, but I can't let Evie's teeth chatter.

This doesn't seem possible.

I set the bill down and google "high gas bill" to see what might be causing it. After reading a few articles, I conclude that it's the house's age. It's not weatherproofed for the cold, and we've got drafts everywhere, from pretty much every window and doorway.

The articles all give suggestions for how to make the house more energy-efficient with caulking and weatherstripping, and I dutifully make notes of what I need to buy, but my heart sinks as I total it. It's going to take almost two hundred dollars of supplies to do enough weatherproofing for the mere *hope* of bringing down the gas bill.

I drop my head against the wall, trying to ward off the first whispers of hopelessness. Even with all my big plans and careful saving, I won't be able to start my car fund for another two months. At least.

It's too much. I have a sick kid, a decrepit house, and a mortgage that is already squeezing me even with my most conservative budgeting.

Tears burn behind my eyes, but I learned a long time ago that once they start, they don't stop, so I close my eyes tight and take deep, even breaths until I feel the pressure behind them go away. Then I open them and grant myself some self-care by streaming a comfort watch on my laptop through my library account: Rock Hudson and Doris Day in *Pillow Talk*, a movie I can not only quote from memory but also draw from memory. Those mid-century modern sets are delicious.

Evie wakes up once, and I get her to drink about four ounces of water and eat a cracker. It's not enough, but I'll wake her again in two hours and get more water into her. I know that matters more than anything right now, especially since she hasn't peed since I got her from school.

When the movie ends, I go online and look for open jobs. I need something part-time to supplement my salary. I've filled out my third application, this one for a cashier position, when someone knocks on the door.

I hurry to open it before it wakes Evie and find Bill and Lisa standing there, Lisa looking worried, Bill looking almost . . . angry? It's an expression I've rarely seen on his face. Lisa is the one with a temper.

"How's Evie?" Lisa asks.

"She's been sleeping most of the day. Still has a fever but it's dropped some. No vomiting since school."

"How come we had to hear about this from Gary?" Bill asks.

"I wasn't going to drag you back from your celebration for a flu."

"But you thought we'd be okay with letting our grandkid sleep on the back room floor?"

"Bill, I'm sorry. I didn't think you'd mind if I set her up back there." I'm shocked that he's mad. "I'll pay for the air mattress and sleeping bags—"

He cuts off my words with a slash of his hand. "I'm not upset that you made her comfortable back there."

I look at Lisa, at a loss.

"Honey, he's upset you didn't call us. Grace would have. Tabitha would have. We wish you felt like you could have."

I fall quiet, not sure what to say to this, so I step back for them to come in.

They settle themselves on the sofa, Lisa resting a hand on Bill's knee as if to comfort him. "We love you," she says. "We don't want to stress you out any more than you already are, but we wanted to make sure that you know we care."

"If you didn't feel like you could call us, I wish you would have at least shut the store down and brought her home," Bill adds gruffly. "Gary would've called you when he showed up for his shift. It wouldn't have hurt the store. Hell, you've seen me do it several times since you've worked for me."

"I'm sorry," I say, meaning it so much it's an ache in my chest. "The last thing I want to do is make you feel bad. I just felt like we'd finally been able to move out and quit relying on you so much, and in less than a month, I'm already failing at independence. I'm so thankful for all your help while I was finishing school. I didn't want you to think I expected that from you forever."

"Paige." Bill says my name on a heavy sigh. "You're not a burden."

Lisa nods. "I raised two of the most stubborn girls to ever walk this earth, and you've got them both beat. It's why you've been able to do so much in two years, but it gets in your way too. It's not serving you right now. Let us help. We want to."

I want to lean into that reassurance. But I have been nothing but someone else's problem to solve for almost eight years since my parents died and I came back broken, broke, and pregnant.

First it was Noah. Now it's Bill and Lisa. I can't be someone else's problem anymore. "I will never, ever be able to thank you for everything you've already done for me. And I promise that I will tag you in the next time something like this happens. But for the most part, wherever I can, I need to stand on my own. I need to know I can do it."

"You've proven it to us a hundred times over, Paige. You've got so much grit you're number twenty-four sandpaper."

It's such a Bill analogy that it wins a small laugh from me. "I'm really sorry, Bill. We absolutely love you guys. I will do better at leaning on you, but only if I really, really have to."

"We'll take it," Lisa says. "But just know you never need a reason, honey."

"Can we check on her?" Bill asks.

"Better let her sleep, but I'll have her FaceTime you when she wakes up."

"Fair enough." He climbs to his feet and helps Lisa up. "Let us love you, Paige-girl. We're better at it the older we get."

Lisa holds out her arms for a hug, and I accept it and murmur a promise to let them, but to myself, I give a second, silent promise. *I will be deserving of this kind of love.*

"Stay home tomorrow," Bill says.

"I'll work if he needs me," Lisa adds. "Evie will want you and no one else."

The house is quiet for a couple more hours after they leave. I'm thankful for the time off to take care of Evie, even though I can afford time off less than ever. I settle back in my spot in her room, getting a full cup of water down her the next time she wakes up, then helping her when she throws it up fifteen minutes later.

I really, really hate the flu.

She's sound asleep when there's another knock on the door. It's after dinner now, and since I doubt it's Bill and Lisa, my heart picks up. It has to be Henry. Maybe he noticed a lack of Christmas cheer when Evie didn't leave a gift for him before school this morning. Maybe he's even ready to forgive me.

I hurry to the door, but when I throw it open, I find two vaguely familiar people standing there instead. Maybe I've helped them at the store?

"Hi," I say, smiling. *Please don't be here to ask me about my eternal salvation. Or to sell me anything.* "Can I help you?"

The woman gives me a tight smile, and that's when it clicks in my memory: this lady and her husband were the couple who got passive-aggressive about my light display the other day.

"We're here on behalf of the concerned residents of Orchard Street. We've hoped for several years that when this house sold, it would go to someone interested in restoring its character in a way that reflects our neighborhood values. Since that doesn't seem to be the case, we've come to present you with this petition. We hope you'll consider our position and rethink yours."

I take the clipboard she's handing me out of habit, like when Evie hands me something and suddenly I'm carrying around her trash.

"Have a good evening," she says as she and her husband turn to leave, and somehow, I doubt that she means it.

I stare after them for a minute, feeling like I just witnessed someone get struck by a truck without realizing it's me yet.

Then I close the door and lean against it, reading through the petition.

We, the homeowners of Orchard Street, request that the owner of 341 Orchard please revise your Christmas display to better suit the aesthetic of the street. In particular, the excessive traffic your display has drawn is untenable and degrades the quality of life we enjoy on our quiet street. The influx of vehicles is disruptive, and the style of your decorative choices is at odds with the spirit of Orchard.

We realize these are subjective parameters, so we tender the following list of changes to give you specific, actionable steps you can take as a demonstration of your commitment to community and long-term goodwill:

1. *Reduce the number of lights by half*

2. *Remove any plastic yard decorations*

3. *Choose a unified color theme and stay with it*

4. *Remove the more amateur display elements, e.g., the hand painted Christmas scenes*

5. *Turn off light displays at 8:30 PM*

For examples of how to create a more coherent theme, please visit the Main Street store windows with particular focus on Handy's Hardware, which uses color in a tasteful and pleasing way.

Signed,
Concerned Neighbors

I can't even enjoy the irony of them directing me to my own window display as a model for what they want; a white-hot anger is burning its way through my chest.

The list of names is long, and at the moment, I don't even want to look at them. Instead, I slap the paper down on the back of the sofa and march down the hall and out the back door, straight to the shed where I have four more bins of unused lights because I couldn't find anywhere to put them.

Believe me, I'll figure it out now.

So help me, if I have to climb every branch of the tree in the front yard to wrap it with lights, *I will*.

How *dare* they? This crazy patchwork of light and color looks like it sprouted from the imagination of a seven-year-old because it *did*. It's the realization of every Christmas decorating wish she's ever had, all come to life in what should be our most special Christmas—the first in our own home.

I march around the front of the house and thump the bin onto the porch, whirling with my hands on my hips to decide where to start, my chest heaving as I struggle to control my angry breaths.

A car drives past slowly, windows rolled down to check out our lights, then another. And beyond them, the warm light shines from the windows of the houses across the street, most of them trimmed with single strands along their eaves and occasionally around the doors and windows.

Damn right we don't fit their aesthetic.

But as I stoop to unlatch the lid of the bin, I pause, then straighten. That had been a long list of names on the petition. Most of the street, I would guess. Do I really want to antagonize all of them by doubling down?

If it were just for me, YES.

But I don't want their disdain to bounce back on Evie.

I push the bin aside with my foot and slowly head back into the house, picking up the petition, reading through the names. Do I want to make this a list of enemies my first month in our house?

My eyes fall on the final name on the list, and my breath catches. The neat black letters strike me with the force of a gut punch.

The final signature belongs to Henry Hill.

Chapter Twenty-Five

Henry

I WATCH CONNIE AND Walt march up Paige's front walk, and I pause, stuck between the kitchen and the living room with a hot bowl of soup in my hands.

Perhaps I shouldn't have signed it. But when they knocked on my front door yesterday, I had to agree that their requests were more in keeping with the tone of Orchard. And furthermore, I'd told Paige all of this. I told her before she even bought the house.

Yes, Evie's excitement over each new feature was hard to resist.

But the rubbernecking traffic is annoying, and it will only escalate to miserable as the word gets out and more and more people crowd Orchard.

A glance to the street and the cars already rolling past firms my resolve.

We deserve to have our peace and quiet.

I sit on my sofa, eat my soup, and listen to the silence in my house. It's been louder this week.

"Everything okay, Henry?"

I look up at Leigh who I have once again failed to notice come into the office.

Too distracted by thoughts of Paige. Of her smothering her laughter in the bathroom. Thoughts of the satisfaction I felt when I signed that petition. Thoughts of how satisfied I tried to feel as I watched the neighbors march it to her door.

Thoughts of how that moment wasn't satisfying at all.

I'm trying to label the feeling I've had since watching them arrive and leave instead, and I've narrowed it down to one I don't like: shame.

"Henry?" Leigh prompts me again.

I shake my head, embarrassed. "Sorry. A lot on my mind."

"You've been pretty distant this week. Anything you want to talk about?"

I'm about to say no out of habit, but I pause. I've got a trained psychologist sitting in front of me, someone whose job it is to make sense of behaviors that don't make sense to the rest of us civilians.

"Can I ask for your opinion on something? Your professional opinion?"

She leans back in her chair, her posture relaxed. "Sure."

"I've been having issues with my neighbor. We've had a few disputes about her aesthetic choices." Leigh's lips twitch at this but she says nothing, and I continue. "However, lately we'd been getting along. A truce of sorts. We've even broken bread together, as it were."

"You mean you've eaten meals together?"

"Yes. Otherwise, she and her daughter only eat Hot Pockets, so I've had them over a time or two."

"That does help with community relations."

I nod. "I thought so. I thought we'd perhaps even become . . . friends. On Sunday, I invited her over for cocoa." I stop and meet Leigh's eyes. "I make excellent hot cocoa."

"I'll need to verify that for myself."

"Very well," I say.

"Henry. I'm kidding."

"Oh. Right." Why is it hard to tell when Leigh is joking when it's so easy to figure out with Paige? Especially when I'm more used to Leigh, frankly. Odd. "Anyway, I don't like Christmas." At Leigh's confused expression, I add, "These things are connected."

She nods. "Continue."

"My neighbor knows this. And she asked me why. I'd become comfortable with her, so I told her. She seemed to be taking it rather hard. Hiding her face, shaking."

"Is your reason rooted in a trauma?" Leigh asks, her forehead furrowed.

"No. Just something sad." One of her eyebrows goes up, but she nods for me to go on. "Anyway, she excused herself to use my restroom, and through the vents, I could hear her laughing. She wasn't upset at all. She laughed for several minutes before she came out."

I think about it again, the sound of her muted laughter drifting toward me. It hollows out my chest again, and I feel like my heart is beating too loudly.

"How did you feel about that?" Leigh asks.

I haven't been to a therapist before, but this is what they all sound like in movies. "I wasn't asking for therapy." I try to make my tone as courteous as possible. "I'm more interested in whether my return action was warranted."

"Why don't you tell me about that?" she says.

Despite that sounding suspiciously like another therapy prompt, I comply. "I cut off contact."

"Ah."

I don't like that "ah." It sounds full of understanding, but how much could she possibly understand from the little I told her?

"Did she apologize?" Leigh asks.

"Yes. And she left a note with another apology. And . . ."

She nods in a sign to go on.

"Her daughter is trying to win me over to Christmas. Or was. Leaving gifts and things on my doorstep with cards and notes. But perhaps I've gotten through to them since I didn't see anything yesterday or this morning."

"But you looked for it," Leigh says. It's not a question. She thinks for a moment. "Your reason for disliking Christmas . . . you don't need to share specifics, but is it something that people would generally find sad?"

"I suppose."

She falls quiet for a moment. "Your neighbor, does she laugh a lot in general?"

"She jokes a lot." She's certainly made me laugh even when I wasn't in the mood to.

"But does she *laugh* a lot?"

I think about it. "No, not really. She smiles a lot, but I've only heard her outright laugh a few times."

"Have you ever heard her laugh that hard before?"

I scowl. "One time she accidentally painted me. Ruined a sweater. That got her going." The more I think about it, the more I realize Paige has issues. What was I thinking, telling her my hardest stuff? I must be lonely in ways I don't necessarily recognize consciously.

"Would you describe either of these instances as uncontrollable laughter?" Leigh asks.

"Yes. It was highly irritating."

"Irritating or hurtful?"

"Irritating," I insist, because it feels slightly pathetic to admit that the second time, it hurt quite a bit.

Leigh appears to mull this for a bit too. "Do you know if your neighbor has sustained any serious emotional traumas or possibly major stresses in the last couple of years?"

"She lost her parents in an accident when she was in high school, I believe. But that was some time ago. As for lately, I wouldn't know. I've known her barely more than a month. She's a single mother without a co-parent. And I believe she recently finished her college degree."

"How long ago was high school for her?" Leigh asks, her gaze suddenly sharp.

"She's twenty-six, I think."

Leigh's face relaxes. "That's not too inappropriate."

"For what?" Almost as soon as I ask the question, I realize what she's thinking. While it is strange that my first lengthy conversation with Leigh is about another woman, there's no romantic context here. "It's not like that with us. I'm almost ten years older than her."

"Sometimes people's life experiences make them old souls. She probably acts and thinks older than twenty-six. Besides which, speaking in terms of the brain, she is a fully grown, fully shaped adult."

My mind strays to an unhelpful place when Leigh says, "fully shaped," a phrase one might use in reference to Paige after seeing her in jeans.

But that is entirely beside the point.

"It's not like that," I repeat. "My interest is . . . elsewhere." Is that too big of a hint? Or is it far too subtle? Why am I so bad at this? Before I can spin out any further, Leigh has moved on with her analysis.

"All right. You've described someone who sustained a major trauma in her life with the sudden loss of her parents at an early age, who was fairly recently under a great deal of stress finishing a college degree as a single mother. Plus she's just purchased a fixer-upper house. Do I have all that correct?"

"Yes."

"And twice now during a stressful interaction with you, she's had a fit of uncontrollable laughter."

I nod. *Reluctantly.* I don't like the way she's building her case, as if Paige might have a solid defense.

"Honestly, Henry, it sounds like a trauma response. It's a lesser-known one for sure, but sometimes when a person's natural default is toward laughter anyway, it masks a reaction that's attempting to happen at a deeper level, a reaction that might hurt them. The person laughs because it feels like a safer release valve for big emotions, but if you know them well, you'll sense a slight hysteria to it.

"It's a sign of anxiety and can sometimes become its own problem because the very nature of being uncontrolled stresses the patient to the point that they begin to fear social situations that may provoke the response. There's not a great deal of documentation on this, but in general, this reaction tends to develop during a time of extreme duress and to fade as circumstances settle down."

"Or she's simply rude."

Leigh smiles. "Always a possibility. You're in a better position to say than I am. I'm not a therapist, but clinically, if I were looking at these facts in a case study, it would read as a trauma-induced response to me."

I'd intended to ask Leigh if signing the petition was fair on my part, but I don't need to. I suspect I know what she'd say: no. That there is more to the story of Paige's behavior.

At some level, I know I'm not justified. It's why I feel uneasy about signing. It was petty.

But it may have been even more harmful than I realized if Leigh is correct about Paige's laughter—bizarrely—coming from a place of trauma or even just heavy stress.

Is it possible I've made a bad situation worse?

What if Paige really meant it when she said she was sorry?

Chapter Twenty-Six

Paige

EVIE BOUNCES BACK QUICKLY from the flu the way little kids do. By Saturday, she's well enough to spend the day in the living room with me, tired and cuddled on the couch, but awake more than asleep. We watch some of my favorite old Christmas movies, including *Miracle on 34th Street*.

I don't know if I'm lucky that Evie likes old movies as much as I do, or whether she likes them because I've had her watching them since she was old enough to sit still for them. Either way, it makes me happy, especially when I introduce her to a classic like *The Wizard of Oz* and watch her eyes light up at the technicolor wonder.

We enjoy our rare Saturday together. It's almost a mini-holiday, minus the flu. It's going to be a very long time before we get to do this again. Six months at least. But I don't want to ruin it by telling her that, or even thinking about it myself. I'm going to enjoy these last two days off with her.

She's a big bright spot, but also the only bright spot, and still a sick bright spot at that.

The dim spots almost overwhelm me if I dwell on them too long. Like when she wants to leave a gift for Henry on Saturday afternoon, but I talk her out of it on the grounds that I don't want her to spend too much energy and undo the rest she's been getting. I can't bear to tell her that these gifts will also go unacknowledged because of the way I acted.

Or any time I catch a glimpse of our yard through the windows. It's literally bright, especially at night, but I haven't added anything to the decorations. I won't take a single one away, either. Still, I think about the petition every time I see them now.

There's the weight of expenses and the feeling of my goals slipping further away.

And then there's Bill and Lisa. The Dubs stop by each day with gifts for her. A Christmas coloring book and a box of sixty-four Crayolas that makes even me want to color. A new pair of Christmas footie pajamas Evie insists on wearing immediately.

They only stay a short while each time so they don't tire her out, and they always make sure I'm taking zinc to ward off the flu myself before they go. I promise I'm taking it and remind them that I got a flu shot, but Lisa especially fusses anyway. But none of it feels right.

It's been strained since they showed up on Thursday, upset that I hadn't called them when I had to get Evie out of school. I've managed to alienate or hurt pretty much everyone.

I don't care about the neighbors. I did care about making things right with Henry until I saw his signature on the petition. And I have no idea how to fix things with Bill and Lisa. It feels like it will take more than words, but I don't know what.

I'd be paralyzed with self-loathing if it weren't for Evie's hour-by-hour improvements. She, at least, is the one thing I get right, even if it costs me the goodwill of my neighbors. It's not like any of them ever showed up to welcome us to Orchard anyway.

Sunday, Evie wakes almost her usual self. She's tired but she's had no fever or nausea for twenty-four hours. By noon, she's itchy to do something besides watch movies, and I'm stir-crazy too.

"How about if we go to the diner for lunch?" The diner is the least expensive place in town but still a rare treat, and her eyes light up.

"Yes, Mama! Let's break out of this house!"

"Wait a minute," I say, tickling her sides. "Are you saying this house is jail?"

"No," she gasps between giggles, "but it smells like being sick, which is yuck."

"You're right. Let's air this place out and go treat ourselves."

"Yay!"

Twenty minutes later, we're in clean clothes and on a leisurely walk to Main Street. We leave our windows open to let the air circulate, and I refuse to think about how much it will cost to heat the house again.

Evie wants to see the Handy's Hardware window, and I have to disappoint her with how little progress has been made since she last saw it. "Don't worry, Eves. I'll get back to it tomorrow when I go to work."

The Sunday brunch rush is over at the diner—a deliberate strategy on my part—and we choose a booth where Evie can watch the happenings on Main Street. The server brings us menus and a coloring sheet for Evie. Once Evie is absorbed filling it in, I slide from the booth and hurry to the register to speak to Cindy, the manager.

"Hey, Cindy," I say.

She smiles. "Paige, right? From the hardware store."

"That's me."

"Can I help you with something?"

"I'm kind of hoping I can help you. I'm looking for some part-time work. I waited tables at a diner in Granger for a few years, and I wondered if you might need an extra set of hands on your weekend breakfast shifts. I'm off every Saturday and Sunday morning and a couple of others during the week too."

"Just mornings?" she asks.

I nod. "I have Evie in the evenings after daycare closes."

"It'd be nice to have an extra pair of hands for the breakfast rush." She fishes out a copy of a generic job application from the hostess stand and hands it to me. "Fill this out. I can't guarantee more than weekend shifts right now, but I'll check your references at your old place, and we'll see what we can do."

"Thank you," I say, accepting the application. "I'll get this back to you soon."

"That'll be good."

I step out of the way so she can ring up another customer, and I head back to Evie.

"Look, Mama." She holds up her coloring page to show me her progress. It's an old pickup truck with a stack of chicken crates in the bed. She's colored in the truck with green polka dots on a background of purple. I smile. It's definitely her aesthetic that drove our Christmas display.

"I love how bright it is," I tell her. "You use color in such a fun way."

"Thank you." She settles down to color more.

Despite the weight of all the things that are wrong right now, it soothes my nerves for a bit to watch her doing her Evie thing, nearly her old self. With plenty of fluids and an early bedtime tonight, she'll be good to go for school tomorrow.

"Well, hello there, Redmond ladies."

I look up to find Miss Lily standing beside our table, smiling. "Merry Christmas, Miss Lily."

"And to you," she says. "Missed you in church this morning."

"I've been sick," Evie tells her.

"She came down with the flu on Thursday. This is the first time I've let her out of the house, so we're seeing how she does with a short adventure."

"I'm glad you're feeling better, Evie," Miss Lily says. I love this about her, that she knows Evie by name. "I'm here for an adventure too. I decided it's the perfect day to spoil myself with a peppermint milkshake."

"Would you like to join us?" I ask.

"I would indeed."

She settles into the booth beside Evie, who gives her a smile and returns to her coloring, absorbed in her masterpiece.

"How goes it with your new place?" Miss Lily asks, and despite my best effort, my face falls. Her forehead wrinkles in concern. "Not well? Is it Henry Hill?"

I don't know what it is about Miss Lily, but I find myself incapable of polite conversations with her. Every time she asks how I'm doing, I tell her the truth for better or worse, and today is no different. In fact, it's almost like the universe knew I would need to unburden myself and nudged the town wisewoman in for a milkshake.

"He's been challenging," I say. "But to be honest, I believe that may be my fault."

"How so?" she asks.

I take a quick glance at Evie, but she's oblivious, carefully working on outlining the crates before coloring them orange.

"He finally told me what happened to his grandmother, and I . . . laughed." It sounds even worse coming out of my mouth in such stark terms.

Miss Lily's expression is startled, though she finds her composure quickly. "That does sound unfortunate."

Her good opinion matters to me, and Miss Lily can be trusted with this kind of information, so I explain the circumstances of Marley Ellis's accident.

"Oh my," she says when I finish. "I hadn't heard the details. Only that there was a freak accident and a head injury."

Why couldn't I have taken it the way she did? Calmly, with compassion? With recognition for the tragedy? Why couldn't I—

Wait. Miss Lily's lips twitched. I saw them. I narrow my eyes, and they do it again.

I test her. "Miss Lily, his grandma got run over by a—"

"Don't." She presses her hand to her mouth. It's as much a plea as a command.

I sit back, feeling slightly absolved, and watch her as she stares at the table for a full minute. Finally, she takes a deep breath and meets my eyes. "That must have been hard for him, so young."

I feel less vindicated now that she's pulled herself together far more easily than I did. "It's made him hate Christmas," I say. "And all of our decorations." This would attract all of Evie's attention if she's listening, but the tip of her tongue is stuck between her teeth as she works on her crates, trying to keep the orange within the lines. "So much so that he joined a petition from my neighbors demanding that we reduce our display and make it more tasteful, in keeping with the rest of the street."

Miss Lily shakes her head. "Too many old people on the street. That's the problem."

I smother a smile, but she catches me.

"Your body can be old without letting your spirit get old," she says. "And your neighbors have. But your Henry . . ."

"He's not my Henry." I say this firmly. There will be none of her matchmaking.

"I don't believe your Henry is old, but he skipped a lot of being a child after losing his grandmother that way. What's more, if I had to guess, he only signed that petition because his feelings were hurt."

"I know." I slump and stare at my hands, my fingers tugging on each other nervously. "I was trying to make it right before he did that. We were leaving him gifts and cards to help him love Christmas again. It didn't work, obviously."

"I assume you apologized?"

"I did," I promise. "More than once."

"Still, that's a hard thing." She stares through the window but more as if she's slipped into a daydream or memory.

"Miss Lily?" I say after a minute.

She turns back toward me, her eyes bright and present again. "He shared his greatest sorrow with you, and he feels like you mocked it."

Each word cuts me. "I wish I could go back and change it, but he doesn't want to hear my apologies."

"No," she murmurs, "I don't believe that's what he's looking for." She leans forward and settles a soft hand atop mine. "Do you ever share your greatest sorrow with anyone?"

"Noah," I say.

"But I'd guess he has the same sorrow, does he not?"

I nod. "My parents. He misses them too."

"Neither of you speak of it often, but I suspect that it might help Henry feel more understood if he had that insight into you."

The idea makes me uncomfortable. "He was so angry."

"Or hurt?" she asks. "Because he showed you his soft underside and thinks you didn't understand?" She squeezes my hand. "Be vulnerable. Let him know that you understand how he feels better than your actions showed him."

"He'll probably close the door in my face."

"He may. At the very least, if he does, he'll feel like he's gotten some control back. It's within your power to grant if you're willing to take the risk."

"But if he does that, it won't help us be friends again."

"*If* he does that, you'll be right. But maybe he won't do that. And since nothing else you've tried has worked, and since his friendship seems to matter to you, you may risk more by doing nothing."

The server arrives with our orders, and the smell of french fries breaks Evie's concentration at last. She shoves aside her coloring page and dives into her food with relish. Miss Lily and I chat about mutual friends, Christmas Town, the window at Handy's which she informs me she loves, and everything but Henry.

When we've all eaten until we're full, she insists on picking up the check.

"That's not why I invited you to sit with us," I protest.

"I know. But my grown grandchildren aren't around nearly as much as I'd like, so it makes me happy to do this, if you'll let me."

I smile. "I can't turn down such a gracious offer. Thank you."

"My pleasure. Merry Christmas, Redmond girls."

"Merry Christmas," we chorus, Evie's face delighted. She loves to say Merry Christmas. Miss Lily excuses herself and heads to the register to pay, and when Evie finishes her last chicken strip, we also head home.

"I'm so relieved you felt good enough to eat your whole lunch," I tell her as we walk.

"Me too. But I'm tired now. Can I take a nap?"

"Yes, ma'am," I tell her. "I think that would be very smart of you."

"Me too," she says, yawning. "And that way, you'll have plenty of time to talk to Henry and fix everything."

And my jaw drops as she skips ahead, not looking tired at all.

Chapter Twenty-Seven

Henry

I read the text again.

PAIGE: Can I come talk to you and tell you a sad, sad story I never tell anyone?

It's not normally the kind of invitation I receive. Not that I receive many invitations at all. But if I did, this one would distinguish itself. I don't know what it says about me that hearing a "sad, sad story" is irresistible, but so it is.

Paige and I have taken far too sharp of a turn from the path toward friendship to fix that, but it will at least give me a chance to apologize for signing the petition. I text her to come over.

A few minutes later, she knocks, and I open the door to let her in. She walks past me, that familiar smell of vanilla wafting up, and I resist the urge to reach up and touch her hair. Why? Why would that be my impulse, given that I haven't spent even a second running my fingers through it? *Pull it together, Henry.*

"How are you?" she asks, stopping and turning.

"Fine." I wave her to the sofa and take an armchair. Last time we were both on that sofa, it didn't go well.

She sits. "How do I start a conversation where I puke up my emotional guts? Is there some sort of preface to that?"

"Your text was, I suppose."

"I suppose," she repeats with a small huff that's almost a laugh. "Here we go then. First, I'm sorry I laughed when you told me about your grandmother. It's not funny. Nothing about it is funny. But ever since I finished my degree, I keep having these laughing fits, and they stress me out. I'm sorry you lost her. It's really sad, and I understand why Christmas is hard for you."

I nod. She sounds utterly sincere. "I appreciate that."

"But there's more," she says.

"The sad, sad story?"

She gets up and runs her fingers through her hair, dropping them and leaving it a mess. Again, I feel a strong desire to reach out and touch it, to perhaps smooth it.

"In the spring of my senior year, my parents died in a car accident. It was awful. Our family was already small, just the four of us. And just like that, we were half as many. I went through the end of the school year in a state of shock, doing things on autopilot. That worked for me. I was a good student, and I could regurgitate what I needed to for tests. My grades stayed up, I graduated, and it was that final day when it hit me. When I looked out and only my brother was there. No parents."

I can't even imagine. I may not have the most expressive parents, but I would miss them fiercely if I were to suddenly lose them.

"I got into UVA." She flicks a glance at me to see if I'm impressed.

"You must have been a very good student."

She nods. "My parents' life insurance money came about a week after graduation. A hundred thousand dollars. It should have been enough to pay for me all the way through school, but the idea made me angry. That what would make it easy for me where Noah had struggled was blood money. I didn't want it. I wanted my parents. And when Noah handed me the check from the insurance company, it unlocked all the feelings I hadn't been processing after their deaths."

She returns to the sofa but settles on the edge and hugs one of the throw pillows against her chest, quiet for a minute. I don't know if I'm supposed to talk or ask something here, but I don't know what to say, so I say nothing.

Eventually, she starts speaking again.

"From the second I had that check in my hand, all I felt was anger. That doesn't even feel like a strong enough word. Rage. *Rage*." She squeezes the pillow then flings it aside. "I would be terrified to even feel a fraction of that again. It took over, and suddenly Granger was too small to hold it. The house was too small. The town. The state of Virginia.

"So you left?"

"So I left, as fast as I could. I went straight to New York. I wanted to be a set designer, and Manhattan is the center of theater. So many colleges there offer degrees in production design."

"That's why you're so good at the store window," I say.

"You've seen it?"

"I have. I knew it had to be you. It just felt like you." I don't know how to explain it other than that I could see Paige in the story of that window when I spotted it the other day. The use of color. The subtle humor in the details. The theme of bringing something bland to life. It's all Paige. No question.

She nods. "Yeah. The problem was that I couldn't pull myself together enough to apply to a college. I couldn't even get a job at any of the theaters as an usher or ticket-taker. I stayed in a hostel for a few nights, spending the days looking for theater jobs, but the giant invisible chip on my shoulder got in my way.

"Eventually, I met up with this girl who invited me to stay at her place, sort of this millennial communal loft in Brooklyn, one of the ungentrified parts, where you had to fight off the rats to claim your spot on the floor or sofa. That's the first place that felt right to me. Or that I felt like I deserved."

"Deserved," I repeat. "Why deserved?"

She smiles over at me, even if it's tight at the corners. "You're being way nicer about this than I was when you told me your story."

I lift and drop a shoulder. It's true, but it also doesn't matter to me right now.

"I don't know if I can explain why I felt like that's what I deserved. It was like I didn't want to spend the insurance money on a single thing that would make me happy when I only got it because they died. It didn't make sense."

"I think I understand," I say quietly.

"It was a miserable headspace," she says. "I doubled down on it. I paid for everyone's alcohol and pretty soon, for their drugs. It was hateful money, and it gave me vicious satisfaction to spend it that way. To waste it. To not let it make anything meaningful of their deaths, because their deaths were senseless. And as a bonus, sometimes I could get high enough not to feel miserable."

She heaves a deep sigh and keeps her eyes trained on the Persian rug beneath the coffee table. "I don't like remembering those times. I can't remember a lot of it, honestly. But it went for a while, and it turns out that people are always happy to help you spend a lot of money in a hurry or do anything else you want to do to forget how bad you feel. And suddenly you're broke, your paid friends evaporate like your empty bank account, and you're pregnant."

I'm so used to experiencing Paige as a jolt of energy, somewhere between a breath of fresh air and a jack-in-the-box, depending on the day. But to see her wilted, pressed down by the weight of memories, is awful. It's like watching a bounce house deflate and fold in on itself.

"You don't have to tell me any more," I say. "You don't owe me this story."

She glances up, a glimmer of a smile playing across her mouth. "But we're about to hit the dramatic turn. I can't stop now."

I don't want to put her through one more second of this, but at the same time, I want her to know that I'm listening. I follow an impulse I don't completely understand and go to her on the sofa, pulling her up, then slipping behind her to settle into the corner, and pulling her back down again, nestling her in the vee of my legs. She holds herself stiff for a few seconds, then slowly relaxes, leaning back against me.

"Is this all right?" I ask quietly. "I think I'm trying to quite literally show you that I have your back."

She draws a deep breath, and I can feel her slight frame expand before she releases it. She nods. "This is good."

She falls quiet for a while, another minute or two, and I rest my hands on her shoulders and feel the rise and fall of her breath. Finally, she takes a slightly deeper one and speaks. "I came back. To Granger. I had to panhandle for a couple of days to get the money. Those were the worst three days of my life, and I never want to be that low again. I got together enough for a bus ticket, and I came home and found Noah. He took me in.

"I hadn't taken anything or even had a drink from the second I found out I was pregnant. He paid for rehab, which was expensive. He helped me get Medicaid so Evie could be born safely and have insurance. I got a job waiting tables, and I tried to take care of as much as I could, but I still could not have gotten through those first five years without him."

I give her shoulders a soft squeeze. "That all sounds really hard."

"It was," she says simply. "In so many ways, remembering that time feels more like telling someone else's story, like someone else lived it, because I don't recognize myself in that lost and angry girl. Anyway, the next two years were way better. I convinced Noah that he could leave without worrying about us, largely because Bill and Lisa insisted on 'adopting' us." She makes air quotes around the word.

"Why air quotes?"

"They love their daughters and want them to be happy, and if that meant taking in me and Evie so Noah felt like he could separate and be with Grace, they were willing to do that."

That's not how it's read to me any time I've been around them, but Paige is the one who lives this, so I don't contradict her.

She turns, slipping to her knees on the floor and settling her elbows on my knees, her chin in her hands. "I mostly feel like I've healed. Done the work. Turned it around. But about the time I finished my degree, this laugh thing started happening. It happens at the worst times too. I can't stop it, and I don't know why I do it, and I'm so sorry I hurt you."

I have this impulse to stay utterly still so I don't scare her into flitting away, but I have an even stronger impulse to connect with her, so I do. She's tucked her hair behind her ears, but an escaped tendril rests against her cheek. I touch it, then curl it around my finger and slowly unwind it, letting it trail across my hand and drift back against her skin.

"You're forgiven," I say. "I'm sorry for being stubborn about it. And for signing that petition. I shouldn't have done that."

She closes her eyes and drops her head to my knee. "That petition," she grumbles to the floor. "I get it, but it's super annoying."

"What are you going to do about it? Please don't take the decorations down."

She straightens. "I have to. I had to give myself a few days to get over being furious, but honestly, I want Evie to have a good experience on this street, and that means appeasing the neighbors. I hope Bill isn't too disappointed."

"Bill?" I frown, not following.

"He gave them to us." She waves her hand. "It's okay. I'll figure it out." She climbs to her feet and holds out a hand to pull me up. The spell is broken, and not even the warmth of her hand in mine can bring it back.

"So, Evie has had the flu for a few days, but she's feeling better today. She wants to get back to her campaign to convert you to Christmas. I can hold her off if you want."

I shake my head. "No, it's fine. She may be making more progress than she thinks."

Paige tilts her head and smiles at me. "Yeah?"

"Yeah."

"Don't say yeah. It sounds weird when you say it."

I slide my hands in my pockets because they twitch with the need to touch her again. "What should I say instead?"

"I don't know. The real Henry Hill would say 'affirmative' or something."

"Affirmative," I say.

She nods. "Better. Thank you for hearing me out." She turns toward the front door. "Bye, Henry." Then she stops and pivots, sliding her arms around my waist.

I've always been an awkward hugger, but perhaps because I didn't see this one coming, my arms come around her on instinct, my hands settling with open palms one above the other on her back. It's the perfect position to mold her to me so I can feel every inch of the hug. My breath stops, caught off guard by the way every nerve ending is responding to her.

This is . . . electric.

If she feels it, she doesn't say. She nestles in closer for a few seconds, and just when I'm sure my hands must be unbearably warm through the cotton of her long-sleeved shirt, she slides away from me and gives me a small wave before disappearing through the door.

I look after her for a full minute at least, then down at my hands, frowning.

The list of things that happen around that woman that I don't understand continues to grow.

But she's done what she can do to smooth things over. And I know how to mend the last of the rift between us, because it's the part I caused.

I fetch a jacket and head into the growing dark.

Chapter Twenty-Eight

Paige

WHAT WAS THAT?!

That "meeting" with Henry . . .

It went better than I was afraid it would, for sure. I didn't even know if he'd agree to hear me out. I hated sitting and telling that story, but for as judgy as Henry often seems to be about things, he didn't seem at all judgy about this. Interested. Compassionate. Supportive.

Not pitying. Not like he was trying to be a white knight and save me. It was like he was taking the pieces and letting it flesh out the puzzle that I must be to him sometimes.

I feel . . . seen.

But what was that touching thing? The cuddling? The moments at the end that felt like they were about to tip into something more?

That can't be my imagination. Granted, it's been a long time since I've been in a relationship. I can barely remember the last time I kissed someone. But am I affection starved to the point of imagining things?

Maybe. But I am not the one who sat me right in Henry's lap, his muscular thighs around me, his hard chest against my back, his soft breath riffling my hair while he listened.

I definitely didn't imagine all that.

What does it mean? That's what I don't know.

I'm afraid I know what I *want* it to mean.

I want it to mean that I'm a bright part of Henry's day. That it's not my imagination when I sense him checking me out when I'm walking away. That his touches were about comfort but also about wanting.

In so many ways, Henry might as well be as old as Ebenezer Scrooge himself. His stodgy wardrobe. His formal vocabulary. His old man documentary habits.

But his new, dark scruff gives his staid, preppy look a sexy edge that makes him seem his actual age and not forty-something. Dad vibes? Gone.

Sitting there, talking, I was hyperaware of how wholly he concentrates on things—in this case, me. His intense stare as he listened made me feel like he was taking in every part of me, seeing me as a whole, inside and out.

I don't know how I missed what a good listener he is too. I think of professors as blowhards. People who like to hear themselves talk. That's not Henry. Maybe it's his field that makes him such an engaged observer, but he seems far more interested in everyone around him than he does in hearing his own opinions.

It's slightly addictive.

I realize as only a recovering addict can that *Henry* is addictive. His smell. The broad line of his shoulders. The lean lines of his body. I would give up every Christmas present for the next five years to see that man in a pair of shorts just once.

Or not. It might cause me to spontaneously combust.

This has to be because I'm man-starved. How else could this come out of nowhere?

Except . . . it hasn't. Not really. These observations have been building on each other for weeks as I see new facets of him. It was just the surprise of his touch that's forced it into hyperfocus.

I *like* Henry Hill as a *person*.

I *want* Henry Hill as a *man*.

Oh, this is bad.

He and I don't make sense. We're too different. And what happens when we inevitably break up? *Evie* gets hurt. Henry needs to continue to be a benign and kindly presence in her life, just like he's been almost from the beginning.

Besides, I could be reading him totally wrong. Henry may feel nothing toward me but friendly affection. He's obviously still growing his beard for Leigh the Office Goddess or whatever she is.

I stress about this all the way through a viewing of the Jim Carrey *Grinch*, a movie I usually love to dissect for the way its set would work far better as a theater piece than a movie. I barely even notice.

Evie insists on putting the finishing touches on her next gift for Henry, the Christmas coloring page that she chose specifically because it had no Santa or reindeer in it, since I told her those things made him sad. Instead, she's colored a woodland scene of evergreens, but decorated each with a different theme, adding butterflies to one, cats to another. It's color chaos and so Evie.

She sleeps well and seems practically her usual self in the morning, cheerfully clambering up to Henry's porch to leave her picture, then chattering beside me as she holds my hand on the short walk to school. There's no skipping; that's the only sign that she's still a touch fatigued.

I drop her off and head straight for the store. Luckily, I'd employed an old theater trick for the window display when I set it up; the backdrop is two-sided. On one, the black and white drawing. On the other, the full color version. It's segmented into twelve-inch panels so I can flip each one around, which I do as soon as the street is clear of pedestrians, so I don't ruin the illusion.

From inside the store, the back of the set has a false cover, a cheerful green and red sign encouraging shoppers to "Let Handy's Help Your Holiday!" with simple line paintings of items we carry.

The customer flow is normal for a Monday, but it feels more hectic than usual because I have three days of back office work to catch up on. I leave tired and not quite caught up, but it feels better than missing another day of work.

Bill came in after lunch to work until closing, and our vibe is slightly off, but I can't put my finger on it. He acts the same as usual, but a couple of times I catch him studying me with a puzzled, even slightly sad expression before he moves on with whatever he's doing.

All in all, I'm glad to fetch an extra-tired Evie from daycare and take our short walk home.

We're turning up our walkway when she perks up slightly. "I'll turn on the lights."

I squeeze her hand and clear my throat, not sure I've found the right way to approach this, but I can't avoid it anymore. "Evie, about the lights—"

"Hello, Evie."

We turn to see Henry standing in his driveway where it borders our yard. His appearance sends my heart racing in a way I can't chalk up to being startled. It would be so much easier if I could.

"Hey, Mr. Henry," Evie says.

"I like the picture you left for me this morning."

"I decorated the trees special."

"I noticed. I was really impressed."

"But did they make you happy?"

The simple question makes me want to gather and squeeze her. She's not trying to impress anyone; she's trying to make people happy. Why do grownups always forget this lesson?

"They did," Henry says. "Very happy. What are you up to this evening?"

"Early bedtime for this one," I say. "She's still tired from her flu. We were just going to talk about our Christmas light display."

"We were?" Evie asks.

"About that," says Henry. "Could I speak with you for a minute, Paige?"

I frown at him even though I know he can't make out my expression in the dim light. "Sure. Let me get Evie inside for a bath."

When she's in the tub, the lights in the house giving warm light, I step out on the unlit porch.

"I brought you something." His voice is a tad hoarse, like he's nervous. He hands me a sheaf of papers, but it's too dark to read them.

"Sorry, I can't see, and I don't want to"—I drop my voice so Evie doesn't hear—"turn the lights on because of the petition."

"If you turn them on, you'll see that it's all right."

"Henry?"

"Trust me."

I sigh and crack open the front door, reaching inside to flip the porch light. It brings every bulb on the lawn and house to life. Henry only smiles, and I shoot him a questioning look before looking down at the papers.

It's another petition.

"Henry, I don't—"

"Just read it, Paige." His voice is patient but with a note of almost giddiness in it. "Giddy" is not a Henry preset, and my curiosity overtakes my tiredness.

"We, the homeowners of Orchard Street—ugh." I stop reading. "These words don't lead anywhere good."

"Keep going. Trust me," he repeats.

I do, but silently, not wanting to hear the hateful words aloud.

We, the homeowners of Orchard Street, accept the proposal of the owner of 341 Orchard to turn your light display into a charitable effort. We further accept your amended hours in the spirit of compromise.

On Monday through Thursday, only lights on the house will be lit. On Friday, Saturday, and Sunday nights, the full display will be on between dusk and 9 PM. Signs placed at the streets intersecting Orchard will encourage a donation of canned goods or cash for the Presbyterian Food Pantry to benefit less fortunate Creekville families during this holiday season.

Due to the high interest from the surrounding community in your display as currently constituted, we do not require a revision as it seems to appeal to the many visitors to Orchard.

We do ask that you please update your invitation on the community page to reflect the new donation request and hours for the full display.

Signed,

Your Reasonable Neighbors

I reach the signature and look up at Henry, stunned into silence. He's grinning at me in the most un-Henry-like way.

"They all signed it. Every one of them. They love the idea of benefiting the church food pantry. Even Connie and Walt signed it. I started with them. Look."

He points to the first two names on the list. Beside Connie's name, there's a note in elegant script. *We love your windows at Handy's.*

"This was your idea?"

He nods, his face still excited but now with a touch of shyness. "I hope it's okay. I'll understand if you still want them on all the time. I'll figure out how to explain it to everyone. But—"

"This is perfect," I tell him. "I can't believe you did this." *For me. I can't believe you did this for* me. Mixed with the gratitude is a small sliver of guilt because once again, someone else has to come in and fix things for me.

But it has, without question, solved a major headache, and I can go to Evie with a Christmas light proposal that she'll be thrilled to get behind.

"I kind of assumed you'd be able to make the adjustments so that there are fewer lights during the week. I hope I didn't overpromise."

I shake my head. "No, that's an easy fix."

He looks relieved. "I'm glad you're okay with all of this."

I slip my arms around his waist and squeeze him tight. "More than okay. Thanks, Henry."

Like yesterday, his hands settle into exactly the right spots on my back, like they were perfectly sized and placed to fit just so.

"You're welcome," he murmurs into my hair.

We probably have at least three neighbors watching us hug it out on the porch. I can't even begin to guess what they think is happening, but I don't care. I'll stay here forev—

"Mama? I'm done," Evie calls through the open door of the hallway bathroom.

I step back from Henry. "I don't know how to repay you for this, but I think I know where to start. How about once I get Evie down for bed, I'll text you and you can come over?" I realize too late that it might sound like a hookup invitation, so I trip over my words trying to clarify. "For nothing bad. Or naughty, I mean." Oof, no, "naughty" is *so* much worse, I realize when he pulls back enough to look down at me with a hint of confusion. "I have an idea for Project: Makeover, that's all. I'll tell you about it when Evie's asleep."

He releases me and steps back, slipping his hands into his pockets. "Sure, the project. Sounds like a plan."

"Okay, I'll text you," I repeat.

He's already retreating down my steps, and who can blame him? I just asked him to come over for something naughty.

I shake my head and go to Evie, helping her dry off and get dressed in warm pajamas. After two stories and a couple of Christmas songs, she nods off, and I tuck in her blanket and turn out the light before heading to my own bedroom to change. I'm always seeing Henry at my worst. Work clothes I've worn all day. Mismatched pajamas.

It's not like I'm going to dress up at 8:00 PM to stay in my house, but I do switch into yoga pants and a soft red cotton sweater. I've decided I can't turn on the heat until it's down to sixty degrees inside, and we're hovering a bit above that, so I pull on thick wool socks and pad out to the sofa to nestle under a blanket and text Henry that Evie's asleep.

He sends back a thumbs up. It's the first emoji he's used. Henry doesn't seem like an emoji guy.

A few minutes later, he knocks softly at the door.

I open it and flip off the Christmas lights as he comes in. "In the spirit of neighborliness," I explain to his questioning glance. I wave him to the sofa, and he sits, not exactly comfortably, but not like he's perched to run, either.

"You mentioned an idea?"

I sit on the other side of the sofa. "How's it going with Leigh?"

He gives me a long look before he rubs a hand across his jaw. I can hear the rasp from five feet away, and it's doing something for me.

"It's going," he says. "Your tips worked."

"Tell me." *Don't tell me. My tips were stupid. I should have never given them to you.*

"She noticed the scruff."

She'd have to be dead not to.

"And I've been distracted, so I ignored her on accident, but it worked the way you said it would. Suddenly, she's talking to me more. Asking me more questions. Taking it past chitchat."

That twenty-first century *tart*.

No, no, I lecture myself silently. *Men aren't scarce resources, and we don't fight other women for them.*

I still kind of hate her.

I stare at Henry as he talks, and the super senses keep firing. He smells so good. How did I not notice? And why had I ever thought he was average-looking? Shame on me for being so easily fooled by his V-neck sweaters. Henry is dead sexy and it's *killing* me.

"Paige?" He's looking at me strangely, and I make a split-second decision that I may live to regret, but I cannot, will not, talk myself out of it.

"Sounds like it's going well." I'd meant to strategize with him on his outfit for the faculty party, the next phase of his glow up. Then I was going to help him figure out how to ask her out for a date after he showed up looking like a snack.

But I throw all of that out the window in favor of a new plan. An insane plan. A plan I can't talk myself out of.

Maybe it's because it's the end of a long day and I've given myself ideas with my slip of the tongue earlier. Maybe it's because his shampoo or something smells amazing. Maybe it's the memory of his warm body framing mine yesterday.

Maybe it's that damn scruff.

Whatever it is, I can't resist the pull of my Very Bad Idea.

I rest my arm on the back of the sofa and lean forward slightly. "Are you nervous?" I ask softly.

He gives me a startled look. "N-nervous? About what?"

"About all of this working. You've got to be ready."

"For?"

"Anything." I flutter my hand in a careless way. "Sudden changes in conversation. Or she could have strong ideas about where she'd like to go for your date. Are you ready to go with the flow?"

"Yes." But he says it like he's in a slight daze.

Or under a spell. My spell.

I scoot forward several inches. "Good. Because there are all kinds of possibilities. You need to be in the moment, flexible."

He nods. "I can do that."

"Can you, Henry? What if, for example . . ." I trail off, pretending to think.

"What if what?" His throat sounds a touch dry.

My long-buried wild and restless instincts take over, the ones that fling caution to the wind like a leaf in the December gusts that stir the yards along Orchard.

"What if it goes really well? Great conversation. Great dinner. Great vibe. And you get to the end of the night. You'll walk her to her door like a gentleman, I assume?"

"Of course."

"So?"

He raises his eyebrows, looking both confused and . . .

Spellbound.

I scoot forward a few more inches and smile. It's been so long since I've flirted this way, since someone stirred my interest enough to play like this. *Addictive.* The word flashes through my mind again. I push it away.

"So how's your goodnight game?"

"My . . . goodnight game?"

"Right. Your goodnight game. Can you deliver a goodnight kiss that will make her beg you to stay?" I am definitely going on someone's naughty list as I watch his Adam's apple bob up and down. His swallow is almost a gulp.

"I . . . yes. I can do that."

I lean forward, my eyes soft and concerned. "Are you sure? Because you'll want to be good enough that she wants to invite you inside, but you, of course, won't go."

"Right." He swallows again, his eyes on my mouth now. "Why won't I?"

"Any theater kid could tell you the answer to that," I say, leaning forward. At this point, we're barely a foot apart, and I reach out to let my fingers graze the button placket on his shirt. "Always leave them wanting more."

I walk my fingers down the buttons and let my hand fall away before leaning back as if I'd been up to nothing at all. "See how well that works?"

"No."

I meet his eyes in surprise.

His narrow slightly. "I'm not sure I understand how this works at all. In fact, I'm full of self-doubt." And yet he sounds the most sure of himself he's been since he walked in.

"You'll be fine," I say, suddenly feeling a flicker of nerves along my spine.

"No, you're right. It's really important for me to get that moment right. Nail it, let's say."

"Let's." I stare at him in open fascination. Something subtle has shifted about him, but whatever it is, it has also shifted the balance of power between us. Maybe a firmer set to his jaw? Or a glint in his eye? I can't stop looking at him.

"I'm going to need coaching."

It's my turn to swallow hard. "Coaching?"

"Coaching." He leans toward me, closing the distance again, lifting his hand and settling it on the curve between my shoulder and neck. "Like, for example, is this a good opening move?"

My fingers drift up to touch his warm hand. "Yes, that's a good opening."

"Then next I'm thinking maybe something like this." He exerts the lightest pressure with his fingers against the back of my neck and draws me toward him with no effort until his mouth is by my cheek. "What do you think?" he says, his words barely a whisper that tickles my skin.

I give a small shiver. "That's a good second move. Then what?"

It's a dangerous question. He doesn't move for three full seconds, and my heart pounds fast enough to fill the silence with several beats as I wait for his answer.

But instead of words, he draws back, his lips tracing along my skin until his mouth meets mine and brushes across it.

It's a feather-light touch that burns.

"Oh." I say it so softly, and it's swallowed up by his next breath. There is a split second where I realize now is when I back away.

Except I don't.

This time when he brings his mouth to mine, I kiss him back, my hand coming up to cup his jaw and let my thumb run over the scruff I've been dying to feel.

It's another soft kiss until it isn't, until lips aren't enough, and his tongue brushes against mine in an exploration that steals the shallow breath I have left. He tastes like he smells, warm, rich, and complicated. Layers of sensation.

I make a sound—a squeak, maybe, or a whimper, but it's swallowed up in the rough groan that rumbles from him, a sound of want. Of need. I feel it all the way to my core.

This was such a stupid idea, like shooting off bottle rockets in a drought-dry field. The explosions of sensation are that intense, and the heat spreads that fast.

I rise to my knees, straining for more, and he does too, circling his arm around my waist and pulling me toward him. We fit together as perfectly this way as we did yesterday on his sofa.

"Paige." His voice is low as he murmurs my name against my throat, sending a new shower of sparks down my spine.

What is happening? I don't care as long as it doesn't stop.

There's a sound intruding from somewhere until I finally register Evie's plaintive, "Mama?"

I freeze. Henry's hands go still.

"Mama?" She's calling me from her room, and I realize she's been coughing. That's what was trying to penetrate the fog of . . .

I slip from Henry's grasp as he settles back onto the couch, and I duck into Evie's room to find her coughing again.

"My throat hurts," she says.

"Okay, sweetie. I'll bring you some cool water. It'll help."

I dart into the bathroom and fill the cup I leave for her at night. She struggles upright and drinks it all before sinking down to her pillow again.

"Better," she says.

"That's good, Eves. I'll refill it and leave it for you in case you cough again."

She nods, already more asleep than awake. I do as I promised, letting the cup fill slowly as my mind races, clear now that I'm beyond the effects of Henry's . . . smell?

Pheromones are the pirates of common sense.

When I walk back into the living room, Henry is standing behind the sofa, as if he's only been waiting for me to come back so he can leave.

He opens his mouth to say something, but I cut him off, panicked.

"You'll be fine." His eyebrows draw together. "On your date. With Lulu." I'm borderline babbling, but I need us to reverse course, *fast*. The only plan my scattered mind can come up with is to play this all off.

"My date," he repeats.

"Right. With Lulu."

"Leigh." His voice has gone very flat.

"That's what I said. You shouldn't have any problem. The party is this weekend, right? Friday."

He watches me for a couple of seconds. I'm not sure what he's looking for. Maybe evidence that he didn't imagine those few minutes on the couch. But whatever he sees, he nods.

"Yes, Friday."

"Remember, black button-down shirt, gray slacks. I'll text you a picture of some shoe choices. And some conversation starters. You've laid the groundwork, so it should be pretty easy to find a natural opening to ask her on a date."

He gives me another long look. "That's what you think I should do."

I nod like a bobblehead. "Definitely."

He nods. "Cool."

A hideous yowling followed by scratching sounds on my front door fills the awkward lull.

"What in the world?" I start to move toward it, ready to do battle with anything messing up my gorgeous new paint job.

"Wait," Henry says, turning to open it. "I think that's for me."

He opens the door and we both stare at a black cat who is sitting on my porch, staring back at us.

"It's Cat," he says.

"I can see that it's a cat."

"No, I mean it's *Cat*. I forgot to put food out for him tonight. I've been training him to come get food every morning and night."

I look from Henry to Cat and back again. "It's cute you think *you've* been training *him*."

Henry looks from Cat to me and back again. "Fair point."

"Do you think he'd come over here if we put food out for him once a day? Like maybe we could give him breakfast?"

"Probably, but how is Evie going to feel about walking out to decapitated animals every morning?"

"Uh, not great."

"I better handle his meals then."

I nod. We've run out of things to say, which means the only thing left to talk about is what happened on my sofa. But I would love to not do that. I'm debating how to head off the conversation when Henry makes it simple.

"Good night, Paige."

He walks out without waiting for me to say anything, and I sit down. Like down on the floor, my knees no longer supporting me.

I press my finger against my still-tingling lips where his scruff marked me. *Marked* me.

I still feel him with every one of my senses.

What have I done?

And more importantly, how do I undo it?

Chapter Twenty-Nine

Henry

PAIGE IS AVOIDING ME.

It's not subtle. I've seen her heading toward her trash cans only to turn around and disappear into her house when I step out of mine, her bulging garbage bag still in hand.

Evie isn't avoiding me. So far this week, I've found a pinecone tied with a yarn bow, a box of staples that has no staples but does have a soft black feather in it, and a rock taped to a note telling me to put it in water to make it shiny.

Cat isn't avoiding me. I take too long with his breakfast on Wednesday morning, and he yowls and knocks again.

But I understand Paige's retreat. I have no idea what to say to her either. Principles of anthropology, cultural anthropology, and paleopathology stuff have all ceded ground to Monday Night on Paige's Sofa, which plays on repeat in my mind. That's unfortunate since grades are due by noon tomorrow, which gives me less than twenty-four hours to pull myself together.

I have never been thrown for a loop by a kiss until now.

I try to tackle it from a scientific angle. What had caused that kind of chemical reaction? Proximity plus opportunity? That can't be it, or I would have experienced other kisses with the same level of . . .

Conflagration.

Damn. That woman, as my students might say, is fire. And for a handful of desire-drenched minutes, I had embraced the burn.

I should regret that, shouldn't I?

She's far too young for me.

Except . . . hearing her story, watching the way she handles herself—she may only have a few years on my students, but she has lived twice their lifetime in experience. Either she doesn't feel young to me, or she makes me feel young. I'm still not sure which statement is truer. All I can say for certain is that we connect in a way that makes those differences disappear.

The only thing that's perfectly clear in all of this is that she regretted it nearly as soon as it happened, and that she would very much like me to turn my attention elsewhere. Like to Leigh.

Even a couple of weeks ago, this would have appealed to me. But the more coaching Paige has done on how to win over Leigh, the less interested I've been in succeeding.

It's a quandary. Since Monday night, I've been clear on who I want. But since about three minutes after I figured it out on Paige's sofa, so had she: not me.

I'm sure she has reasons. Some of them I can even guess. It would be awkward if things didn't pan out since we're next-door neighbors. It might confuse Evie. And the age gap must cross Paige's mind.

The question is how to proceed. Her reasons are all good ones. Certainly it's already awkward with her fleeing into her house carrying full trash bags simply because I've exited my house at the same time.

I suppose the most logical play here is to follow her lead and pretend that our kiss was part of her coaching.

That mind-blowing, reality-bending, gut-tightening, fire-starting kiss.

Yes, well.

Coaching. All part of the coaching. It does allow us to put the moment at a distance. It means I should continue pursuing Leigh, even if I'm not quite sure Leigh realizes that's what I've been up to.

Perhaps she does. We've spoken more this week than we have the entire year, and I feel comfortable enough with her that I don't forget basic conversational skills anymore.

That's why on Friday, at 5:40 PM, I pull on the black button-down shirt Paige ordered me to buy and tuck it into the waist band of my flannel gray slacks. She'd sent me photos of acceptable shoes, and I slide on something called "Chelsea boots" in black. I check my reflection. It feels on par with my usual slacks and sweaters, so I'll have to take her at her word that this is a makeover.

The thought gives me an idea. This is an opportunity to nudge us back into safety. She won't be home until after six based on her normal schedule, so I take a picture of myself in the full-length mirror and text it to her captioned, "Project: Makeover Update."

HENRY: Have I gotten this right?

A long pause follows.

PAIGE: Nailed it. Leigh won't know what hit her.
HENRY: I will not hit her. I will not even hit on her. But I take your meaning.
PAIGE: Have fun at the party. I expect a progress report.

That reply comes back far faster.

I leave dinner for Cat and reverse carefully out of my driveway since the weekend light-lookers have already begun their slow crawl down Orchard.

White cardboard boxes flank either side of Paige's yard, courtesy of Connie. She'd embraced the food pantry project and run with it, and now, in addition to these boxes, more sit at either end of the street and on the intersecting street partway down. Each has a large QR code taped to the side for people to donate directly to the food pantry if they haven't brought nonperishable goods.

I hope she updates us with the totals. Based on the traffic queuing, I suspect the pantry will be able to do a fair job of tending to its neediest congregants.

I park on campus and make my way to the art building. The faculty party is being held in one of its galleries, and although I arrive exactly on time at 6:00 for the event, I'm still the only other attendee besides the dean himself.

We chat for a few minutes about the students this semester and the direction of the anthropology classes in the future, potentially even looking at expanding it into a full major. These conversations are easy for me because it's a subject I'm interested in, so perhaps that's why I'm fairly relaxed when Leigh walks in. That, plus a glass of wine.

She's stunning in cream slacks and an icy blue sweater. It all accentuates her Nordic goddess vibe. And yet, my mind immediately contrasts her with Paige's soft sweater and leggings the other night. Leigh's angles are the type of look fashion designers create for, and indeed, she's quite beautiful. But it rather pales against Paige's earthy, easy sensuality, the curves that speak of her motherhood. The inviting softness. The . . .

"Hey, Henry. You look . . . good."

I smile at Leigh's compliment. It sounds simple, but her tone injects it with a layer of meaning I don't miss. This is exactly what Paige coached me for, but now that I'm getting the reaction I wanted, I find the moment falling flat.

Still, I repay it, telling her that she looks lovely.

"It won't be too long before we're strangers," she says. "I can move offices in January, the week before school starts. I'll be out of your hair."

"I haven't minded." It sounds flirtatious, but it's true. She's easy company.

"Still, I bet you're a man who thrives on solitude."

"That used to be true," I murmur, thinking about how much less solitude I've had since the girls next door moved in, and how little I regret its loss.

"What do you mean?" she asks, and I realize it sounds like I'm referring to her presence in our shared office.

"Just that I've been more people-y lately, and it hasn't been terrible."

"I'll take credit for some of that." She tilts her glass toward mine in a light toast.

"As you should." This conversation could not be going better if I had Paige feeding me lines through an earpiece, but I suspect it's due to lack of nerves. That lack is due to no longer being invested in the outcome of this conversation. Strangely, this all seems to be even more enticing to Leigh.

I should ask Leigh out now. There's no more shared office dynamics to worry about should a date go poorly.

But I don't want to.

Why? Because Paige now has my attention?

She doesn't want it. And without her explaining, I understand and accept all of her reasons. For as much as she still berates herself at some level for her impaired decision-making at eighteen, all the evidence I've seen suggests she's done an outstanding job of making the best choices for herself and Evie since.

I need to respect that. And a future date with Leigh sounds better than mooning over a neighbor who has rightly corralled me into a "friends only" pen. What's the term for that? Friend zone.

Very well.

I clear my throat, startling Leigh, who was in the middle of saying something I've missed. "Would you like to get dinner sometime?"

She takes a drink of her wine, eyeing me over the rim. "I would."

"Will you be in town over the holiday?"

"I leave Sunday afternoon for Colorado."

I smile. "They got their snow?"

"They did."

"Tomorrow evening, then. Are you available for dinner?"

"I am," she says, smiling like she's amused by all of this.

I quirk an eyebrow at her. "Something funny?"

"You." She taps her fingers against the wineglass. "You're a surprise, Henry."

"A good one, I hope."

"We'll see."

Another woman in the psychology department joins us, and their conversation turns to shared students.

The rest of the night passes pleasantly enough. I speak when spoken to, and it's less irritating than general social situations because I have shared professional interests with most of these people. Still, my mind wanders often to Orchard Street. How much food has been collected? What is Paige doing?

Am I supposed to tell her that Project: Makeover worked, and I now have a date with Leigh? I would dislike hearing that Paige has a date with someone. What if that UPS driver wears down her resistance? I scowl thinking of it until my colleague, a decently kind man from the sociology department, gives me a wary look.

"Did I say something wrong?" he asks.

"Not at all. My apologies. I allowed some stress at home to creep in for a moment."

He nods and continues with his story about a grant he procured to study ethnography in the mid-Atlantic South.

In the end, Paige settles the question of whether I tell her about Leigh. I've no sooner parked at home and closed the door behind me than she texts.

PAIGE: How did it go?
HENRY: Fine.
PAIGE: ????!!
HENRY: I asked Leigh to dinner. She said yes. I think she liked my shirt.

There's a long silence before the next text comes in.

PAIGE: I knew it would work. Good job.

I don't respond. I don't want to talk about Leigh. I want to . . .
Make out with Paige.
Which . . .
It's unseemly.
Thirty-five-year-old men are not preoccupied with thoughts of makeouts.
It's more than unseemly; it's absurd.

I growl at nothing in particular. Maybe my id. Then I march myself up to
my room to go to bed at old people o'clock and read a soporific book on the
linguistics of the New England fishing culture until I fall asleep.

I wake late for a Saturday but still early enough to stave off any testy
demands from my feline overlord. I set out Cat's breakfast of shredded
chicken and wonder briefly if I've whetted his fowl appetite by serving
poultry so often when I find a headless wren on the doorstep.

After disposing of it before Evie can see, I set out on my long run, trying to
shift my mindset to looking forward to my dinner plans instead of wondering
what Paige and Evie are up to today. And tonight. Especially Paige.

It doesn't go well.

I return to find another Christmas spirit offering on my porch, this one
much bigger than usual. It's about the size of two stacked shoeboxes, and I
wonder what Evie could have possibly found or made to fill it.

I set it on the table inside and open it to find it filled with an assortment of
goods and an envelope with my name atop it all.

Congratulations on getting a date with Lulu!
I knew you could do it. I open at the store today, so I don't think I'll catch you
before you go out, but I want to make sure I send you prepared.
This is a date survival kit. It has everything you'll need to make sure the
evening is successful.
Can't wait to hear the details!
—Paige

I'm not even sure what's in it and I instinctively hate it, but I sort through
the contents, each labeled with explanations or instructions in Paige's

handwriting. It's crisp and feminine, the kind of handwriting someone would want as a font.

There's a tin of Altoids because "chewing gum looks trashy." A bergamot-scented candle for "pre-date stress relief." There's a roll of antacids in case of butterflies, a canister of cocoa from the fine foods market "in case it goes well enough for you to show off your hot cocoa skills."

When I pull out a small bottle of massage oil, I've had quite enough. I drop it back in the box and close it, not wishing to investigate further. It *is* a rather fascinating inventory of what Paige feels makes an excellent date. I eye the box again then turn away. I'd rather not know.

When Paige opens, she's usually home by 6:30, not that I've obsessively paid attention to her habits or anything. Sometimes you attune to other people's rhythms without trying. However, just before I leave to pick up Leigh, she still hasn't come home yet, and I get a text from her asking me if I'll flip on her Christmas lights.

I do, wondering where she is, then head out for my date, trying to remember that once upon a time, not so long ago, I would have been excited about it.

Chapter Thirty

Paige

SATURDAYS BEFORE CHRISTMAS IN retail are wild. I love it. We've hired two part-timers to help with weekend sales, and all of us are moving just short of a dead run all day. I'm happiest when it's busy in the store, probably because it gives me no time to think about my own problems because I'm too busy solving everyone else's.

Mounting brackets to shore up a fireplace mantel that detached beneath the weight of too many stockings? On it. Locating extra light clips for the customers who have left their decorating to the last minute? I got this.

I zip from one task to the next, happy with the bustle. And yet, it's not quite enough to distract me from wondering if Henry found the date box, what he thinks of it, whether he's nervous about tonight.

Our kiss . . .

Just before noon, Cindy from the diner comes in, still in uniform and scans the store until she spots me. She waves and smiles.

"You still interested in picking up some morning shifts?" she asks.

"Yes. Definitely." Even a single weekend will make sure I can give Evie more than a bare bones Christmas. A few months, and I should make some good progress on a car fund if no major house repairs pop up.

A big if.

"Great. Any chance you can start tomorrow morning? There's a flu going around, and it's taken out three of my regulars."

"I'm pretty sure I can do that. Let me do some rearranging, and I'll stop by the diner and let you know for sure when I'm off work."

"Sounds good. Gotta get back for the lunch rush."

It's midafternoon before I can check in with Bill to ask him about the scheduling changes. I find him in the back room, looking for a leaf blower.

"Hey, Bill. Do you have a minute?"

"Sure thing, honey. What's up?" He straightens to look at me, and I think about how lucky Tab and Grace were to be raised by a father who is always so present.

"Cindy at the diner offered to let me pick up some breakfast shifts on the weekends." His face clouds, and I hurry to placate him. "I know you and Lisa do so much for us already, but I'm hoping you'll be willing to watch Evie on weekend mornings."

"We already do that."

"On Saturdays, but this will mean Sundays too. I just need to build up my savings again and get a car. It's fine not having one until it isn't, like last week. I need to prioritize that."

"You can borrow one of ours whenever you want. You know that."

He sounds faintly hurt, and I smile. "I do. But there's a point where I can't keep depending on you and Lisa to bail me out, even though it's literally what I'm asking you to do again right now."

"Paige, you can *have* the dang car if you're not comfortable borrowing it."

"You embiggen my heart in more ways than I can count. You do." I press my hands to my chest. "But taking the car outright is worse, not better."

Bill blows out a frustrated breath and looks around the back room like he's trying to find something to change my mind. Like maybe a shovel to whack me over the head with. "You just got your time back after finishing school, and Evie loves it. If this is about money, I'll raise your salary."

I shake my head. "I did some research. You're already paying me top dollar for what I do. Honestly, I've thought about it, and waiting tables is what I can live with the easiest. It's hard enough asking y'all to do more babysitting, but if you could, that would be amazing."

He shakes his head. "I've always thought that I lived with the three most stubborn women on the planet, but it's possible you've got an even harder head than they do."

"Sorry." I know I'm frustrating him, but it's important to me to do it this way. To prove that I won't be the burden I was to Noah for five years. To prove that I can fill the gaps in my own life, even if I have to lean on him and Lisa more than I want to while I get to that point.

"I can't change your mind?"

I shake my head.

"All right. We're happy to watch her."

I give a sigh of relief. He's put up less of a fight than I was afraid he would about trying to do more for us. "Thank you, Bill. I'll be the best server ever and earn big tips faster so I can quit sooner and let you out of babysitting duty."

"I don't want out," he grumbles, and he's still grumbling when I head back to the sales floor.

He cuts out of work early, which is fine. Gary and I can handle the customers. I leave an hour later on schedule and detour to the diner to let Cindy know I'll be there in the morning. Then I head over to get Evie.

Normally, when I arrive to pick her up, she's neck-deep in a project with one of her Dubs, either baking or crafting something with Lisa or helping Bill in his workshop.

Today, they're all waiting for me on the front room sofa, looking serious, even Evie, who has Lisa's iPad clasped to her chest.

"Hey," I say, pulling the door closed behind me but not coming any farther into the house. Something is up. "What's going on?"

"This is an invention," Evie says.

Lisa pats her leg. "Very close, baby. It's an intervention."

Evie nods and looks at me, triumphant.

"I'm sorry, an intervention for *what*?" It's not the kind of term a recovering addict takes lightly, especially not one who managed to seek help before getting to this point.

"I talked to your brother," Bill says.

This clarifies nothing. "What does Noah have to do with this?"

Evie turns the iPad to face me, and I realize Noah is in on this too via FaceTime.

"Hey, Paige," he says. I don't answer. I only stare him down, and I hope he can feel my disapproval through the screen. "We're here to pump the brakes because we love you."

I throw up my hands. "*On what*? Can someone please explain this to me?"

"You're addicted to independence," he says.

My jaw drops. "Are you joking? I'm the least independent person in this room, plus your house, plus Tab and Sawyer's house too."

Evie raises her hand. "No, I am."

"That doesn't count, Eves. If you were the most independent person in this room, I'd be doing something wrong."

"But you're about to," she says. Her voice is very small. Lisa slips an arm around her shoulder and hugs Evie to her side.

"What?" I hear the tremor in my voice. "What do you mean, Evie?"

"You're going to work more," she says in the same soft voice.

I shoot an accusing glance at Bill, who doesn't flinch.

"Do you have to, Mama?"

Noah cuts in before I can answer. "No. You don't, Paige. There's nothing wrong with accepting help."

"Especially because we want to give it," Bill says. "You've been one of ours from the first day you worked in the store." His voice is thick, unshed tears lurking in it. "It was obvious. We took you in with our whole hearts way before we did your brother."

"Hey," Noah objects.

"It's true," Bill says, not taking his eyes off me. "We know what it's like to love and raise strong women. You came to us after already doing most of the hard work yourself, and we're just trying to catch up. It breaks my heart that you hold us at arm's length."

The sadness in his voice nearly breaks mine. "I appreciate everything you do for me, Bill. Lisa, you know I do. How can I make you believe that?"

"By not acting like you're keeping a ledger of everything you need to repay," Lisa says. She gives Evie another squeeze and then slides from the sofa to come stand in front of me and take my hands. "If you're doing that because otherwise you feel disloyal to your mom and dad, I understand. Is that it?"

"No," I say, so surprised by this that the word almost explodes from me. "No, not at all."

"If anything," Noah adds, "I'm sure they're up there raining down extra blessings for you both, thankful you're helping."

"Then what is it, honey?" Lisa's eyes are so kind and concerned that for the first time in as long as I can remember, my own eyes well with tears.

I can't remember the last time I cried, but a tear slips out now, and when I speak, it's barely more than a whisper. "I don't deserve this."

"Oh, Paige." She pulls me into her arms. "You do. You are worthy."

"That's the intervention, Paige," Noah says. "You deserve this. You deserve our love and support just because you're you."

Bill pulls me out of Lisa's arms to wrap me in his. "You don't have to prove anything to us. You don't have to earn it from us. We told you, you're our kid until your mom and dad can take over again. And we'll say it as many times as we have to until you believe us."

I press my face into his shoulder, his flannel soaking up more hot tears.

"I love you," he says. It makes the tears fall faster.

"I love you," Lisa says, hugging me from behind.

"I love you most!" Evie shouts, barreling into all of us.

"I think you're okay," Noah calls from the iPad, which is now abandoned and pointed at the ceiling.

For some reason, that's what gets the sob out of me, and Lisa hugs me tighter.

"Evie, come rescue me," Noah calls. "Bring me to your mom."

Evie lets go and fetches the iPad.

"Hold me so I can see her, favorite niece," Noah says. Evie does as directed, and I turn my head on Bill's shoulder enough to meet Noah's eyes. "Paige, repeat after me. I am worthy."

I take a deep breath and straighten. "I am worthy."

"I am deserving."

"I am deserving."

"You are, Mama," Evie cheers.

"I am loved," Noah coaxes.

"I am loved."

Bill and Lisa crush me, and I laugh.

"I will let people help more," Noah continues.

I don't say anything.

"Paige . . ." He prompts. "Say it. I will let people help me more."

"I guess it works in the Balkans."

Noah looks at me like I said it in a Baltic language. "What?"

"Nothing." I consider what Henry said about the well-adjusted kids. "I will . . . try."

Lisa laughs. "We'll take it."

"But I really have to help Cindy at the diner tomorrow. She's down a few people because of the flu, but I promise it will only be until they're back."

"I can live with that," Bill says.

It's going to be hard to accept a car from them until I can save up, but now that I know how much Evie doesn't want me gone for more hours, it's easier than it was. And I'll still look for side work, like maybe going back to the idea of work-from-home jobs I can do while she sleeps. It won't pay as well as brunch tips, but it'll be worth it if it eases Evie's mind.

Bill drives us home after pizza, and I notice that Henry's car is gone. His date must be going well, and I try not to think about it.

Evie and I settle in for the classic Claymation Rudolph, and I hate the Burgermeister even more on this viewing as I snuggle under a blanket with Evie in our too-cold house. First thing I'm doing when I'm done with brunch service tomorrow is installing some weather stripping.

About an hour after I put Evie to bed, my phone rings with an incoming call from Tabitha.

"I talked to my dad and Noah," she says without any preamble as soon as I answer.

"Please, no more intervention. I get it, I get it."

"This isn't about that. Or not directly, anyway. Do you know how I started this cozy little empire of mine?" she asks.

I snort. I love that Tabitha has zero false modesty about her success. "YouTube, right?"

"Right. I started doing cooking tutorials for other college students who were sick of their dining halls, and it grew and grew from there."

"Okay. You know I don't cook, right?" I have no idea where she's going with this.

"Can you hear me rolling my eyes, P? Because I'm doing it loudly."

"She is," Sawyer confirms in the background.

"I know you don't cook, Paige. But what *do* you do?"

"Run a hardware store." I'm still confused.

"And?"

I look around, trying to guess what she's getting at. "Work on my house sometimes?"

"Exactly! And Mom says you've been taking lots of pictures, right?"

"Yeah . . ." I'm starting to catch on.

"So do that for an audience! Start a TikTok where you show some of the techniques you do. You could easily make and post three a day. You take for granted the things you know how to do that millions of other people would love to learn. So teach them! And as more and more of them find you, you start getting sponsors. And *money*. And no extra shifts away from Evie!"

"It's not a bad idea." I scootch up in my bed, my brain starting to whir, thinking back to my branding classes and how to create one for myself. Then I sag. "Except that I bet there's a thousand other people out there trying to do the same thing right now."

"Wrong," she says. "You've got a secret weapon, but we'll talk about that in a minute. You have to lean into what makes you unique. Being a single mom. It's the whole 'sisters are doing it for themselves' thing. You show how someone young can be independent and take on a task like renovating a whole house."

"You think that would be unique enough?" I ask, visualizing it. A series of tutorials is already shaping up in my head. I could even start tomorrow when I do the weatherproofing. It's seasonal and perfect.

"*Yes.* Oh my gosh, yes. Yes, yes, yes. *Especially* because you're young and unreasonably hot."

I start laughing as I look down at my dusty Handy's shirt. "Not lately."

"Always," she corrects me. "Own it."

"Is that my secret weapon?"

"No, I am." There's such a note of smug triumph in her voice that I laugh again. "I have a massive following. When you get a good backlist of videos, I'll blast you on all my socials and you're going to get a huge running start. Then it's up to you to keep them. Think you can do that?"

"Totally. I'm going to wear booty shorts and knot my shirts above my midriff."

"You're messing with me."

I grin. "I am."

"You're going to do great."

"Tab?"

"Yeah?"

"I feel really good about this idea. Thanks."

"Sure. Let's call it payback for that shirt you let me borrow last summer."

I hang up on another laugh and roll over onto my stomach. This could work. I have to explain so many things to Evie or customers at the store that I've gotten pretty good at teaching people in the simplest way. I'm sure there are a million tutorials on how to be an influencer, not to mention watching other influencers to figure out how to differentiate myself.

I can film a bunch of these when Evie's at school so I don't have to work on them when we're together. And maybe, just maybe, with Tabitha's support, I can start earning.

I'll still find ways to let Bill and Lisa take care of us too. I take a deep breath. *I am loved. And I am worthy. And I deserve it.*

I tuck my pillow beneath my cheek with a happy sigh. A few days ago, I was in a low I didn't know how to climb out of. I'd offended Henry, alienated my neighbors, failed my kid, and hurt Bill and Lisa.

Now, it's all better.

Almost.

I turn away from my window so I won't be tempted to peek at Henry's house for evidence that he's home.

I'll figure how to get us back to a friend footing.

And then I'll do the hard part: convince myself that it's what I really want.

Chapter Thirty-One

Henry

"Tell me about your neighbor."

"Pardon, what?" I stare at Leigh across the table at the very nice restaurant we agreed upon for dinner.

She smiles and pats her mouth with her napkin to hide it. "I asked about your neighbor. The laughing one?"

I frown, still confused. "What about her?"

"Is she by any chance attractive and available?"

A blush prickles my neck and climbs toward my face, and Leigh has to hide another smile.

"So that's a yes," she says.

"It's irrelevant."

She sets her napkin down and laces her fingers together. I've seen the look on her face when she's stared down a student who comes in with a weak excuse for unfinished work. "Is it, Henry? Because for much of this semester, I sensed some interest from you. But just when it felt like an appropriate time to explore that, I could feel your interest wane. And that coincides with the arrival of the new neighbor."

There are several things in that speech to unpack. "You thought I was interested in you all semester?"

"Weren't you?"

"Yes," I admit. "How come you didn't say anything?"

"Didn't seem smart while we were still sharing an office. Isn't that why you waited to ask me out?"

I smile at her. "Not much gets past psychologists."

She shrugs. "I pay more attention than most. Which is why I notice that you still haven't answered the neighbor question. You've been polite but distant tonight. I wonder if she's why."

I sigh and look down at my plate of half-eaten butternut squash ravioli. "I'm sorry."

"Don't be. It's more fun to watch you all twisted into knots than a run-of-the-mill first date would be."

"I hate feeling obvious."

"I don't know if you are to anyone else, but as you noted, I pay attention. And we happen to be straying into one of my subspecialties, which is human connection. So tell Dr. Leigh all about it."

I do, starting with meeting Paige on the sidewalk and ending with, "and there was . . . possibly kissing."

"By the color of your cheeks, I'm guessing it was pretty good."

Why am I blushing like a debutante? This is asinine. "Better than good."

"That's what I like to hear," she says. "What are you going to do about it?"

If there is such a thing as a frustrated shrug, that's what I give her. "What *can* I do about it? She's made it clear she'd rather I was safely back in the friend zone."

"You mean because you let her think you were into me?" She arches an eyebrow at me.

"I am." She arches the other one. "Fine. I was."

"Uh-huh. Did you clue her in that your interest in me has faded?"

It feels harsh when she says it that way. "It's not you," I say. "It's me."

She sighs and shakes her head. "Honestly, Henry, do I look like I care?"

I study her face for a moment. "You do not."

"Correct. In fact, I'm very invested in this neighbor saga. What's your next move?"

I slump. "Nothing. If she's not interested, I have to respect that."

"Once again, Dr. Hill, I must point out that you've offered no evidence that she isn't interested." She signals for the waiter. "I'll take the check, please. This one's on me, Henry, for the sheer entertainment you've provided tonight."

"Glad you find it funny."

"I'd like an invitation to the wedding."

"Ha ha."

She leans forward, her eyes sparkling. "But Henry, that wasn't a joke."

I have no idea if my dinner with Leigh went well or horribly. It's a matter of perspective, I suppose. But I lie awake for a long time, wondering how long the soft glow of the light behind Paige's bedroom curtain will stay on.

I'm not prone to insomnia, but I wake up on Sunday feeling like I'd barely fallen asleep before the sun slanted through the curtains.

I spend a couple of minutes talking myself into a run until I hear faint noise outside. I slip on a pair of joggers and an old race T-shirt, then head downstairs to investigate.

Evie, Paige, and Bill are in an animated conversation in her front yard. Bill appears to be tugging at one of the painted Christmas backdrops, and Paige is waving her hands like she's not thrilled with him.

I debate for a minute, but there's no real question about whether or not I'm going out. I'll take any excuse to see Paige.

"—want them," Paige is saying as I shut my door behind me. "Stop. Leave them."

Evie looks from one to the other like she doesn't know what to think, but her expression is curious, not upset.

"They're mine, and I'm taking them back." Bill doesn't sound upset either, but Paige looks even more annoyed when he pulls the plywood from the ground.

"Good morning," I say, walking over and wishing I'd taken time to put on shoes or at least socks. It's probably in the forties this early in the morning. "What's going on?"

"I'm taking my Christmas stuff back," Bill says calmly.

"Is there a problem?" I ask with a glance at Paige's exasperated face.

"Noah tipped me off that maybe she didn't want these displays after all. And Evie mentioned something about a petition."

Paige looks down at Evie. "You knew about that?"

Evie shrugs. "I know about lots of things."

"The thing is, Henry," Bill continues as if they haven't spoken, "we've recently discovered that Paige doesn't think she can tell us honestly when she does or doesn't like something or we might quit loving her, as if that's a thing." He snorts. "So I'm making it easy on her and taking back my Christmas paintings." He pats the plywood. "I missed them more than I thought I would."

"I love them, Poppa Dub," Evie says.

"Then you can come over and help me put them up in my yard while your mama is at work for no reason."

"Bill, come on. You don't have to take them back," Paige says.

"Do you love them?"

"Well, I don't hate them."

He snorts again and totes it to his truck.

Right then, Connie and Walt reach us, clearly returning from their corgi's morning walk as he pants and plops to the ground.

"Morning, Paige," Connie says. "Reverend Huff says they've gotten five hundred dollars in donations in the last two nights from Christmas light peepers."

"That's great." A smile lights Paige's face, though it fades as she watches Bill positioning the plywood in his truck bed.

"Can I ask what's happening here?" Connie continues. "You aren't taking it down, are you?"

Paige's mouth drops open in surprise, and Connie has the grace to look abashed. "I know I'm the last person you'd expect to ask that question, but honestly, I've—we've—gotten used to it," she says when her husband clears his throat.

"Um, well, I'm glad to hear that," Paige tells her. "But honestly, they're Bill's to take if he wants to."

"I'll leave them if you say you love them," he calls.

She presses her lips together.

"That's what I thought," he says, sounding cheerful. He walks back to the yard and pulls on the next one.

"Bill," Paige says, her voice firm.

"Yes, honey?"

"I would please like to keep the lights."

He pauses in his tugging. "You would?"

"Yes, please. All of them. I love them."

His face creases in a grin. "You bet."

"I've got some extra bins I can give back though. I ran out of places to string them."

"Deal," he says, happily toting the next backdrop to his truck.

"Kind of a shame," Walt says.

Paige smiles. "Don't worry. I have some ideas I want to try after work today."

"Glad to hear it." Walt and Connie move on with a wave and a smile, their dog panting behind them.

Paige glances at her phone. "Speaking of work, I need to be at the diner in ten minutes. Be good for the Dubs, Evie."

"I will, Mama."

"Bye, Bill. Bye, Henry."

Paige takes off, and she's almost around the corner before I realize she doesn't normally work on Sunday. "Wait, why is she going to the diner?"

"Some people have the flu and she's helping, but only for a day or two or three or maybe four," Evie says.

"Oh."

"But then she's going to be an influencer," Evie adds.

This doesn't clear things up.

"Can I come see Cat?" Evie asks.

"I don't know if he wants to be seen."

"I'll try until Poppa Dub is ready to go."

"Hey, Bill, I'm sorry. I should have already offered to help you with those. What can I do?"

He lets go of the next cutout long enough to wave me off. "It's not hard. It's fine if Evie goes to see the cat if you're okay with it."

"Sure. Let's see if he's in the utility room." We walk up my driveway, but Evie stops when we reach my car.

"That was a little bit of a trick, Mr. Henry. I know Cat probably won't come out."

"I see. Why the trick?"

"I really do know lots of things," she says. "If I pretend I'm busy doing stuff, adults talk in front of me, and that's how I learn stuff."

"Good strategy." I make a mental note: always assume Evie is listening.

"Like when Mama and I went to the diner for breakfast last week. And we saw Miss Lily. And they talked about you."

I'm so torn here. I want to know everything that was said, but it's absolutely unethical to pump this child for information. "I'm glad your mom has someone to talk to."

"Don't you want to know what they said about you?"

I shake my head. "If your mom wanted me to know, she'd tell me herself."

Evie gives what sounds like a happy sigh. "And that's why I'm going to tell you. She likes you big-time. Probably loves you, even."

My stomach and heart attempt to switch places in a giant somersault.

"Evie," I say gently, "I don't think your mom would like you telling me all of this."

"Oh, she won't," Evie says. "But I asked Unc on FaceTime, and he said I should definitely tell you."

"He did?"

She nods.

I consider this for several seconds. "Okay," I say, still not sure I'm on solid ethical ground here. "What did he want you to tell me?"

She scrunches her face like she's trying to remember. "Ummm, oh, I know."

I'm going to have a heart attack waiting for these details.

"He says Mama is really good at making sure other people get what they want and very bad at saying what she wants." She scratches her nose. "Did the practice kissing help you with your other girlfriend?"

I choke on my own spit and can't answer, but Evie isn't deterred.

"Did it?"

I shake my head. I have no words.

"My mom thinks you want Lulu. Do you?"

I shake my head again.

"Then you better tell her. My mom. Because I think she wants you for herself, but she won't say it if she's trying to help you get Lulu."

"Evie?" Bill calls. "You ready?"

"Yes, Dub. I'm coming," she calls back. She gives me a long look, a look that sees more than any of the adults in her life give her credit for, but I won't underestimate her again. "Can you fix this, Mr. Henry?"

I give a slow nod, the glimmer of an idea shaping up in my mind. "I think I can."

"Good," she says. "Tell Cat bye for me." Then she waves and runs around the corner of the house to her grandpa.

I have a massive amount of manual labor to do and several phone calls to make to find out how long I have to do it.

But I'm ready. Willing. Able.

And on fire.

Just like any man in love.

Chapter Thirty-Two

Paige

I CAN'T BELIEVE I did this job for five years.

It's taken until well after 1:00 for the "brunch" rush to die down. I remember the mechanics of waiting tables well enough, and I've got a plump wad of cash in my pocket thanks to generous tips. But I'd forgotten how sore my feet could get and how much my lower back could ache.

Also? My hair smells like onions. I forgot how I was desperate to wash off that smell at the end of every shift.

Truth be told, Cindy probably could have handled the last hour by herself, but she thanked me so profusely and begged for just a little more time, so I'd stayed longer. Now only two tables are occupied, and I'm ready to go. I'm also more thankful than ever for Tabitha's influencer idea and determined to be the best student of how to make it work than anyone in the history of ever who has not wanted to go back to waiting tables.

I'm folding my apron and getting ready to walk home when Bill calls.

"Hey, honey, I'm sorry to ask, but Gary called and it sounds like that flu found him. I took Evie with me to do some errands in Roanoke, and we won't be back for a couple hours. Could you go in and cover for him until I get there and take over?"

Worst "day off" ever. But what can I do? Bill doesn't ask for many favors, and Gary would do it for me. "Sure, Bill. I'll head over right now."

"Thank you, Paige. We'll find you some extra time off during the week."

"It's no problem." Or at least it won't be when I've swung by City Drug and gotten some Advil. I might even treat myself to sitting on a stool behind the Handy's register for a while.

In the pharmacy, I chat with Farley while I pay for my Advil plus the medicine I grabbed for Evie last week. "Bet you're having a hard time keeping your cold and flu stuff in stock," I say.

He shakes his head. "Not really. Definitely selling through a lot of it, but the state health agency already put out a notification that it would be a rough flu season, so I'm stocked up. I do hope this virus finishes up with Creekville soon."

"I just had to cover at the diner for brunch and I'm heading to Handy's to relieve Gary who caught this thing, so I have to say a hearty me-freaking-too."

He gives me a sympathetic smile with my change. I dry swallow two pills on my way to Handy's, where I go through the back and change into a spare store T-shirt before hitting the floor.

Gary is standing by a pellet smoker and laughing with a man I don't recognize when I come out. When he sees me, he quits smiling and gives a couple coughs.

"Glad you're here. I best go home and lie down." *Cough cough.*

I narrow my eyes at him. He coughs again and disappears into the back.

I tie on my store apron, walk behind the register, and lean against the counter, something I never do. But my goal is to let the Advil kick in, then coast until Bill shows up. I'll let the holiday hires handle customer questions and fetch merchandise while I cashier.

It's closer to three hours before Bill makes it into the store. By now, my back is better, but I'm dealing with bone tiredness.

He walks in with Evie, apologizing before the front door even swishes shut behind him. "Sorry about that. Had to run around more than I thought I would. Evie's going to hang out with me until dinner, if that's all right. Said she wants to earn pocket cash for Christmas presents, so I'm going to have her do some sorting."

Grace and Tab both grew up doing this too, and I nod. "Sounds good. I'll see you at home." I take off my apron, hug them both, and walk out into the dusk, so glad to finally be getting home. I'll make sure to crash on the sofa, so I'll hear Evie when she comes home, hopefully with a foil-covered plate of leftovers for me.

It's nearly full dark when I turn onto Orchard, and the street is already filling with cars. I smile when I notice a couple of people jump out of their vehicles to scan the QR codes on the boxes, and again when a teenage boy climbs from a minivan to deposit a bulging grocery sack inside. Henry and Connie make a formidable team, though it might horrify Henry to hear it.

Speaking of Henry . . .

I squint, trying to make sense of what I'm seeing ahead. Normally, my house is the brightest spot on the street, but I haven't had a chance to flip on the lights. Yet it's still really, really bright.

As I get closer, my confusion only grows. That's *Henry's* house practically glowing up there, and is that . . . no. It can't be.

I pick up my pace, my tiredness suddenly disappearing. *It is!* His yard is full of holiday inflatables. Every single one we carry at Handy's, in fact. There's a snowman so tall it's squished beneath the branches of his front yard sycamore. There's a grinch in the act of stealing away with a bag of presents, Santa riding a dinosaur, a gingerbread man who is terrifying at this scale, his head even with the roof line.

And lights! So many lights! Outlining the front door and every window, wrapped around all the columns, every bush, and along the eaves.

I reach his driveway at practically a jog, and that's when I spot Henry himself, standing outside in a light jacket like he's waiting for me, hands slid into the front pocket of his jeans, his glasses reflecting red, green, and gold Christmas lights.

"Henry?"

"Hello, Paige."

It slays me, the hello. I love the formality of it. Evie and I may have loosened him up in some ways, but I love that he still gives a full and polite, "Hello."

"What's going on?"

He glances over his shoulder like he's only now noticing that he has taken the crown for tackiest holiday display. "Oh, that?" He turns back to me. "I guess Evie won me over to Christmas."

"Is that all?" I say, amused. Happiness bubbles up in my chest like the Christmas punch Lisa makes. For all that we may have driven him crazy for the nearly six weeks we've been living here, it's nice to think we've brought him some holiday cheer. He deserves it.

"It's not all, actually. But maybe we should turn on your lights for your admirers, and then I'll tell you the rest."

"Okay." I'm curious to the point of impatience, but I hurry up my walkway and turn on my lights too. This wins a cheer from the passing cars.

I cut across the lawn—easier to navigate now that Bill has reclaimed his cutouts—to Henry, who crooks his head toward his house, like he wants me to follow. He leads us to his front porch and settles on the front step, scooting over to make sure I have room beside him.

"So about my date last night," he begins.

My heart sinks, and the words spill out of me. "I don't think I want to hear about it, Henry."

He's quiet for a beat. "Why not?"

I shrug and stare out at his yard without seeing. *Because I wanted that to be me. Because I don't want you going out with her. Because I've been lying to myself for a good while now about how I feel about you.*

There are a dozen reasons I could give him and not a single good reason I should give any of them. This is messy. But I'm too tired not to tell the truth. I sigh, and it's defeat. "Because it will make me sad."

"How did you know it went badly?"

I blink at him, and he's studying me with an intensity that sends a shiver down my spine. A good one. "It went badly?"

"Very badly."

I consider this. "Maybe I do want to hear about it."

"Sadist."

"More like rubbernecker. So tell me."

He rubs his palms on his jeans. "I couldn't concentrate, so the conversation prompts you gave me were useless. In fact, I was so distracted that Leigh finally called me on it."

"That's too bad." There is a shameful note of glee in my tone. "Why were you so distracted?"

"Dr. Leigh diagnosed the problem. She's pretty good at her job."

"How nice for her." I can't stand this woman.

His mouth twitches. "She thinks I have a thing for my neighbor."

But she might be a pretty good psychologist.

"Do you agree with that diagnosis?" I hold my breath, hoping I know the answer. Hoping I suddenly understand why he's corrupted his yard with inflatables.

He reaches over and picks up one of my hands, twining our fingers, and my heartbeat pulses in my fingertips. "It's hard to argue with the evidence."

"Which is what?" I'm fully breathless now.

"That I think about you constantly. That if I'm not with you, I want to be with you. That my day is better if you're in it. That you give me all the symptoms of a panic attack but they feel good."

It's so awkward and so perfectly Henry.

I turn toward him. "I make your heart pound?"

"Yes."

"Your palms sweat?"

"Can't you feel them?"

"Your stomach flips?"

"It's awful."

"You get short of breath?"

"So far, only when you kiss me." He stands and pulls me to my feet. "I have one more decoration to show you."

He doesn't let go of my hand but tows me gently to his front door and then through it, shutting it behind us and backing me against it.

"Henry." It's a question. A plea. It's two syllables of pure wanting.

"I think I love you," he says.

"You think you do?" My heart skips a tiny beat. I want him to *know* because I do. I know I love him, and it makes it okay that he's still figuring it out. I'll help him.

"But this is going to take science."

"Wh-what?"

He points above me, and I realize he's backed me beneath fresh mistletoe. "Science. I feel it here." He touches his chest. "And here." He touches his temple. "But there's a final piece of evidence I need."

I reach up for his shirt and pull him down to me.

This is not an exploration like Monday night. This is a reunion of lips that were made for each other.

It's a slow kiss, one that takes its time until it doesn't. One that turns deep and delicious and makes the door propping me up totally necessary.

After countless minutes of the best kiss of my life, I lean back. "Henry, I've got some data."

He gives me a serious nod. "Let's hear it."

"Your kisses make me weak in the knees."

"I've got a diagnosis," he says. "Paige Redmond, you're madly in love with me."

"Are you sure, Henry? You're so cranky. And you have too many V-neck sweaters. Those are not the qualities that a Christmas-loving, rule-breaking neighbor would fall for. How can you know?"

He punishes me with another long, melting kiss before he rests his forehead against mine. "Because, you difficult woman. I've come down with a case of the same thing."

"Wow," I say as hot prickles of joy sweep through my chest. "It's as contagious as the flu."

"Incurable too," he says. "It's chronic." Then he reaches up to brush my hair from my face, his eyes suddenly serious as he looks into mine. "I definitely love you, Paige Redmond."

I sigh. "I hate to admit it when you're right, Henry. But I might probably definitely love you madly too." And then I pause, a suspicion occurring to me. "Did Cindy really need me to work that long?"

He shakes his head.

"And did Bill really need me to cover?" Another headshake.

"And does Gary actually have the flu?"

He pulls me against him. "No. But every last one of them is a sucker for love, and they all bought me enough time to help me set up my yard."

"I love it." I press a soft kiss against his mouth. "And I love you, Henry Hill."

"Merry Christmas, Paige. But I love you more. In fact—" his face grows serious—"I have an important question for you." He clears his throat, and before I can stop him, he's holding my hand and getting down on one knee.

Oh, no. Oh no, oh no, oh no. I will want this someday, maybe even someday soon, but this is *too* soon.

I need to save us both from some horrific discomfort. "Henry, I—"

"I have to get through this, Paige." He clears his throat again, gives my hand a soft squeeze, and says, "Paige, will you go to Christmas Town with me?"

"I can't, Henry," I say in a mortified burst of words, eyes squeezed shut, before I register what he said. I open them to find him grinning at me. "What did you just say?"

He repeats it very slowly. "Will you go to Christmas Town with me?"

I stare at him for a full twenty seconds. Then also very slowly, I answer, "I'm going to kill you."

He's laughing as he climbs to his feet. "Can I choose my execution? Like being smothered by kisses?"

I roll my eyes but reach up and grab the collar of his jacket. "Fine, Henry. I'll smother you with kisses."

And I do.

Epilogue

Paige, One Year Later

"Are you sure you aren't sick of seeing this play yet?" I ask Henry.

"Are you kidding me? Watching Evie as Tiny Tim is the greatest theater experience of my life."

I've been helping as a backstage mom with the community theater production of *A Christmas Carol* every night this week. Tuesday was the absolute chaos of dress rehearsal, and Wednesday through last night, I helped with all the backstage wrangling, including keeping the youngest cast members entertained during the long stretches between their scenes.

Henry bought tickets to every performance and watched from the creaky seats in the small Albemarle High School theater.

Tonight, I get to watch as an audience member, front row center, along with the entire Winters crew. There's still two weeks to go until Christmas, but they all insisted on coming into town to see Evie in her breakout role. I don't know how good Evie is, but I can say with absolute confidence that no one has performed Tiny Tim with such relish in the history of theater.

We meet up with everyone else in the school parking lot, and I'm overcome again with gratitude for this family of mine. In the year that Henry and I have been dating, they've folded him in as easily as they have Evie and me, and sometimes—especially during extra-mushy times of the year like Christmas—my heart feels bigger than my body.

We file into our seats—Henry bought out the front row for tonight as soon as tickets went on sale—and settle in with a flurry of jackets and winter scarves. The only one missing is Lisa, who is taking my place backstage so I can be in the audience.

I imagine Evie all keyed up like she is every night, squirmy in her impatience to go onstage and deliver her lines. Lisa will have her hands full trying to keep Evie from sneaking into the wings the whole show to peek out at the audience.

We've arrived twenty minutes early, and I spend it with my hand tucked into Henry's, listening more than I talk as Sawyer and Noah tease him about his new nickname—Dr. Hottie Hill. It turned up on Rate the Prof after he leaned into the wardrobe makeover I suggested in the spring. He'd tolerated it for about two weeks before he had such an influx of students—especially girls—coming to his office hours that he went back to V-neck sweaters in "self-defense."

Tonight, he's wearing my favorite look, a cream-colored handknit sweater that had been pricy even at the thrift store because of the designer label, jeans, and a truly homely blue and gray winter scarf Evie crocheted for him because he's a "Ravenclaw, obviously." She's deep into a Harry Potter obsession, working her way through the books with Henry, who reads them with her. It's his first time too, and he wears his Ravenclaw scarf unironically and pretty much everywhere.

She made one for me in the bumblebee colors of Hufflepuff, and I hope all her aunties and uncles know that they've got Hogwarts scarves in their future. Two weeks in their future, to be precise, when they come back for Christmas and open Evie's present to each of them. And none of them had better argue with her about the house she sorts them into; she's very confident she's pegged them all correctly.

Grace leans around Noah to squeeze my knee. "The set looks amazing, Paige."

I smile, a flush of pride creeping up my cheeks. I'd volunteered to work on them and ended up being the de facto set designer. I still love managing the store, but it had been fun to immerse myself in the creative challenge of bringing Victorian London to life on a tight budget. If I could do this a couple of times a year while keeping the steady income and the sense of community from working at Handy's . . . man, that's the good life.

I've given up wondering what I did to deserve all this. I would want this kind of happiness and fulfillment for everyone I love, and I spend my time appreciating that they all want it for me too.

Soon the house lights dim, and the stage lights come up. The buzz of audience chatter subsides to first a hum and then a rustling of coats and programs. As the actors appear on stage and the lines I know now by heart begin, I relax into my seat.

Henry does not. He leans slightly forward, his leg bouncing in a soft but very fast rhythm.

"Hey," I say, whispering so not even the actors a few feet away can hear. "You've seen her every night. She'll do great."

He nods, but when his leg continues to bounce, I settle my hand on his thigh, a gentle reminder to take it easy. He does for minutes—even scenes—at a time, and I smile at how similar the play is to my own Scrooge's story, even down to the memory of Henry's Grandmother Marley who helped him find the first sparks of Christmas joy again.

However, by the time we're in the final scene, I give up trying to keep Henry's leg still. It doesn't seem to bother anyone else on our row, all of them watching the stage raptly as they wait for Evie to deliver Tiny Tim's famous words. Henry is sitting ramrod straight, leg bouncing like mad, his hands clasped tightly over the arms of his seat.

"She'll nail it, Henry," I whisper.

He looks over at me and nods, his face serious, then turns right back to the stage. Right on cue, Evie steps to the center of the stage and pronounces the final line of the play. "God bless us, every one!"

The audience bursts into applause and cheers. I know I'm not impartial, but it feels like Evie outdid herself tonight. Probably showing off for her Dubs and aunts and uncles.

"See," I say, after giving an ear-splitting whistle, "she did great!"

Henry nods, but he doesn't even look at me. "She did."

The cast gets a standing ovation every night from the warm Creekville audiences, and normally, they'll take a couple of encores. I watch as the curtain closes and the audience cheers louder until it opens again and the cast bows. After a minute or so, the curtain closes again, and I grin at Henry.

"One more and then we can hug our girl."

He nods again, but he doesn't seem any more relaxed now that Evie has come through without a hitch. Something has him stressed. I'll get it out of him once I've put Evie to bed.

When the curtain opens for the final encore, I stop clapping, surprised to see only Evie there instead of the rest of the cast. That's weird.

She waves at the audience, takes another bow, then makes the "settle down" gesture with her hands. I look up and down the row, thinking I'll meet someone's eyes in shared confusion, but no one makes eye contact with me.

"What's going on?" I ask Henry, as we take our seats.

He shrugs. "I don't know, but no one is giving her the hook, so it must be planned."

"Probably a Christmas Town announcement," I say.

Evie clasps her hands behind her and assumes a stance like she's about to recite the Constitution or something equally grand.

"Thank you for coming to the final night of our production of *A Christmas Carol* this evening," she says in her slightly too loud "projecting" voice. "Tonight, we have a special encore. May I present Mr. Henry Hill!"

My head whips toward Henry, more confused than ever, but he doesn't look at all surprised. He rises and walks to the edge of the stage before he turns to face the audience, still standing on the floor, where the spotlight finds him. His eyes, however, are fixed on me.

"Ladies and gentlemen, I stand before you a reformed Scrooge."

It's his engaging lecture voice. I've sneaked into his class a few times to listen to him, and I love it.

"I forgot the joy of early Christmases when a tragedy erased them, and I spent years loathing the holiday and everything associated with it. That all changed when Tiny Tim, disguised as a moppet named Evie, moved in next door to me with her mother, Paige." He smiles at Evie then over at me. "You may know her as the finest window and set decorator in Creekville."

This earns some cheers and whistles, but I barely notice, because I can think of only one reason Henry would do this, and my stomach flutters like I've got a partridge in a pear tree in there.

"These two Redmond women made a point of winning me over to Christmas last year, and they did sneaky things like leave me thoughtful gifts and delicious treats." Evie beams and jumps down to stand beside him, then gives me a huge wink. She slides her hand into Henry's, something she's done easily almost since the night he confessed he loved me and we'd won him over to Christmas. Two turtledoves and three French hens join the partridge in the fluttering.

"It made my Christmas Present as happy as I could ever imagine being," Henry continues, "but lately I've been wondering about Christmas Future.

How could it ever top any of this?" He stops and clears his throat, looks down at Evie, and nods.

She reaches into the pocket of her Victorian knee breeches and produces a small velvet ring box. The audience buzzes.

I press my hands to my stomach. The whole flock is here. I've got calling birds and geese and swans a-swimming in there.

Henry turns back to me. "I realize the only way that Christmas Future could ever be bright was if these Redmond women were in every one of them. Paige, could you come here?"

I stand and walk toward them, tears already trembling on bottom lashes, threatening to fall, but I sniff them back. *Keep it together, Paige.*

When I reach him, Henry draws Evie around to stand next to me, then drops to one knee, and there's another cheer from the audience.

"Paige and Evie Redmond," he says, "one of my favorite rituals in every culture is marriage."

This pulls a laugh from me, because it's so Henry, but it's a purely happy laugh, no threatening panic beneath it. That hasn't happened in months and months.

He opens the ring box to reveal a simple golden ring. It's exactly what I would have picked for myself. "Would you two do me the great honor of becoming my family and permanent Christmas Future?"

Evie clearly had not expected a proposal for herself, and she looks up at me with wide eyes.

"What do you think, Evie?" I ask.

She nods hard enough to give herself whiplash.

"Good call," I say. I look back to Henry, love shining up from his warm brown eyes.

I reach down and cup his face in my hands, loving the soft scrape of the stubble he keeps for me. "Very well, Henry Hill. But I'll see your Christmas Future and raise you a forever."

"That means yes, right?" Tabitha demands from the front row.

"It means yes!" Evie shouts, and I barely register our standing ovation as Henry surges to his feet and seals the best Christmas ever with a kiss.

For a bonus scene in Paige and Henry's future, please visit Melanie's website.

AUTHOR'S NOTE

At the end of 2006, I had a very strange three months: my dad died six weeks before I got married, and my mom died four weeks after the wedding. It's fine. I've grieved. And I have a strong personal faith that helps when I'm sad sometimes. But during that time, I developed a bizarre laughing reaction, just like Paige's. After about a year, when things began to settle down, the laughing did too, thank goodness! It's reappeared for short periods of time during times of duress, like the day I finished all my coursework for my master's degree.

In the years since, I've been diagnosed with an anxiety disorder which is now managed, but it took years before I realized that my levels of anxiety were much greater than most people experience. If any of this sounds familiar to you, consider this a gentle sign to connect with a professional. I started with a therapist and eventually a physician's assistant specializing in mental health. It's been life-changing in the best ways, and now I'm healthy and happy, *and* myself. It's me. Just not . . . anxious.

I wish this kind of peace and clarity for everyone, and I'm cheering for you if you're considering a step toward managing your own well-being. You deserve it and you can do it!

Acknowledgments

Special thanks to Josi Kilpack and Marisa Whitaker for answering real estate questions. All errors are my own! Thank you to Jennifer Moore and Becca Wilhite for their speed reads on this! Thank you to Brittany Larsen for thinking deeply and pushing for more character development. Thank you to Jenny Proctor for the cheerleading and commiseration and the help. Always so much help! Much appreciation always to Jen White, Tiffany Odekirk, Aubrey Hartman, and Teri Bailey Black for listening to scenes over and over until I get them right. Thank you to the Zoom crew for keeping motivated, especially Ranée Clark, who laughed when I told her what I intended to do with the book and said, "YES." Thank you to Kenny and my kiddos who do so much to help and support me, and for whom I do this all.

About the Author

Melanie Bennett Jacobson is an avid reader, amateur cook, and champion shopper. She lives in Southern California with her husband and children, a series of doomed houseplants, and a naughty miniature schnauzer. She holds a Masters in Writing for Children and Young Adults from the Vermont College of Fine Arts. She is a three-time Whitney Award winner for contemporary romance and a USA Today bestseller.

Made in the USA
Coppell, TX
27 December 2022

90855016R00135